He had come to prison at the tender age of eighteen; now, four years later, he was leaving with an education a man could get nowhere else. He had learned the hard way that, if you were going to live a life of crime, go for the big buck. Now he was ready. By this time next year, he planned to have the city of Detroit all wrapped up.

Holloway House Originals by Donald Goines

DOPEFIEND
WHORESON
BLACK GANGSTER
STREET PLAYERS
WHITE MAN'S JUSTICE,
   BLACK MAN'S GRIEF
BLACK GIRL LOST
CRIME PARTNERS
CRY REVENGE
DADDY COOL
DEATH LIST
ELDORADO RED
INNER CITY HOODLUM
KENYATTA'S ESCAPE
KENYATTA'S LAST HIT
NEVER DIE ALONE
SWAMP MAN

Special Preview of *Street Players*—page 301

BLACK GANGSTER

Donald Goines

BLACK GANGSTER

An Original Holloway House Edition

This edition reprinted 2007

Printed in the United States of America

BLACK GANGSTER
ISBN 978-0-87067-984-1

WWW.HOLLOWAYHOUSEBOOKS.COM
OR
WWW.HHBOOKSTORE.COM

BLACK GANGSTER

1

THE SUN WAS SHINING through the bars on the window as Prince, tall, slim, and black, got up from his bed and paced back and forth in his cell. He stopped in front of the small calendar he kept on the wall and smiled. It had been a long time, but he had managed to keep his sanity. Suddenly the sound he had been waiting for reached him loud and clear.

"Break one!" The yell was sharp and, before it had diminished, the sound of over a hundred steel doors opening together drowned it out. "Break two!" came the yell again, followed by another hundred iron doors opening at the same time. Voices were raised in harsh humor as over four hundred men joked and argued back and forth. "Break three," the break man screamed as he reached the third gallery.

Prince glanced into the small mirror hanging over his facebowl, reached up and patted down his large afro hairstyle and then rushed to the front of his cell and snatched open the steel door. Then he stepped out on the gallery, slamming the door behind him with the experience of a convict who has been jailing for a long time. He quickly glanced back into his cell to see whether his bed was wrinkled. It was more a reflex motion than any real concern for the appearance of his cell.

Prince fell in step with the man in front of him. "How you feel, baby, gettin' up this morning?" the white inmate who locked next to him asked. From the sound of the man's voice, there was no way of telling whether he was black or white. This was not unusual in prison. Many white men after spending a lot of time behind prison walls adopted the mannerisms of black men.

"What's happening, Red?" Prince replied easily as they started down the concrete stairs. Glancing down from the third-floor gallery all you could see was a line of blue-dressed men.

"Break four!" came the yell as the break man let out the men locking on the fourth gallery. The sound of a hundred steel doors slamming shut came to their ears as they hurried down the stairway.

"Stop that running down there," a guard yelled from his gun tower. The gun tower was up on the fourth floor, built down from the ceiling, away from the gallery. The only way a man could reach it was from the roof. A prisoner could spend a lifetime behind the walls and never come close to seeing the inside of a gun tower. All he would ever see would be the bright steel of the gun barrel sticking out of one of the many slots.

The inmate guilty of running slowed down after he reached the friend he had run to catch up with. They began talking loudly as they continued on towards the line of men lined up on the base, the bottom floor. The sound of so many voices talking together was like the hum of a million bees. The old silent system had been abolished many years before. Now inmates could talk on the way to chow, while sitting in the dining hall, even while standing in the line as they went to eat. Jackson Prison, the largest penal institution in the United States, was becoming modern.

The men lined up and the guards waited patiently until the men quieted down before opening the doors and allowing them to file out quietly. Guards walked up and down the line speaking to individual prisoners.

"What's wrong, Jones, you ain't hungry this morning? You there, Collins, keep the bullshit up; we got all fuckin' day. If you don't eat, it's your own damn fault." From close association, most of the guards spoke the same language the inmates used. "I guess don't none of these boys want to peck today," the sergeant said loudly. He rubbed his huge potgut and laughed. None of the guards working the floors, or blocks, or yard, were allowed to carry any form of

weapon. There were no more nightsticks or guns at
the guards' sides. If violence occurred, it was up to
the guard to get his ass to cover or under one of the
gun towers.

The line of men soon quieted down enough to satisfy the guards. They started filing out the large doors
of Three Block. The other eight blocks inside the
prison walls had already eaten.

Prince walked beside Red, shooting the bull until
they reached the mess hall. Then, by tacit agreement,
the men split up, blacks going in one side of the huge
mess hall, whites in the other side. The men segre-
gated themselves in the mess hall by personal choice,
blacks eating on one side, whites on the other. Here
and there you could see a sprinkling of whites sitting
with blacks. In most of these instances it was a white
homosexual sitting with his man, or when it occurred
on the white side, a black homosexual sitting with his
white man. At times, it would just be friends sitting
together, but it was more than likely to be lovers
together.

At all times during the meal, the men were kept
under surveillance by the men in the gun towers. At
the first sign of any disturbance, long-barreled rifles
would appear in the gun slots. It was a known fact
amongst the inmates that the guards would shoot, and
shoot quick. It didn't take much to give them cause
for target practice. In prison, a man quickly learned
that, at the beginning of any fight, you got the hell
clear of the fighting area, because when the guards
started to fire, it would be right into the crowd of

fighters.

Prince ate quickly and left the mess hall. It was yard time now, so he had a few hours until it started to get dark before locking back up. He searched through the gym first, looking for his older friend, Fox. The gym was full of men playing basketball on the two courts, plus men in the weight pits, lifting iron over their heads, trying to build muscles up so they could impress their girlfriends when they got out. On the benches lining the walls men sat huddled over, playing chess and checkers, cigarettes stacked up beside them to bet with.

Prince retraced his steps and walked over to "Las Vegas," a large area with wooden tables and seats. Here the men gambled from the beginning of yard time until it ended, winter or summer. In the winter you could find them huddled up in their coats, betting boxes of cigarettes as if they were real money. To them, they were money; in prison, cigarettes take the place of currency. You could buy everything from a homemade knife to a sex act with one of the many queers who lived like beauty queens inside the prison walls. All it took was cigarettes. To have a quick relationship with one of the younger, prettier queers, it would cost two cartons of smokes, any brand. Older homosexuals would sell themselves for five packs on up. The prices varied with the merchandise; any sissy, no matter how ugly he might be, could find a boyfriend. From eighteen up to eighty, if they had a hot head or whatever else it took, somebody inside the prison walls would gladly become his man.

Fox saw Prince coming and stepped away from the poker game he had been watching. "Hey there, guy, I been lookin' for you."

"Yeah, Fox, the bastards fed us last today," Prince said as he walked up to his associate. Fox was in his late thirties, with the appearance of a man in his early fifties. His eyes had deep circles around them, while there was a thinning out of his hair that came with old age. His face was slightly bloated, and his pale brown skin had a burned look about it, as though it had seen too much scorching sun. He was short, about five-seven, with a growing paunch. His gut hung over his belt buckle.

"Let's walk around awhile." His voice was firm and strong.

Prince fell in step with the older man. He had grown accustomed to Fox's way of speaking long ago. He was not necessarily used to people talking to him in this manner, but he had long ago learned to accept certain things if he thought that they would one day pay off in his favor.

They walked side by side around the yard. As they passed the stands Prince waved to Red, who was sitting with some hillbillies playing guitars.

"Goddamn, it's more fuckin' woods with guitars inside this joint than it's roaches in the city," Fox said and removed his hankie to wipe sweat from his brow. "The goddamn hot weather brings them out with them funky guitars like flies."

Prince laughed and continued to walk without comment. He was used to hearing Fox curse over just about everything inside the prison. Fox had done nine years on a twenty-year sentence for sale of heroin. He would be going up for a special in another month, and with his good record Prince was hoping that he made it. With the release of Fox, his plans would be falling right in order. He needed that good connect that Fox had with the dagos. A good heroin connect with Italians would make a young, fast black man rich.

"Hey, Prince, you got a minute?" an elderly black man called.

Both men stopped and waited for the older man to catch up. "I just wanted to find out if you could let me have a couple of packs, Prince. I got some good spud-juice lined up, but it takes five packs to cop."

"I'm sorry, Dad. I done gave away all my extra stuff," Prince answered politely, smiling and revealing evenly spaced white teeth.

The old man shook his head and walked away. "I should have remembered you're gettin' up in the morning," he answered over his shoulder.

"I just can't understand why you waste your time fuckin' with them deadbeats, Prince," Fox said as he coldly watched the older man walk away.

"He wasn't always down and out, man. He's just gettin' old now, and times done passed him by," Prince answered, then added, "I remember him from the old neighborhood, Fox. He used to always have time for us kids when he was doing good. He'd pull up in that white Caddie he drove, and we'd always be able to hit him up for a few dollars."

"He was a goddamn fool," Fox said harshly. "When

he caught his case, that nigger had big money. More than the average nigger ever sees in a lifetime. Now look at him. Anytime a old man's fool enough to leave all his money with a young bitch, he's supposed to get took."

That was true enough, Prince agreed silently. He had the same thoughts. Not only any old man, but any young one, too. Still, it didn't stop him from being kind to the old man. He believed kindness was the sweetest con of all. Ever since he had been here, he had used a pleasant front, picking the men around him so subtly that they never knew he was using them. It had taken him two weeks to pick the little knowledge out of old Dad. Now he knew how old Dad had gotten rich, which people he had gone to to get the connections he needed to get his whiskey stills made. All of this and more was written down in his cell.

He knew just the people to go to for sugar connects, where he could buy twenty thousand pounds of sugar without any static. In fact, when his woman had come up to visit him last month, he had had her check it out, and now it was all set up, ready for him to get it out and put the business into operation. He smiled silently as he remembered her last letter. She had mentioned that she had a hundred thousand pounds of sweetness for him whenever he got out. The guards who censored the mail would have never realized that she was talking about sugar stashed away in an empty slum house.

"I don't know how that old bastard made the kind of money he was supposed to have made off of corn

whiskey anyway," Fox said as they started to walk
again. "It ain't that kind of money in no whiskey, in
this day and age. This is the sixties, not the roaring
twenties."

You know-all bastard, you, Prince thought coldly.
Just continue thinking that way. "Maybe you're right
at that, Fox," he said, agreeing with him as he always
did whenever he knew there was no point in starting
a useless argument.

There was a crowd in the middle of the yard, so
they stopped and watched it for a few moments. Two
men stood closely together, while another man stood
in front of them with a bible. It was just another mar-
riage going on. Almost weekly in the large prison,
some homosexual was getting married to another man
behind the bleak walls of the prison. It had become
so regular that few people stopped to watch it.

"Goddamn punks!" Fox cursed loudly, his words
carrying to the men in the rear of the crowd.

"Hey, Prince," one of the men yelled from the
crowd. "They passing out ice cream and pop as soon
as the wedding is over."

"That's all right, Bull. I got some script. We might
stop at the store on the way around and pick up something," Prince replied with humor. "Unless you want
some of their cream," he said to his companion.

"I'd rather be dead first," Fox replied with his usual
impoliteness. "You know me better than that, Prince.
That shit is for these goddamn parasites like Bull.
Whenever you hear of something being given away,
you'll find him in the front of the fuckin' line. I wish

they would give away some shit sandwiches. He'd
probably be right down front for that, too."

Prince glanced down at his companion. Again he
wondered how the man had survived nine years
behind the walls without getting himself killed. Fox
bitched about anything and everything. If he wasn't
crying over the food, he was complaining about the
lousy movies that came inside the prison once a week.

"About that favor I been asking you about, Fox. You
goin' do that for me?"

"I don't know, Prince. I gave it a lot of thought,
man, but it just ain't right. I can't send you to them
people like that." Before Prince could interrupt, he
continued. "You just wait until I get out, baby, and
we'll go over to the Big Apple together."

Prince remained silent for a minute. It was no more
than he had thought would happen. He had never really believed that Fox would give him the connection
in New York, but he had kept on trying until his last
day in prison.

"Yeah, man, yeah. I didn't believe you'd act like a
true friend, Fox," he said, some of his anger displayed
in his voice. "After fuckin' around with me for over
three years, Fox, you still don't trust me enough to let
me get this thing off the ground for us. By the time
you get out, man, I could be done made fifty grand."

"Hold on there, Prince, just hold on. Look here.
When I go to the board, if I don't make it, I'll write
and let you know. Then all you got to do is send your
woman up to see me and I'll give her the information
you need."

"Sure, baby, sure," Prince answered and turned his back and walked away. If it happened, cool, but if it didn't, he had other irons in the fire. By this time next year, he planned to have the city of Detroit wrapped up. It wasn't a bad dream for a young man of twenty-two. He had come to prison at the tender age of eighteen; now, four years later, he was educated with a schooling that a man could get nowhere else but in prison. He had learned the hard way that, if you were going to live a life of crime, go for the big buck. Now he was ready.

2

THE GREYHOUND BUS roared through the outskirts of Detroit. Prince twisted around in his seat and
pretended to stare out of the window. He tried to
ignore the slim, blond man next to him. They had both
been released from the prison at the same time that
morning. After reaching the bus station they had been
left alone, but for some reason the young white man
hadn't wanted it that way. He continued to stay close
to Prince. When the bus arrived, he had followed
Prince to the back of the coach and sat beside him.
Prince stretched out his long legs as a bell went off
in the back of his mind. "No, it couldn't be," he told
himself and tried to push the thought out of his head.

After leaving queers alone for four years while in prison, it couldn't be possible for one to try to pick him up on his first day out. He went back over their conversation slowly, looking for a hint of the truth. For the first few minutes of the ride, they had talked about the prison, then they both had started speaking about their futures. After a few minutes of this, Prince attempted to change the conversation back to prison. He had quickly grown tired of talking about choppers. After twenty minutes of being told how to turn some kind of 1957 motorcycle into a chopper, he turned his back on the boy in disgust.

Here was a sonofabitch twenty-five years old, he thought, who believed all you had to do was get a fuckin' motorcycle and you had it made with all the bitches in the world. This bastard is queer as a three-dollar bill, Prince told himself coldly as his eyes turned a frosty gray. All this crap about motorcycles is a fake-out. He listened to the young man's voice go on and on until he finally decided to put an end to it.

Prince turned back around and stared the young man in the eyes. "How would you like to go to a motel when we get in the city?" Prince asked sharply.

Now that it was out in the open, Prince could see the man's desire. His hesitation was only a fake-out. "What? I mean, I don't do those kind of things," the young man replied uneasily. He was nervous, and his hands shook slightly as he lit a cigarette.

"Don't give me that shit," Prince answered harshly. "You been had before. I been trying to place you ever since we left the joint, and now I got you pegged. You used to be Eddie Townsend's woman in the joint. Don't bullshit me, 'cause it won't do you any good."

The young man shook his head. "That's not true," he said. "You really must have me mixed up with someone else."

"Bullshit!" Prince answered coldly. "What did you say your name was? Johnnie. Yeah, that's right. They used to call you Johnnie-may. I remember your little fine ass now."

Johnnie dropped his head, too frightened or ashamed to speak. He dropped his eyes, afraid to return Prince's stare.

Now that Prince had hit on the right track, he continued more ruthless than he needed to be. He wanted to browbeat the kid. "You know you been had, Johnnie boy, ain't you? So why you want to start acting like a man now? You didn't act like one while you was in the joint, did you?" He laughed harshly, the sound of his laughter filling the coach.

The young man's eyes searched Prince's face with desperation. He muttered brokenly, "They made me do it. They made me, I swear to God, they forced me to."

Beginning to tire of his little game, Prince said flatly, "I knew there wasn't no way for no fine young blond bitch like you to go behind the walls and come out without being touched up." His words beat at Johnnie like a tattoo. "Why did you come on with all that motorcycle crap when you sat down here anyway, boy? Was that your way of making me think you're bad or something?" Prince shook his head. "Well anyway, boy, you ain't got to worry about me. I don't use. I don't care if you're a punk or not. It don't make me any difference one way or the other."

Prince didn't even glance around when Johnnie got up and walked to the front of the coach. He bent down and spoke softly to the driver. At the next red light the driver pulled over. With his small shoe box clutched under his arm, Johnnie jumped from the bus.

Prince watched him depart, carrying the accumulation of junk that he had collected while in prison. As the bus pulled away, Johnnie started to wave, then caught himself and looked away. Prince smiled to himself as he stared at his own reflection in the window. His heavy eyebrows seemed to meet as he scowled out at the passing scenery.

In a few minutes the bus was parking in the terminal. Prince grabbed up his few belongings and pushed his way to the front. One woman complained loudly as he pushed his way between her and her children. He glanced back over his shoulder and caught her with an icicle glare. For years he had waited and thought of the day when he would return home. In none of his wildest dreams had he imagined being cursed out by some woman on his first day out. For a brief moment, some of the ruthlessness he kept concealed beneath a front of good humor revealed itself.

The woman glanced away from him quickly and busied herself with her four children. As she bent down to straighten out one of her kids' jackets, Prince got a glimpse of a full black bosom and his anger left.

It had been years since he had seen anything close to a woman's breasts, and the sight was rewarding enough to restore his anticipation. He continued on his way, elbowing a fat salesman out of his path as he hurried down the steps of the bus.

Once free from the pushing of the crowd of departing passengers, Prince stopped and allowed himself to breathe deeply, enjoying the taste of freedom. He stared around as if it were his first time in a big city. Any passerby would have taken him for a country boy on his first trip to a large city. His face lit up with a broad smile as he stared around at the milling crowd of people. His happiness was easy to see.

Suddenly he spotted a group of teenagers standing off to the side. People seemed to be giving them a lot of room. He waved and started to make his way in their direction. The leader of the group was standing out in front of them, posing, and scrutinizing the passengers with as much disgust in his stare as he could possibly manage.

A look of recognition appeared in Roman's eyes as he noticed Prince breaking through the crowd. "Over here, baby," he yelled loudly. The gang rushed forward to meet Prince. They crowded around him, banging him on his back roughly.

Prince shook the hands of the boys and girls surrounding him, then stepped over to where Roman stood all alone, watching the group of teenagers. As Prince held his hand out towards Roman, his mind went back into the past. It had been over four years since they had parted company. On that occasion they had been locked up in the bullpen in the city jail, each man sunk deep in his own thoughts. Both of them were aware that neither one of them would likely get out for a long time. They had been caught red-handed, with a car full of stolen television sets.

"Glad to see you, Prince," Roman said softly, his black eyes flashing with concealed amusement. He was medium in size, just under six feet, with slim, boyish shoulders. What caught the attention immediately was his keen features. His sharp nose was set off by the constant sneer on his tightly clenched lips.

In height, Prince towered over him. As the two men stared at each other, Prince held his hawklike eyes on Roman until the smaller man dropped his eyes. "Did you take care of everything like I told you to, Roman?" he asked quietly.

"Everything's been taken care of, Prince. We've just been waiting for you to get out so we can really stretch out."

Prince smiled slightly. Neither man spoke further until they left the station and entered the parking lot. One of the girls screamed sharply, then began to curse loudly.

"Goddamnit, Joan, can't you act like a young lady instead of some fuckin' whore who happened to be out for the night?" Roman yelled over his shoulder at the cursing woman. "You bitches can't go nowhere without cussing like goddamn fools."

"Prince," she called, "this sonofabitch here should be locked up in a goddamn cage somewhere." She pointed her finger at one of the members of the gang who was bringing up the rear.

Brute, the man she pointed out, grinned broadly. "Her ass is softer than cotton candy," he said loudly, to the amusement of his friends.

She stopped and pulled her sweater up, then removed a large knife from her bra. With a well-practiced, swift motion she pointed it towards Brute. "You put your fuckin' hands under my dress again, Brute, and I'll cut some of that fat off your lard-ass."

"Don't tell me a friendly little feel goin' cost Brute some of his ass?" one of the other members remarked, as they joked back and forth.

Joan, a tall, underweight, light-brown-skinned woman, kept up a steady flow of curse words until they reached the cars. She was pretending to be more angry than she actually was. Most of the men in the gang had had her at one time or another. What she really hoped to do was impress Prince. Knowing that he had just come home from prison, she hoped that he would end up spending the night with her. It would really be a feather in her cap if she could bed down with the big man. In her daydreams she could see herself as his number-one girl. She stared at his broad back as they stood beside the cars. She preferred tall black men, and Prince fit the bill perfectly. To her, he was the most handsome man she had ever seen.

Roman opened the door to a beat-up '62 Ford. "We ain't got but the two cars, baby, but I know things are going to change now that you're back home." He nodded towards the older car parked beside the Ford.

Joan forced her way into the car with Roman and

Prince, pushing ahead of the two other girls who were trying to get in with them.

"The rest of you broads get in the other car," Roman ordered, after three girls climbed into the backseat. Everyone wanted to be close to Prince, the women most of all.

"Damn, baby," Roman exclaimed, "it seems as if all the bitches got hot pants for you, Prince. When your old lady gets out, she's goin' have big fun kickin' these back-stabbing bitches in the ass."

"Yeah man, they ain't never had no cherry before, and they think this is a cherry they'll be getting," Prince replied and laughed. He tossed his arm over the front car seat.

Roman, sitting between Prince and the driver, moved slightly to avoid his arm. "I should have put one of the broads up front," he said.

Shortman, a muscular, narrow-faced man, drove expertly, taking most of the side streets to avoid the downtown traffic. He turned on Michigan Avenue and followed it on out until he reached the slums. It was swarming with Mexicans, Italians, and other foreigners. Shortman slowed down in the worst part of the slum quarters and parked in front of the Roost.

The Roost was the main clubhouse of the Rulers, the best organized and most vicious young gang of teenagers Detroit had ever encountered. After convicting Prince and sending him to the state penitentiary, the police department's vice squad had made the blunder of thinking they had broken up this highly organized gang. After months of crime, the rumors began to come in that Prince was still running the organization, even though it was from behind prison walls.

Prince, waving right and left, led the way down the cellar steps into the Roost. Music blasted out of the open door. The couches along the walls were occupied by young couples locked in each other's arms. At the end of the room, ten young men wearing identical outfits were sitting on soft stools beside a long bar watching a girl swing her hips along with the beat of the music.

One of the men at the bar spotted Prince weaving through the crowd. He rose, walked over to the wall, and hit the light switch, flooding the room with light. A low mutter of discontent welled up, only to die down as Prince put his hands on his hips.

"If there's anybody in here who's not a gang leader," he said loudly, "step outside until after this meeting is over." Some of the fellows sitting by the wall began to leave, followed by their girls. Two of the men sitting at the bar stood up.

Prince waved them down. "All the members of the Rulers stay," he ordered. He waited until the door closed behind the last lagging person.

"Okay," he began, looking out over the still crowded room, "now we can get down to business. I guess all of you already know just about what I'm going to say, but you're not really hep to what the rewards are going to be. I hope that by the end of this week each of you will have your own private car for business and pleasure alike. From here on nobody makes a move without the okay of their district leader." He stopped speaking to make sure everyone was paying attention. "Before, you guys were fighting over such small things as what turfs or blocks each gang ruled. That kid shit is out." His voice carried the conviction that he wouldn't accept any interference. "In case any of you studs out there with twenty or thirty punks in your gang should happen to think you're a little too strong to have to take orders, look around you."

Slowly, Prince lit a cigarette. "Each man and woman here has at least ten followers in his gang. For those of you who can't count too goddamn good, there's at least sixty people here, not counting the broads, so that would be about six hundred studs. Are there any comments?"

"Yeah," a tall redheaded boy said. "If we can't make a score when we want to, man, how in the hell are we going to make our pocket money?"

"Don't worry!" Prince replied. "After today all of you are on my payroll. Each gang leader will receive fifty dollars for every ten members in his or her club."

"Say man," one of the guys yelled from the back suspiciously, "just what the hell we going to have to do for this money?"

"Don't worry," Prince assured him, "you won't have to do no more than what you've been doing. The only difference is that this time you'll be organized."

"Well, Prince, what about us?" one of the girls asked.

"The same goes for the women. You won't be called on to do much more than you're already doing."

"Just what do you mean," a slim girl standing on the side asked, "by too much more?"

"From here on out," Prince answered abruptly, "anytime one of you girls becomes strung out on drugs, we'll find a whorehouse for you to work out of before some pimp gets his hands on you. Also, whenever you find out one of the debs in your gang is screwing everybody and everything, that's whorehouse material, and the organization wants to know about it." He stared coldly at the women until they looked away.

"Now," Prince said softly, "there's one more thing you had better know. From here on out, whenever you see someone wearing one of these outfits," he turned and pointed at the outfits his gang members wore, "you can spread the word that there is going to be a hit made somewhere in this city. Other than that," he added significantly, "you'll never see them wear anything but silks or sport clothes."

He waited until he was sure they understood what he meant, then continued. "We're going to start an organization that almost every one of us in this room will sooner or later take a part in. All of you are aware of the rising cry of the sixties—'Black is Beautiful.' Well, we are going to jump on the grandstand with all the rest of the organizations that use this as their rallying cry. Before the month is out, we'll be backing a group of our own called 'F.N.L.M.' Those letters will mean 'Freedom Now Liberation Movement.' Behind that organization we'll be able to manipulate a whole lot of squares that ordinarily wouldn't go along with our program."

Prince removed a handkerchief and wiped the sweat from his brow. "There's no reason now for me to explain to you why we need this front or what we are going to do with it. All you need to know is that one day soon we'll be behind it."

He dropped his cigarette on the floor and stepped on it. "I haven't run down everything yet, but whatever else I've got to say to you, I'll get in touch with you over the phone. Sometime tomorrow the person who will be giving you your orders will stop by each of your clubhouses and you can get your questions answered completely."

Turning his back on the crowd, Prince said wearily, "I want all the members of the Rulers to meet me at my apartment within the next hour."

He turned abruptly and started through the crowd, followed by some of his more intimate friends. Behind him, a murmur of subdued voices whispered back and forth. It was as though a giant had just left their presence.

3

PRINCE STOPPED ON the sidewalk, inhaled the fresh evening air, and let his eyes rove over a couple of the young miniskirted girls as they passed by. They flirted with him boldly, switching their firm hips. Prince continued to watch them as they walked down the street. He hoped the short skirts would stay in style for another two or three years.

"I'll be damn glad when Ruby gets out," Prince said sharply. The sight of the girls had aroused his desire more than he wanted to admit.

"They gave her ten days last week for driving without a goddamn license," Shortman replied quickly, not aware that it was about the hundredth time someone had told Prince the same thing that day.

"She should get out Friday, Prince, if she don't go and fuck up some kind of way," Roman added as he came up behind them.

Prince turned and glanced over his shoulder. Most of the members of the Rulers had come out of the club to form a crowd behind him.

"Well, let's get over to my place before we get picked up for loitering," Prince said and laughed pleasantly. Before the words were out of his mouth, young men and women began to pile into cars up and down the street. The elite of the gang scampered for seats in the car with Prince and Roman.

Brute, Fatdaddy, and Apeman used a flying wedge to monopolize the backseat. Danny, a vicious-natured young man in his early twenties, got in under the steering wheel.

Prince squeezed in the front seat between Roman and the driver, then twisted around. "What's been happening, Apeman? You look like you're trying to catch up with Fatdaddy in pounds," Prince said and grinned at the dark-skinned, hairy-armed man. Apeman, huge and brutal, grinned back. On his wide face the grin looked like a sneer, but it wasn't. He had been dedicated to Prince ever since grade school. There was a bond between them that Apeman held dear.

Among the three large men in the backseat of the car there was a constant challenge over which was the roughest. Fatdaddy might have exceeded the other two men by a few pounds, but when it came to viciousness, they were equal.

As the car moved away from the curb, Prince settled back in his seat and fell silent, thinking over some things that Roman had said to him earlier. He had spent four years planning, so Roman's objections were nothing new to him.

Prince spoke his thoughts out loud. "I didn't just start thinking about this thing, Roman. I been kicking your objections around, man, and I can see where you're coming from. I know when things get rough somebody is going to talk, but by the time we get finished with whoever does talk, it will be quite a while before somebody else tries to snitch on us again."

Danny gave a sharp bark that went for a laugh. "Yeah, baby, if there's one thing a nigger fears, it's the thought of someone sticking a blade between his shoulder blades." His harsh laughter sounded again. To people who did not know him, it would have been a chilling sound. But to these men who lived beside him, he was just being himself. They all knew that he was a dangerous man, but they considered themselves just as dangerous, if not more so.

Roman laughed. "What are you going to use to enforce this fear, Prince," he asked sardonically, "the fearsome three sitting in the backseat?"

Brute spoke up. "I don't see what's so goddamn funny about that, Roman. You ain't the big wheel in the show no more, so be cool. Prince might give us the go-ahead and you'll see just how efficient we can be."

"Sweet Jesus!" Danny exclaimed. "I wouldn't mind helping out the fearsome three if that's the case."

Roman frowned at Danny. "You better keep your lip buttoned, punk," he said, "or you might find yourself unable to close it."

With a casual gesture, Danny removed a straight razor from his pocket. "The only reason I've followed you up to now, Roman," he said, "is because I've had my orders from Prince; other than that, boy, I'd have stuck my razor in your ass long ago."

The roar of laughter from the backseat caused Prince to intervene. "Okay, killer," he said coldly, "all of you will get a chance to show your best hands before it's over, so be cool."

The group in the car fell silent. Prince reflected on his closest men as the silence held. Roman was a good man, smart, but he lacked the ruthlessness it took to rule such a gang. When they had been in the city jail waiting to go before the judge, it was Roman who had come up with the idea of flipping a coin to see who would take the weight. Prince lost, so he had pleaded guilty, stating that Roman had accepted a lift not knowing that the stuff in the backseat of the car was stolen.

It had been doubtful whether or not the judge believed him, but they realized that if Prince stuck with his testimony, it would have been impossible to convict Roman, so they released him.

"What's this black power bit, baby?" Danny asked suddenly.

"You should know as well as I do," Prince replied. "With all this black awareness coming to light, we're going to ride to the top of the hill on it. Once we get organized, we'll be able to function smoother and faster. I was in the joint when all that burning and looting jumped off in '67, but I'm here now. With the organization we're fixing to start, we'll be able to sway the people, start fights against the Man. Keep pounding it into the people's faces about police brutality, which there's always plenty of. All we got to do is keep it before the people's faces, and every time the pigs do something to a black man that stinks, we'll be on the case and cash in on it."

Danny hesitated briefly, then said, "I don't like the idea of frontin' our people off, Prince. They catch too much hell already without us stickin' a dick to them."

"We ain't goin' front them off, baby," Prince replied quickly. "If anything, we'll be showing them the way. Today is the year of the black man's revolution. Whenever a revolution jumps off, somebody gains, so why not us during this particular one?"

Danny pulled up and parked in front of a row of apartments that resembled modern motel cabins.

"This joint here," Roman began, "is the best...."

"Knock it off," Prince interrupted. "I don't want no excuses. If this is the pad you copped for me, it's too late now for you to start trying to clean up; you should have thought about it and handled it before I came home."

They entered the dinky apartment single file. Prince glanced around at the cheap furniture. The end tables were burned from cigarettes left carelessly around.

"Roman," Prince said softly, "do you really think all the members can fit into this death trap?"

Roman laughed self-consciously. "Yeah, man. They can all get in here. I would have gotten something bigger but, man, I just didn't have that kind of bread."

Cars began to pull up in front of the house, and the first group to arrive called back and forth to friends in other cars. The few girls mixed in the arriving crowds squealed loudly as they came in the door. Brute, standing beside the door, was giving everyone in a skirt a pinch on the rear.

The room quickly filled with whispering, laughing teenagers. Prince slowly raised his hand for silence. Immediately, the room became as quiet as a tomb.

Roman, watching, fought back his anger. After being the leader of this gang for over four years, he still couldn't command that kind of respect.

Prince pulled up a chair and propped his foot on it. "All right," he said quietly, "let's get down to business. I've already split up the districts that each of you will collect from. If any of you should run into any trouble trying to collect any money, contact Roman, Danny, or Chinaman."

"Collect the money from who?" Shortman asked, dumbfounded.

Prince glanced around the room, noticing the puzzlement on the faces staring at him. "Each of you will collect your money from the people that attended the meeting tonight at the club. They in turn will collect theirs from all the business places in their districts."

"That sounds like the old extortion bit, Prince. Ain't that just about been wore out?" one of the members asked.

"Yeah, it's been used time and time again, but not the way we are going to do it. There ain't enough pigs on the police force to handle all the trouble we goin' send their way. Sometime tomorrow, Brute, Apeman, Fatdaddy, and a few more of you will pay a surprise visit to most of the business places in the inner city. It don't make no difference if it's owned by black or white, they all get the same treatment."

Prince pulled a cigarette from his pack and tossed the empty package on the floor. "After you begin tearing the place up," he continued, "I'll send the gang from the neighborhood around to stop you. Now, if the storekeepers don't get the message, we'll just put his or her John Henry in our little black book and when we pay our next visit, they'll never forget it, 'cause we'll be playing for keeps."

"Damn, Prince," one of the members said, "they'll have so many policemen there when we go back, you won't be able to see past the goddamn uniforms."

"Don't worry about the cops," Prince replied. "They won't be able to stay there forever, and we got all the time in the world to wait. I got one of the best young lawyers in the country, so we won't have to worry about any bullshit arrests. As long as we got plenty money on hand bond won't be any problem. In case someone should take a fall, though, they won't have any worries. We'll take care of their people for them as long as they're away, plus put up a large nest-egg for them so that when they get out they'll have some nice money waiting."

Prince waited until he thought his words had sunk

in before continuing. "Our largest income will come
from dope and corn whiskey. I've already picked out
which of you will be my collectors on the drugs being
sold in this city. After tomorrow not a drop of horse,
dexies, or reefer will be sold in this town without us
getting some part of the money. All the dealers will
have to pay protection to operate."

Again he waited to see the effect of his words. "I
know a lot of you don't know anything about corn
whiskey," he said as he removed a small notebook
from his back pocket, "but it's big business." He
flipped open a page. "Last year alone, in Detroit, there
was over five million dollars made off of homemade
whiskey."

It was a staggering sum to most of the young people in the room. They whispered back and forth until
Prince interrupted. "That's right, five million, and here
in this city, it's a black man's racket. Now, what we're
going to do is monopolize the whiskey business. In
three months, if we can get big enough, not a drop of
whiskey will be sold unless we make it."

Roman stepped up beside Prince, a small notebook
in his hand. "So far, we got eight whiskey stills ready
to be put up, plus all the corn and sugar we'll need."
He ran his finger down the page. "We got six houses
rented, with the stills inside the house, waiting for
operators. As far as customers go, we got fifty customers who'll take from twenty gallons down to five
gallons from us at a time."

Prince nodded his head, pleased. "Homemade
whiskey brings ten dollars a gallon, or if the customer

buys over twenty gallons at a time, we'll let it go for eight dollars a gallon." Prince read from his notebook. "Shortman will be in charge of the operation. He will have four of you as his lieutenants. Each one of you will have a district. Your job will be to see that the members of whatever gangs are assigned to you produce enough whiskey to keep your side of the city up until we can get more stills in operation." Prince stopped and flipped a page. "Each still should be able to produce at least thirty gallons of whiskey a day. In seven days your quota will be no less than two hundred and ten gallons. At ten dollars a jug, you can add it up yourself and see how much money we'll be making."

Prince's plan had left the people in the apartment stunned. At first, his ideas had been unbelievable to most of them, but the longer he talked, the more the magnetism of his personality won them over.

"Tess," Prince said, speaking to a tall brown-skinned girl wearing a high natural, "I want you to take over absolute control of all the debs until Ruby is released. Your main job will be to see that most of the girls take at least two tricks a night someplace where the boys can roll them without too much trouble. Danny will be working right beside you, so you won't have too much to worry about. The main thing is that, as soon as your girls lead a trick off, you make damn sure that girl gets the hell out of that neighborhood."

"That," Danny said, "don't seem like too much of a job to me, just taking off some drunk chasing his hard around."

Prince laughed harshly. "Don't worry," he said, "there's more to it than that. We're going to need as many stolen cars as we can get for various jobs. Sometimes when we have a large job on hand, you'll have to detain some poor trick while the boys borrow his papers to go along with his car."

Danny laughed. His admiration for Prince was obvious. "Yeah, man, I can dig it now. Just keep the trick under wraps until after the sting goes off."

"That's right, baby," Prince replied. "You got the picture now. Whatever men you might need, just let me or Roman know, and you can have them."

Prince glanced around at all the astonished faces. The magnitude of his plans had jolted them out of their fantasies of toughness.

"I didn't bother telling you," Prince said, his voice harsh, "but it goes without saying: there's no such thing as quitting. You're all in it 'til the bitter end— if it should happen to go that way."

Preacher, a tall brown-skinned Negro wearing a midnight-black silk suit, stood up. He casually displayed the exquisite jewelry on his wrist with a swift motion of his left arm. "Prince," he began, "I'm having a little trouble down in the Hastings projects."

"Oh! And how is that?" Prince asked.

"Well, to begin with," Preacher said, "everybody here is hip to the stud I'm having trouble with. The stud thinks he's a little too big for this thing you're trying to work out of, Prince. He also told me to tell you not to come down in the projects with that shit of yours, 'cause he don't want to hear it."

Prince studied Preacher coldly. "How many guys does he have following him now?"

"I'd say he's got at least a hundred, if not more."

"If something happened to Dave, Preacher, who would fill his shoes?" Prince asked softly.

"That's easy," Preacher replied. "You're lookin' at him right now."

"Can I depend on that?" Prince asked softly.

"You can damn well depend on it, Prince. Once Dave is out of the way, I'll be the big dog down there."

The meaning of the conversation was not missed by anybody in the room. Everybody knew that Square Dave was big not only in his own neighborhood but anywhere in the city he chose to go.

A young girl with hair bleached bright blonde yelled, "Say, Prince, when are we going to start celebrating your homecoming?"

"Soon, honey, soon, but first we're going to take care of the business at hand," Prince said sharply. "So, first of all, I want all of you to put your Ruler outfits on, and then I want you to make sure you're seen all over the city."

"That means there's going to be trouble in the city, don't it, Prince?" Shortman asked.

"You hit the nail on the head, baby boy, that's just what it means," Prince replied. "Make sure all of you have an airtight alibi. Stay in the lights wherever you've taken a notion to be. Make sure you're seen, but make sure you can prove where you were at, too."

4

IN A PENTHOUSE ACROSS town in the heart of
the city, two identical blondes dressed in skintight
black satin dresses swayed to the beat of soft jazz. A
door opened from one of the bedrooms and a young
man stepped into the wall-to-wall carpeted living
room.

"Jesus Christ!" he exclaimed. "Don't tell me you
two are still doing that funky dance!" He stared at the
two women in disgust.

"Can we help it if we like to dance?" one of the
blondes replied. "Tony," the other woman called,
shaking her hips meaningfully, "come dance with
me."

Tony ran his hand through his wavy, jet-black hair, and stared at the woman who had spoken to him. "Why don't you go into the bedroom and wake Racehorse up if you want somebody to dance with you," he said without anger.

"Donna better not wake up my old man," the first blonde said loudly. She stared at her sister, daring her to go into the bedroom. A silence settled on the room as the sisters stared at each other. They had both come a long way from that small town in upper Michigan. Yet they stuck together, neither one trusting the other but true to each other in their own way.

"Don't worry," Donna answered, running her hands through Tony's hair. "I got me a pretty little wop to play with."

"You keep running your mouth," Tony said roughly, "and I'm going to slap some of the goddamn lipstick off you." He turned to the other woman. "Rhonda, why don't you go wake up your old man and find out whether or not he wants to go out for dinner or stay cooped up in this damn joint."

"Shit, Tony," Rhonda replied in a frightened voice, "you know how mad my old man is when I wake him up. Why don't *you* try waking him up?"

"Gee whiz, Rhonda," Donna yelled, "you act like you can't even talk to your man without him jumping all over you."

Rhonda drew a long breath, letting it out slowly. "I don't care what you say, I'm not about to go into that bedroom and wake Racehorse up. If you want to find out where he wants to eat, go ask him. But don't expect me to do it."

Donna laughed sharply. "I sure wouldn't let any man have me that frightened of him."

"Watch your mouth," Tony warned. He pushed her hand away from his hair.

"Well, I mean it," she continued. "If any man had me that afraid, I'd sure do something about it."

"Like what?" he asked, suddenly interested.

Not heeding the warning glitter in his eyes, Donna continued, "Well, for one thing, I wouldn't let no man whip me the way he beats her up. I don't care if I had to wait until he went to sleep, I'd fix his wagon."

Before the words were out of her mouth, Tony had slapped her viciously across the face. "Why do I always have to warn you about running off at the mouth, woman?"

Donna, holding the side of her face, screamed at him. "What the hell did you go and do that for? You sonofabitching bastard!"

Tony swung and knocked her down with one blow, then removed his belt and began to beat her. She squirmed on the floor, screaming in pain. "Please, baby, please! I didn't mean no harm!"

Rhonda, screaming, ran into the bedroom for Racehorse. A harsh, masculine voice responded. "Bitch, if you don't get the fuck out of here with all that goddamn noise, I'll get up from this bed and kick a mudhole in your ass."

Rhonda left the bedroom door open as she turned and fled back to the safety of the living room. In panic, she jumped on Tony's back in an attempt to save her sister from the brutal beating.

Without even a struggle, Tony pulled her from his back and pushed her onto the floor beside Donna. His face was twisted into a snarl as he swung the belt down on the two screaming women.

The shrieking of both women filled the apartment. The commotion finally produced what Rhonda was hoping for. Racehorse appeared in the doorway. He stared at the spectacle before him. There was a look of exasperation on his ebony face.

He looked as out of place as a housewife at a stag party as he stood in the doorway in a velvet black robe; around his head was the bright yellow scarf he wore when he slept to keep his processed hair in place. After observing the scene quietly for a few moments, he spoke up. "What the hell are you planning on doing, Tony, beat them until the police come up and pull you off of them?" He stared at the two women squirming on the floor, their skirts above their hips, red welts on their thighs from Tony's belt.

Tony was too absorbed in the beating to lay off immediately. With difficulty, he gained control of himself and stopped.

"If you can't get along with them fuckin' whores, Tony, why don't you just put their fuckin' asses out?" Racehorse asked coldly. His eyes were bleak as he stared from one woman to the other.

"I didn't do nothing, daddy," Rhonda yelled as she scrambled up from the floor. "Please, honey, it wasn't my fault," she pleaded. "I was just trying to stop him from beating up my sister. He looked as though he was trying to kill her, daddy."

Racehorse stared at her. "All you white whores are crazy," he said harshly. "You should know better than to interfere with their fights. Whatever they do, it don't have a damn thing to do with you, you understand that, bitch?"

"It won't happen again, daddy, I promise!" she cried, nodding her head vigorously. Her bright red lipstick was smeared and there was a dark mark over her right cheekbone. Her blonde hair fell down around her shoulders as she tossed her head back and stared up into Racehorse's face.

Racehorse gave her a slight shake. "You better make sure it don't, 'cause if it does, I'm puttin' your ass out."

Tony gave Donna a kick before he turned and spoke to the tall Negro. "I'm sorry, Race, about beatin' your woman, but the bitch put her ass in where it didn't belong."

Racehorse shrugged. "The bitch was wrong, so she got what she was lookin' for."

The phone began to ring and Racehorse walked into the bedroom. In a moment he reappeared in the doorway with the phone in his hand. "Tony," he said, "come in here for a second, will you?"

Tony followed him into the bedroom, closing the door silently.

"Don't worry," Racehorse spoke softly into the receiver. "We'll take care of everything."

He hung up the receiver and walked over to the dresser, pulling out the bottom drawer. After removing some shirts, he pulled out two snub-nosed thirty-eight automatics.

Racehorse examined the pistols carefully before speaking. "That was Prince, Tony. He's got a little job for us to do down in the projects on Hastings."

"Damn," Tony said lightly. "He didn't waste any time, did he?"

"That's right, baby. I figured he would get home sometime this week, but I sure didn't think we'd be going into action this fast."

Laying the guns on the dresser, Racehorse walked over to the closet. "We got to take an hour to get to Wilkins and Hastings. By then a hot car will be sitting there waiting for us. I told Prince that we didn't want a driver, Tony. I figured that you and I could handle it better by ourselves."

"I dig that," Tony answered. "The less people know about it, the better off we are."

Racehorse took his time dressing, putting on a black suit. He stuck both pistols down inside his belt and stopped in front of a floor-length mirror to make sure the guns didn't bulge. His dark brown eyes were unreadable as he studied himself closely. Sharp hawk-like features stared back at him from a cold black face.

"You about ready, Tony?" he asked, his voice trembling slightly with excitement over the coming job.

"Yeah, Race, I'm just about ready. I got to pick up my hardware from my room, then we can pull up."

Forty-five minutes later a black coupe pulled up in front of a crowded tenement. A tall black Negro leaned out of the car window and spoke to one of the kids playing on the steps.

"What the hell do you want with Square Dave?" a cocoa-brown-skinned girl asked from the top of the steps. She was about thirteen years old.

The young Italian driver spoke quietly to the sharp-faced Negro next to him. Before the Negro could answer, a tall, husky, pleasant-faced black man came out of the apartment building. The girl at the top of the steps nodded toward the car.

"Them guys want to see you, Dave," she said in a small voice.

Dave stopped for a moment, then started on down the steps. The motor of the black coupe leaped to life. People walking up and down the trash-littered street stopped in their tracks and looked around. From dilapidated ruins that still passed for houses, people peered out, smelling trouble with the built-in instinct of the oppressed.

A warning flashed through his mind, and Dave hesitated. Flames of death streaked from the car window as shot after shot found its mark. As Dave staggered the rest of the way down the steps, the coupe roared away from the curb, leaving behind the beginning of murder and the promise of terror.

A clamoring crowd gathered around the dying man as two young hoodlums, dressed alike, pushed their way out of the crowd. The sounds of the distant sirens grew stronger as the street lamp's glare fell across the sinister looking R's on the backs of the men's jackets.

5

THE STIFLING AFTERNOON heat began to carry foul odors up from the gutters and alleyways. Charles Morales, a detective from the homicide division, took a handkerchief from his pocket and wiped the sweat from his brow. To a stranger, he could have passed for a well-dressed insurance collector, but to the inhabitants of this neighborhood, this short, powerfully built middle-aged man, with his bullneck and bowed legs, spelled cop, with capital letters.

Morales, glancing up and down the street for his partner, missed none of the poverty with his piercing blue eyes. He saw his big, red-faced partner coming out of a tenement building, and from the way he walked he could tell his partner hadn't had any luck. Waving disconsolately, Detective Gazier went into the apartment building next to the one he had just left. Morales shook his head sadly. Gazier was a good policeman, but he was just too short-tempered. For homicide, a policeman had to have patience. He wondered again how long it would be before the captain finally transferred one of them to another partner. He wished he had a rookie to work with. That way, you didn't have any problems. A rookie would listen, whereas with an experienced man like Gazier, it was hard to do things any other way besides the ingrained way.

The two officers continued to work the street, each man taking a different side. Half an hour later they met up at the police car. "The hell with it!" Gazier said, his voice rising from anger he had held inside all day. "These goddamn people down here don't want no help, Morales."

The smaller officer watched his partner, half amused. "It's not that they don't want any help, Gazier, it's something else. I don't know why, but these people are scared."

Both officers stared at each other. Neither man liked the way the other worked. Gazier believed that Morales was too easygoing, while Morales believed just the opposite of his partner. The days of cops whipping the people they arrested were in the past. Morales knew that Gazier still believed the best way to get a confession out of someone was to kick the shit out of him. But in his heart he thought this was an outdated policy.

Gazier laughed sarcastically. "I don't know how in the hell that could have happened. This is black bottom, and these niggers down here don't fear God, let alone some person putting fear into them."

Morales said heatedly, "Listen, I went to that boy's house and talked to his mother and father. From what I could gather, the boy's sister was standing at the top of the steps when those punks killed Dave. She was going to talk last night until somebody got a note to her father, and that was the end of that."

"Did you get the note?" Gazier asked.

"No, her father burned it, but he said they threatened to kill the girl if she talked, and that if they couldn't reach her, any of the other nine kids would do just as well."

"That's a bunch of bull!" Grazier said. "These niggers are all alike; now they're trying to make a big play out of a damn gang killing."

Morales managed to control his temper. He wondered just how in the hell did he happen to get such a fool for a partner when there were so many bright young officers working out of their station.

"Well, Sherlock," Gazier said sarcastically, "where do we go from here?"

Some children were crossing in front of the car. Morales waited until they had reached the sidewalk before pulling away from the curb. "We'll take a quick run back to the station and have us a small chat with those two punks we picked up last night. I still don't think we'll get any more out of them, but we can give it a try."

"You're probably right, Morales, as long as you treat those punks like they're in church, you're never going to get anything out of them."

"Just what would you like to see me do?" Morales asked. "Should I start kickin' the shit out of every kid that comes in front of me the way you do, Gazier?"

Gazier replied hotly, "Maybe if you start using a little force, you might get better results."

Morales drove the car into the police garage and parked before he answered. "Being an officer of the law, Gazier, does not give you the right to abuse the rights of others, just because you're in the position to do it."

"Don't worry about me!" Gazier snapped as they walked up the steps and entered the station.

A policewoman came toward them pleading with a young brown-skinned teenager. "Listen, Ruby," she said, "I've talked with your mother and she said that she would be glad to have you back home."

The tall, chocolate-colored young woman stopped and spit deliberately at the policewoman's foot. Putting her hands on her hips, she leaned back on her high-heeled shoes in a provoking manner. Her lips curled in a sneer, and sparks leaped from her jet-black eyes. "I wouldn't sleep under the same roof with that drunken bitch if my life depended on it. I'd rather peddle ass for a quarter a throw before going back there."

"Now, Ruby," the policewoman cautioned, "if you leave with that attitude, you'll be back."

"You were with me in the probation office," Ruby said. "My probation ended when the back money I owed was paid up, so ya ain't got nothing on me. I'm as free as a goddamn bird, so keep your lecture for some girl who has to listen to it, 'cause I don't care to hear that shit." She turned and walked away.

The precinct elevator stopped in the lobby, depositing two young men in black leather jackets.

"Well," Gazier stated loudly. "There go our pigeons."

"I wonder," Morales said wearily, "how those boys got out so soon."

Chinaman, a tall, slender Puerto Rican, spotted Ruby going towards the door. "Say Ruby-do," he yelled, "don't tell me, baby, these squares are just cuttin' you loose."

Ruby stopped at the door. "Chinaman!" she yelled. "What the hell are you and Shortman doing down here in this craphouse?"

Chinaman grinned, showing a row of perfect white teeth. He sneered. "Some would-be detectives picked us up down in the bottom last night for loitering."

"For loitering," Ruby repeated loudly, before breaking up in laughter. "Not you!" she managed to say. "Maybe Shortman, but I can't imagine them pickin' you up on a charge like that."

Chinaman ran his hands through his thick black hair before answering. "I wish your man thought like that, baby," he said.

"I hope these bastards didn't give you no hard time, Ruby," Shortman jeered.

Detective Gazier stepped up and pushed the boys in their chests. "Listen, punks," he said, "I don't know how you got out so soon, but if you use one more swear word in here, I'll lock your goddamn asses up again, and that goes for all three of you."

"Big deal," Ruby said sarcastically. "Just listen to the big man, will you?"

"That goes double for you," Gazier snarled at her.

"Don't worry about these young people," a well-dressed young man said from behind Gazier. "I'll see to it that they leave quietly."

"And just who in the hell are you?" Gazier asked grimly as he wheeled around.

The young man stepped back and removed his glasses before replying. "I happen to be these young people's attorney. Is there anything strange about that?"

"Well, if that's the case," Gazier growled, "you better get them the hell out of my sight if you don't want them locked up again."

"Don't worry, officer," the lawyer replied, nodding his head for emphasis. "We are leaving now."

They walked out of the building in a tight little group. The lawyer, seeing a cab at the curb, waved it down. He smiled at the people with him, reached in his pocket and removed some white cards. "These have my home address on them. I would appreciate it if one of you would make sure that Mr. Nelson got one."

Ruby accepted the card. "I'll be sure to give it to Prince. Thanks a lot for what you did for me."

After the cab pulled away from the curb, Shortman swore. "Damn," he said, trying to read the card.

Ruby laughed. "That's pronounced Antares Noetzold; the 'Att.' stands for 'attorney.'"

It was twenty minutes before the cab reached its destination. The driver turned down a raw dirty street along the waterfront. The surrounding tenements and shacks were still overcrowded with kids of Mexican and Italian descent. Chinaman and his partner stepped out of the cab in front of a huge, grimy warehouse across from some deteriorating piers. Ruby leaned over the seat and gave the driver an address. As the cab shot away, she waved at the boys as they entered the warehouse door.

On the North End, Danny turned off of Davison and drove down Lumpin Street. He stopped in front of a dirty gray frame house. The front yard was barren of grass. There was an old tree that had died years ago; now it stood withered and shriveled like the rest of the neighborhood.

As Prince climbed out of the car alone, an alley cat leaped from the broken-down porch and ran towards the rear of the house. He stared at the familiar surroundings. A cold chill ran up his spine and he shook it off. He hadn't remembered it as quite this bad, but children seldom realize just how unpleasant their environment really is until they gain some experience to measure it by.

Prince knocked on the door lightly, then pushed the screen door open and stepped inside. The two elderly people sitting on the aging couch glanced up, surprised.

"Hi, Grandma, Grandpa," Prince said quietly as he walked across the tiny front room.

The old brown-skinned woman peered over her glasses. Her face was a thousand wrinkles, her head full of gray hair. As she stared over her glasses, her eyes twinkled. "Jeb, Jeb, will you look who's here. Why, I believe it's Melvin." She stared more closely. "It sure is. It's Mildred's boy, Melvin." She tried to hurry across the room to embrace him.

Prince held the thin old woman in his arms. He thought, wistfully, she don't weigh over a hundred pounds. All during his prison term, she had been one of the few people who had written to him. On rare occasions, she would send him a few dollars and say that God had allowed her to hit the number for a few dollars. She never had more than a few pennies to put on a number, so he knew when she sent him two or three dollars that she had given him most of the hit money. At those times he had almost felt like crying.

"Boy, when they let you out of that there jail?" his grandfather asked loudly.

Prince stared across his grandmother's shoulder at the old man who had given him so much hell in the past. He would have liked to take that frail neck in his hands and choke the life out of the evil little old man who had made their lives so unbearable.

He managed to smile. "Hi, Gramps, I got out this week."

The old man snorted. "Huh, well, we sure ain't got no room for you here. That's just what I told that white

man when he came around last year asking if we had
some place you could stay." He stared at Prince angrily. "My old age pension ain't enough to take care of
us, let alone you eatin' up everything in the house."

Prince fought back a sharp retort. "I don't want to
live with you, old man, if it was the only goddamn
house in the world. I just come out to say hello to
Grandma, that's all."

"Don't take on like that, Jeb," the old lady said
quickly. "We ain't seen Melvin in years."

"He just like his ma was. She wasn't no damn good
either. Sleepin' with everything in pants. I don't need
him or nothing like him in this house." The old man's
voice rose. "When they found his ma dead in that
room, the best thing that could have happened was for
him to have been dead too."

"Come on, son," the grandmother said, taking his
hand and leading him towards the kitchen. "Let's go
out back and talk a little. Don't pay no attention to
what Jeb says. He's always evil as hell about something."

Prince followed her, glaring angrily back at the older
man. When they reached the kitchen, he reached in
his pocket and gave her fifty dollars. "Here, Grandma,
I know that old sonofabitch don't give you no money."

She stared at the money as though he had a snake
in his hand. "Melvin, what I'm goin' do with all that
money? I ain't got nothin' to spend that much money
on." She thought about it for a minute, then asked,
"Where you get all that money, boy? You ain't did
nothing wrong, have you?"

Prince smiled at her. He had known she would ask something like that. "No honey," he said and gave her a little squeeze. "They got me a job before they let me out, you know how they do? So, I worked all this week and this is my check, part of it anyway. Here," he said and pushed the money towards her.

She removed ten dollars from the bills. "This is all I need, Melvin. I can get me a chew and play a few numbers with the rest."

Prince walked around her and went to the stove. He opened up one of the pots and dropped the rest of the money in on top of some cold grits. "Well, if you don't want it, just burn it up whenever you warm them grits up." He walked back past her, stopping to kiss her on the cheek.

"I heard them lids in there, mama," Jeb yelled. "You ain't feedin' that boy, is you?" He glared at Prince as Prince came out of the kitchen and stalked out of the house.

Danny started the car and remained silent as Prince slid beside him. They talked very little as they went back across town.

6

ROMAN PACED BACK and forth in the spacious bedroom of Prince's new apartment. Suddenly he stopped and stared down at Prince, who was lounging in a large Hollywood bed. "What the hell can you be thinking about, Prince? You been home just two fuckin' weeks and the whole city is in an uproar. We got to slow down, man. Already the cops done raided the Roost twice."

Ruby laughed unpleasantly. "Just listen to your second in command, Prince. He sounds like he's ready to give it all up, just because the pigs stopped by asking questions. And if he don't stop all that walkin' he's going to wear out our goddamn rug, baby."

Prince ran his hand through her long black hair. "We got damn near every pusher in this city paying us now, Roman. So what do you want us to do, let some tough bastard who thinks he can get away without paying us off the goddamn hook?"

"Listen, Prince," Roman replied, "this guy ain't no punk. He's been supplying the whole west side with drugs for the past three years."

Prince pushed Ruby away and stood up. He pointed his finger at Roman. "Now you listen, Roman, and you listen good, 'cause I ain't goin' say it but once. You take your ass down to the Roost and make sure everybody down there puts on his outfit. Then you make sure they spread out all over the city so that everybody will get the wire that there's going to be a hit made somewhere in this city today." Prince sat back on the bed, sure his point was well made.

Ruby rolled back into his arms while he talked. "After you're finished with that, Roman," he continued, "you call down to the warehouse and have the boys send over five hot cars for immediate use. Make the drivers put on their jackets. I want the whole city to know that the Rulers are making this hit."

"Okay," Roman finally agreed, "but just who in hell am I going to use to fill up those five cars? There ain't enough guys in the Rulers free."

"Don't worry," Prince answered, "I've taken care of all that. Send Little Larry up to Ed's Drive-in on the Heights. Steve and that gang of rich punks he runs with will fill up one of the cars."

"Ain't you kind of leery of those white kids,

Prince?" Ruby asked. "You know the first time something goes wrong, they'll tell everything they know."

"Don't worry, honey. For one thing, the people they deal with all have nicknames, plus most of the business is transacted over the phone. I'm keepin' them 'woods so far in the dark, they won't be able to bust each other."

He grinned up at Roman. "Oh, yeah, Roman, I almost forgot. I'm having fifty silk suits dropped off at the Roost tonight. The merchants on the west side sent them to us to show their appreciation for our protection, so keep somebody there to look out for them, baby."

Prince moved his arm down Ruby's back, causing the sheet to slide and leave her partly revealed. "Send two cars down to black bottom to pick up Preacher and some of his bunch," Prince ordered. He bent down and ran his tongue in and out of Ruby's mouth playfully. "Send the last two cars over to Danny," he directed, as he ran his tongue around her neck. He stopped suddenly and sat up in the bed. "Roman, are you sure this guy deals from the rear of Downbeat Poolroom?"

"He not only deals from there, Prince, but he pays guys to sit up in the front window and mash a button they got rigged up whenever trouble shows up."

"So you really think this Alfonso is going to fight, huh?" Prince asked softly.

"There ain't no doubt about that part of it," Roman replied. "Alfonso ain't scared."

Prince's voice turned harsh. "I don't give a damn if

he does fight, you just have those five carloads of punks piling out and into that damn poolroom at six o'clock sharp. You'll have Fatdaddy, Apeman, and Brute leading the way, so you shouldn't have any trouble. You tell them three big bastards that I said I want them to go after Alfonso personally. You make sure there ain't no mistakes, Roman, even if you have to be there yourself."

"I'll handle everything," Roman replied uneasily. A lot would depend on what happened this evening. Even his position of second in command.

Ruby lit a cigarette for Prince. "Tell Brute for me," she said, "to carve my initials in that punk's face." She laughed harshly.

"I'll tell him," Roman answered gloomily as he walked towards the door. Prince's laughter followed him into the hall as the door closed behind him.

Prince turned and crushed Ruby's lips to his own in a brutal embrace. Nothing else mattered for the next few minutes except her body, which cried for his caressing hands, though they hurt her in the urgency of his own aroused desire. She twisted and met him halfway. Small animal sounds escaped her as he gripped her tightly. Their breathing became harsh, the sounds loud in the spacious room. With an abrupt scream, she attempted to slip from his grip, but he held her tightly until he reached his peak. Her moans of joy changed to words of endearment as he slipped from her sweaty body and stretched out beside her.

The shrill sound of the phone ringing forced Prince to move. He picked up the receiver. "Yeah,

Shortman," he said as he recognized the voice. He listened silently for a minute.

"Listen, man, I put you on that job because I thought you could take care of it," Prince said sharply into the receiver. "If you got that many customers, man, you can't ignore them to take care of just one. I don't care if he does want two hundred gallons. What you got to do is split up whatever whiskey you got, Shortman. Make sure all your customers get some of it. Give the guy who wants the two hundred as much as you can, but be sure to take care of the rest of the people." Prince slammed the telephone down in disgust.

"I got to think for everybody," he sighed, then stretched out on the bed next to Ruby.

She rubbed her hand across his forehead. "Everything will work out all right, honey."

"Yeah, baby," he replied, sarcasm in his voice. "Just like it worked out when they brought me that goddamn broken-down baseball player. I asked everybody to try and find me a fuckin' man I could build an organization around, and what do they come up with?" He answered his own question. "A goddamn broken-down ballplayer."

"Okay, daddy, you ain't got to repeat yourself ten times before I get the message. The only thing I don't understand, Prince, is what was wrong with the ballplayer. He was black, intelligent, plus he'd been to college. What else could you ask for? That's what you wanted, someone with an education behind him."

Prince looked up at her as she rested on her elbows, staring at him curiously. He smiled briefly; she was so lovely that at times she almost took his breath away, with her delicate, cameo-perfect features. She returned his stare with widening brown eyes. He ran his hands over her honey-colored arms until she drew back with a laugh.

"Stop, baby. I know what that's leading up to. First, explain to me why you don't want the man."

He pulled her down and kissed her slowly. Ruby finally managed to slip out of his grip. "Is that the only answer you're going to give me?" she asked. Her voice sounded like music.

Prince laughed lightly. "Okay, baby." He released her arm. "Dig this now. First, if we used the ballplayer, we wouldn't be able to control him. The man has got too much pull, baby. He's still tight with different honkies that got pull. Just because he was in that car accident, it didn't break off his contacts. He still goes to functions that are slanted towards Whitey. He gets coverage in the newspaper whenever he opens his goddamn mouth on anything."

Prince held up his hand, cutting her off. "I know, it sounds like that's what we need, but it's not. If we could control him, yes, but since we can't, no. He gets ballplayer insurance for his accident, so he's not dependent on us for money. What we need, and what we must have, is an angry black man who needs cash money. Do you understand what I mean? If we get one dependent on us for money, we can manipulate him like we want to. Not like he wants to." His voice had risen slightly.

"Okay, I understand now," Ruby replied. "You

know, Prince, I was just thinking."

"I'll bet!" he replied quickly, rubbing her arm.

Ruby pulled away. "Prince, seriously now. Have you given it any thought about being the head leader of this thing you want to get started?" She rushed on before he could answer. "You're black, tall, too, so all you'd have to do would be to let your hair grow out longer. You know what I mean, let your natural get that look that Whitey thinks all militant brothers wear." She stopped hesitantly, then continued. "You can speak in front of a crowd of people, so that ain't no problem."

Prince gave her a startled glance, but it was instantly obliterated by his usual self-contained smile. "I've got too many things to take care of now, honey. Where in the fuck would I have time to organize and lead a black militant group?"

"You could do it if you tried," she replied wryly. "Just think a minute, Prince. If you were the leader, you would always have an excuse for whatever happened."

He had already thought about it. The only trouble now was how to accept the idea without giving her too much credit for coming up with it. He had thought about taking over the leadership of his future militant organization on many occasions but had denied himself the opportunity because of the work involved. Now, since Ruby had brought the matter up, he was sure he could work out a solution just by giving her a lot of the work.

"I'll tell you what, honey. I'll let you take care of

getting the hall rented for our first meeting, plus getting everybody lined up. If you have any trouble, come to me."

Ruby stared at him with respect as he began to outline her duties. She listened to him closely as he explained step by step what had to be done. As the beauty of his plan began to unfold, she had to force herself to smother a smile. Her ultimate interests were nearly as ambitious as his were, but as she listened to Prince she realized he was opening avenues she had never imagined possible.

As Roman left the apartment, his steps were uncertain and wavering. He realized that he would have to carry out Prince's plans, but of one thing he was sure. No matter what happened, he would not be one of the actual participants. There was no way for him to avoid the fact, he reasoned coldly, that he was frightened to death of some of Prince's grand schemes. There was logic in most of them, he admitted, but he wasn't fooled. Prince was using them all as though they were chess pieces. Roman was aware that he was not being used as a pawn, not even as a knight or rook. Prince had reserved a special slot for him. He was being used as the strong piece on the board, the dominating queen. Before the king could fall, which Prince considered himself, the queen would more than likely be toppled; but the fact still remained that the queen would be given up to protect the king.

Roman started the car up and drove slowly across town towards the warehouse. He glanced at his watch, still deep in thought. It would take a lot of arrests before either Prince or himself became vulnerable, but he decided to make sure there were more people than even Prince had thought about in front of him. He stopped at a phone booth. Better to deal through a phone, he decided, and called Preacher. In a matter of minutes he had given Preacher all the responsibility for the hit.

He walked back to the car, smoking nervously. He wondered what his woman was doing. He decided to drive over to his apartment and wait there for the results of the orders he had passed on. If everything went off as he planned, he had nothing to worry about. If it didn't, well, he'd worry about that when it came up. The idea of what had happened to Square Dave flashed through his mind and he shivered from a cold stab of fear.

The afternoon traffic was beginning to get heavy so he drove faster, almost running a red light. He forced himself to slow down. Dot would be there when he got home, he told himself, but he realized instantly that he didn't care if she was there or not. What he was terrified about was the thought of what he had set in motion.

The "big three," led by Brute, stepped out of a cab at the same instant as a black sedan with six young men in it pulled up to the curb. The evening sun shining in the distance seemed to grow dimmer before the formidable sight of the hoodlums. A young kid not yet in his teens stopped in front of Brute and said, "I got a bus on the phone to block up one end of this street. Which end?"

Fatdaddy grinned at the kid. "Take your boys and block up that end," he said and pointed his finger to the south. The kid waved his arm as he went down the street; in seconds he was joined by twenty more kids his age, all wearing turtleneck sweaters.

"I'll bet not one of them is thirteen yet," Fatdaddy said to no one in particular.

Apeman turned and motioned to the four cars that pulled up by the first one. "Take your bunch and block off that end, Danny, since that bunch of kids are handling the other end. You make sure don't no fuckin' cops get close enough until we get finished."

To the idle bystanders in front of the poolroom, the street seemed to erupt with tough hoodlums carrying chains and wearing brass knuckles. When the mass of thugs bore down on them, one tall, scrawny kid turned and ran into the poolroom, giving alarm to the toughs inside. The small group in the poolroom broke up and ran in different directions. Before they could fully arm themselves with pool sticks and cue balls, the mob, led by Apeman, burst through the front door. The lookout man stepped on the alarm buzzer a second before Apeman leaped the counter.

"You bastard you!" Apeman grunted. He swung and shattered the man's teeth with a handful of brass knuckles.

"Ough, ough, oh my God!" the lookout man screamed as he covered his bloody mouth with his hand. Another blow to the head sent him sprawling to the floor.

Brute and Fatdaddy fought their way to the back room, leaving in their wake a trail of human wreckage from the tire irons they swung.

Preacher fell to the floor from a blow from a cue stick. "Goddamnit!" he cursed, as he rolled under the nearest table.

The scrawny kid who had given the alarm was on the floor shrieking, his mouth a gaping, bloody hole. Apeman continued to rain blows upon him. In panic, the boy rolled under the nearest pool table, unfortunately right next to Preacher.

"Well, well," Preacher said as his hand flashed under his coat and came out with his razor. He lashed out, slashing the boy across the neck. Blood gushed from the open wound in the kid's neck, and a scream died in his throat.

At the sight of what he had done, panic welled up inside of Preacher. He stared out at the struggling forms, waiting for an opportunity to escape. He glanced at the dead kid once more.

Somewhere amid the fighting men, someone was weeping. The sound seemed to fill the small confines of the filthy poolroom. The cigar butts and cigarettes that littered the floor now had something to swim around in. Blood. Pools of it.

Preacher made his escape quickly, not bothering to look back.

Brute ran around the end pool table and kicked savagely against the back room door. Fatdaddy, running up, took the door off its hinges with a powerful lunge.

Leaping across Fatdaddy's prone figure, Brute stopped and looked around the empty room.

"Don't stand there lookin' stupid," Fatdaddy roared as he jumped to his feet. "Out the back way, damn it!"

"Goddamn, there's punks lying all over the place," Brute said, glancing over Fatdaddy's shoulder. "We got to get the fuck away from here," he cried in near panic.

"Just be cool," Fatdaddy cautioned, snatching a quick look at the poolroom. "All we got to do is walk out the back door and stroll down the alley. Make sure you wipe your prints off that tire iron, Brute."

Both men walked slowly down the alley until they reached a lot that had once been a building before the 1967 riots. They cut through the debris of the burned-out building and came out on the next street. Fatdaddy smiled as sirens sounded in the distance.

"Pull off that jacket," he ordered as a bus turned the corner. "Lay it across your arm like I got mine."

Brute followed directions. He climbed into the bus behind Fatdaddy and both men walked to the rear and sat down quietly.

Across town in an upstairs flat of a two-family house, Dot watched Roman as he paced up and down. Small specks of gold seemed to dance off of Roman's brown silk suit as the sunlight played tag across his back. "You're the walkingest damn man I've ever seen," Dot snapped.

He turned sharply to her. "Just shut your goddamn

mouth," he snarled, ignoring the tempting view of her crossed legs.

Roman went back to pacing, so Dot picked up a novel and glanced at it. But she couldn't keep her mind on the book. Something had happened, and for some reason Roman hadn't let her in on it. She knew he was upset about something, though. They had been living together for four years now, ever since she turned sixteen. She remembered her father's harsh laugh as she packed her few belongings and left. He had believed Roman would make her a prostitute, but she had known better. Ever since she could remember, her father's brutal advice had kept her aware of what was going on. "Always remember," he used to tell her, "that you're black and poor, so don't never do nothing that you ain't going to get paid for. I'd rather see you selling your ass than out free-fuckin', 'cause whenever you get knocked up, it's goin' be yours to take care of. Ain't no room in this house for no goddamn kids, so make sure you got some way to support yourself and whatever you bring into this world."

When her mother had tried to warn him about talking to her like that, he had snatched Dot by the arm and stared down into her young face. "That shit your mother is talkin' ain't nothin' but neck," he had said. "I'm your daddy and I love you, but I damn sure don't love you more than I love myself. If we was out in a desert somewhere and didn't have but one glass of water between us, who do you think would drink it, me or you?"

She had stared up into his face and realized just what he was trying to tell her. She smiled coldly to herself as she remembered his last warning. While she was packing, he had stepped into her small bedroom and said, "Always remember, Dot, what I been telling you. It's all right to love somebody, but don't never put nobody in front of you. Not even your Jesus, baby. If you do that, you'll have far less chances of being hurt by other people. Look out for you, girl, 'cause ain't nobody else in this world goin' ever love you the way you love yourself."

It had been good advice, she reasoned; ever since that day she had made sure she never did anything unless there was something in it for her. There had been many girls in the neighborhood better looking than her, but she had kept Roman at arm's length until he promised to send her to school if she became his girl. And it had all paid off.

Roman had thought he was getting the best of her, since it didn't cost anything to send her to high school, but when she enrolled in college, he had blown up once she told him what it was going to cost; but she stuck to her demand and he paid her tuition. Now she was in her second year, with more clothes to wear than any girl in her class. Yes, she had to admit, her father's warning had paid off. "Always remember, girl," he used to say, "you got something between your legs that sells better than cotton in New York."

A sharp rap at the door interrupted her thoughts. Roman rushed over and opened it. "Man, am I glad to see you," he said and stepped back, allowing Prince to come in, followed by Ruby and Brute. Fatdaddy closed the door after he entered and leaned against it.

"Pull that short-ass skirt down, Dot," Roman ordered as he noticed Brute leering openly.

Brute, sitting on the edge of his chair, spoke up. "Ah man, it don't hurt nothing to let me look. Do it, Dot?" he asked sharply and smiled at her as she grinned back.

Her small fox-like features had a sardonic sneer that revealed her opinion of men without her speaking it. She enjoyed their discomfort. At times she went out of her way to arouse Roman's anger with her teasing ways.

Ruby sat beside her, crossing her golden brown legs carelessly. "What's wrong, Roman?" she asked softly, her voice sounding like chimes.

"Why don't you check your woman, Prince? We got more important business than to have some goddamn women flashin' their ass," Roman said sharply.

Prince smiled. "I like to see my boys happy," he said quietly, "and besides, Brute seems to be really enjoying himself."

Roman snorted. "I don't know what you could be thinking about at a time like this, Prince. It's been all over the goddamn news all evening, man. Two of them guys died from that rumble and they're looking for at least one more to die before the night's over."

Dot sat up suddenly. She hadn't known they had been responsible for that fight. No wonder Roman had been on edge all evening, she thought.

"So who gives a fuck?" Fatdaddy said, returning

from the portable bar. He gave Prince a drink. "You been carrying on about them punks ever since you heard the news, Roman. What the hell do you want Prince to do, play God and bring them back?"

"Ruby," Prince said sharply, "take Dot in the bedroom and explain to her about the organization we're going to start up." His eyes warned Roman and Fatdaddy to shut up.

He waited until the door closed behind the two women. "Listen, Roman," he began, as though he were talking to a child. "These slums breed poverty and violence, baby. There's so much pain and ugliness in life that that little shit that happened today is only a small part of it. It takes a brutal struggle to get enough money to get above this, that's why them boys got killed today. That happens at times."

"But," Roman said sullenly, "for no reason; the guys didn't even get to Alfonso."

Prince shook his head. "You'd be surprised," he said quietly, "just how much those killings did help us. Right now, Alfonso is somewhere shaking like a leaf. He knows we meant to get his ass and not those kids. By now this rumble is being talked about all over the city, and if we get away with it, without gettin' our fingers burned, this city will be in the palm of my hand."

The pink princess phone rang softly. Fatdaddy bent down and picked up the receiver. He held it out to Prince. "Yeah, baby." Prince's voice was firm.

Chinaman, on the other end, spoke slowly. "Ain't but four of the studs who drove the wheels checked

in yet, Prince. Little Larry was handling the wheel for
them 'woods off the Heights and ain't showed up yet."

"You got any ideas what could have held him up?"
Prince asked sharply.

"Naw, man. The stud should have been back here
an hour ago. All he had to do was to drop them peck-
erwoods off and ditch that goddamn car."

"Maybe he ran into a little trouble," Prince sug-
gested slowly. He balled his fist up, then forced himself to relax.

"That's the way I got it figured," Chinaman replied.
"The stud must have got uptight, somehow."

Prince paused for a moment, his mind working
quickly. "How mellow is this stud?" he asked suspiciously. "It just might cost us our family jewels if this
stud ain't cool."

"The guy's real cool, Prince. Real cool. But if this
happens to be a first-degree beef, baby, I don't know
if he's that strong."

"Yeah, I'm hip," Prince answered coolly. "Dig this,
Chinaman, we better take a few precautions. You get
in touch with the four other studs that did the driving
and send them over to the hideout, one at a time, in
a cab. Have them dress up in suits and ties before
leaving their pads, dig. That way the fuzz might think
it's just another guy going out on a funky date and
leave them alone. After you send the last one over,
you get your ass over here with them until you hear
from me. We might as well put them in hibernation
until the heat is off."

"Okay," Chinaman answered, "but it's going to be

one hell of a party trying to keep them studs cooped up."

"Don't worry," Prince assured him, "Vicky's already over there and I'll be there myself with the rest of the gang."

Prince hung up and yelled for Ruby. When she appeared, he ordered, "I want you to call down to the Roost and have Tess pick up three more girls and head out to the hideout. Tell her to use the '67 Caddie." He hesitated before adding, "Oh yeah, tell her to stop by Billy's apartment and pick up two pounds of reefer to take along."

Brute whistled. "How about me and Fatdaddy going out there, too?"

"No, I'm going to let you and Fatdaddy shack up over at my apartment. Apeman, too, as soon as...."

"Prince?" Ruby called from the bedroom, interrupting him. "Tess didn't know Billy's address."

"Well what in the hell is stopping you from giving it to her?" he yelled angrily. "You been there enough times."

"I just know where the house is, honey; I don't know the address."

"I'll give it to her," Roman said, walking towards the bedroom.

The phone began to ring again. Brute stared around in astonishment. "What the hell!" he exclaimed stupidly after picking up the phone nearest him and hearing a buzz. The phone continued to ring loudly until Prince stepped behind the bar and picked up the receiver of a phone neatly concealed inside the cabinet. He nodded slightly twice, then smiled. "You say the kid sells papers around there, huh. Okay, you find out what peewee gang this kid runs with and reward them. Buy them some new leather jackets or something. Just make sure we give them something this week," he said and hung up.

Prince picked up a piece of paper he had written an address on. "Fatdaddy, you and Brute go in the bedroom with Roman; I'll call ya when I get finished." When the bedroom door closed behind them, Prince picked up the phone and dialed a number slowly.

A female voice answered on the other end. "Let me speak to Racehorse or Tony," he said quietly.

7

CAPTAIN MAHONEY STARED hard at his two lieutenants and said, "I should bust you both. You stand there and tell me you're on the case, but two kids have died already and possibly more before the night's over, and you don't even have a lead."

Lieutenant Gazier grinned sheepishly. "It's only been three hours, Captain; give us a little time."

Lieutenant Morales, well aware of his captain's tantrums, waited patiently for the storm to pass.

"Give you time? You've already wasted two weeks without getting a lead on that colored kid that got killed," Mahoney answered, pounding violently on his desk.

"This is a different situation," Gazier replied. "These kids were killed today in broad daylight with at least twenty punks in the rumble, so there's going to be a leak somewhere, you can bet on that."

Captain Mahoney walked around his desk. "What do you think about that, Morales?" he asked.

Morales stood and looked into the gray eyes of his superior officer. "I believe what Gazier said is true, Pat," Morales said softly. "Too many kids participated in the fight for it to stay quiet."

Mahoney paced up and down the room for a moment. "You can't add anything else to that, Morales?"

Morales slowly lit a cigarette before replying. "I don't think this was just another rumble."

Gazier asked impatiently, "Just why in the hell don't you think so?"

"There're too many little factors in this case, Gazier, that you and I have overlooked."

Mahoney raised his shaggy eyebrows. "What kind of factors?"

"First of all," Morales began, "we have completely ignored the fact that Alfonso Clemente was somewhere in that poolroom when the gang came in."

"So?" Gazier grunted. "What the hell does that prove?"

"Just shut up, Gazier," Mahoney said. "Maybe if you listen you can learn something for a change."

Morales smiled slightly. "Alfonso has dealt drugs from out of that poolroom for the past two years, and the way this thing adds up to me, these punks were after him, not the kids who got hurt."

"That could be," Gazier agreed grudgingly. "There might have been some bad dope sold somewhere down the line to bring this on."

"You got any more ideas along that line, Morales?" Captain Mahoney asked.

"Well, I stopped on my way in, Captain, and checked the records of all the kids who got hurt and especially the two that died, and I couldn't turn up anything special. The only two who associated with each other outside the poolroom were one of the kids we released earlier and the Davis boy, and you know he's expected to die."

"Did you get anything out of the one you released?" Gazier asked sharply.

"No," Morales replied slowly, only his voice revealing the emotion he felt about this case. "The kid didn't have the slightest idea why they were jumped." There was a slightly baffled sound in Morales' voice that the captain was not used to hearing.

"You should have let me handle the kid you had," Gazier stated scathingly. "I might have been able to shake something out of him."

Mahoney stopped Morales' angry reply. "You'd better start trying to think, Gazier, instead of using your muscles. You might just find yourself out of the homicide division." The captain returned to his desk and snapped on his intercom. "Casey," he yelled, "get me the records department, and tell them to send out a pickup on Alfonso Clemente."

A young officer knocked on the door and entered.

"I'm Daniels, sir," he said, "from the Third Precinct."

"Well, get on with it, man, you didn't come here just to introduce yourself," Mahoney growled. "Did you?"

"No sss-ir," he stammered. "This elderly gentleman stopped my partner and myself earlier this evening, and he told us he witnessed the fight down on the waterfront." The patrolman stopped and rubbed his forefinger nervously over his lip before continuing. "He says he saw three big guys with black leather jackets leading the crowd of hoodlums when they ran into the poolroom."

"Is that all?" Mahoney asked quickly.

"No," the officer answered, glancing down at his notebook. "He seems to think he saw a large 'R' on the back of a thug's jacket, but he wouldn't bet on it." The officer pushed back his hair before adding. "Oh yes, the old guy says the kids got out of five different cars, but he can't say what kind they were."

"Well," Gazier growled, "that's a hell of a lot of help."

Mahoney asked, "You think the old guy might be able to identify any of these punks?"

"He says be believes he can identify the three big guys if he ever sees them again."

Morales, standing silently on the side, came alive at this news. "Just where is this old guy you keep referring to, and who is he?"

The officer blushed before stammering a reply. "I'm sorry, sir, the gentleman's name is Anthony Gazura, and he resides at 10995 Twenty-eighth, near Jefferson

Avenue."

"Where is he now?" Gazier asked harshly.

"Why, we dropped him off at his house since he didn't have any more information."

"Were there many people watching when he accosted you on the street with this information?" Morales asked.

"No, it appeared to me as if everyone was afraid and was staying off the streets. There were only about six or seven young kids playing on the whole block, and the rest of the street was completely deserted."

Morales reflected for a moment. "Doesn't it strike you as being kind of queer that, if the parents were staying off the street, they would make their kids come in too?" Something kept nagging at his subconscious.

"What if the kids were from another neighborhood?" the captain said slowly.

Officer Daniels laughed. "These kids were only ten or eleven, maybe thirteen at the most. Hell, I could see them damn good; they were playing right around the car."

"What!" exclaimed Morales. "You mean to say one of those kids might have overhead what that old guy was saying to you?" It had come to him like a flash. The rumors he had been hearing about the consolidation of the various gangs in the city under the rule of one leader.

"I don't...."

Captain Mahoney interrupted the officer's reply, yelling into the intercom, "Casey, send out a call for the nearest car to pick up Anthony Gazura, at 10995

Twenty-eighth." He glanced at his pad. "It's near Jefferson Avenue."

"Have him send out a citywide pickup for any punks wearing leather jackets with an 'R' on the back," Morales said, then added, "believed to be members of a gang called the 'Rulers.'"

Mahoney wheeled around and pointed his finger at Gazier. "You get the hell off your rump and get over to the north side and raid the clubhouse of the Rulers. Don't come back without any arrests. You," he added, pointing at the officer, "you go with him and the boys; I'll fix it up with your sergeant." He turned to Morales, "I got a lot to talk to you about, so make yourself comfortable."

As soon as the door closed behind the department men, Morales asked quietly, "Do you think these kids are that organized, Captain?"

"I don't know, Jim," Mahoney answered. Now that the two men were alone, they spoke to each other with an intimacy born of long association. "I just hope we can get to these punks before there's some more needless killing."

In another part of town a police car pulled up in front of a gray building. "Well, this is the address," the driver said, nodding towards the storefront with curtains over the windows. "They try to make it look a little like a home, anyway," he said.

"Keep the motor running, Al, it shouldn't take but a few seconds to pick the old guy up," the Negro officer said to his white partner as he got out of the car.

Two young men standing in the shadows cursed quietly. "Looks like we got to the set a little late," Tony said, watching the policeman walk up to the front door.

Racehorse turned and stared at Tony. "Dig, poison," he said, "Prince said he wants this cat blowed before God can get the news, man. If you dig it for what it means, baby, too soon won't be soon enough."

Tony laughed unpleasantly. "Well, let's get it over with then, because like you say," he repeated emphatically, "too soon won't be soon enough."

The two men stepped out of the darkness and split up.

The officer called Al turned and glanced at the young Negro speaking to him through the car window. "I don't think there's any such address around here, buddy," he replied to Racehorse's question politely.

"I ain't your goddamn buddy," the young man snarled, then added, "You're just giving me that bullshit because you're scared I'm going to pick up some blue-eyed blonde."

Al pushed back his police cap and stared. Anger began to overrule his usually patient manner. A slight warning crept into his mind, only to be brushed back by instinct.

He stared up at the well-dressed, immaculately manicured Negro. There was something wrong here, he warned himself. The man's appearance didn't match his attitude. No matter how hard you tried, he thought, it was impossible to meet some of these bastards with friendliness. "Why, you smart-ass black bastard," Al began, stopping suddenly as the barrel of a thirty-eight blue-steel automatic appeared in the black man's hand.

"Go on and finish," Racehorse said sarcastically. "I'm gettin' my kicks behind it, man, so you might as well get yours, pig, while you can."

Al's eyes desperately searched Racehorse's face for some sign of alcohol or drug use. But the rigid face, hands, and cold eyes were absolutely unreadable. "Hold it, fellow," he began anxiously, "I didn't mean no harm."

A door slammed, and Al relaxed with a sigh as he saw his partner coming towards the car with a small, gray-haired old man in tow. For a brief moment he appreciated the soundness of the plan to put a black man and a white man in each police car. Then panic gripped him as he saw a small figure come out of the shadows and advance on the two men from behind.

The street erupted with sound as fire leaped from both automatics in Tony's hands. As shot after shot exploded, a fresh burst of laughter came from Racehorse. It flashed through Al's mind in that instant that he would die, and he thought of the young wife he was leaving behind. This was something that happened to other policemen, something he had always thought could never happen to him. It was only reflex that made him grab for the pistol at his side.

Racehorse watched with diabolical joy the officer's feeble effort before pushing his gun into Al's face at point-blank range. Racehorse pulled the trigger, and as each shot went off, he yelled, "Die, honkie, die!"

An old lady ran out from the storefront, calling her husband's name over and over again. She dropped to her knees beside his body and picked up his head as blood gushed from the skull.

Racehorse, wheeling around from the car, pulled the trigger again, just as the old lady leaned over to wipe blood from her husband's mouth. The bullet caught her square in the head, killing her instantly. Racehorse turned and fled up the street after Tony. Reaching the car, he jumped in just as Tony pulled away from the curb.

"Why you gotta go and kill the old lady?" Tony asked incredulously.

"Why the old lady? Why, *paisan*, the same reason we killed the old man, baby, the same reason." Racehorse laughed loudly, relieving some of the tension.

"You're nuts, man," Tony stated flatly. "I mean you're really off your goddamn rocker," he said and burst out laughing. In a moment, both killers were struggling with the insane laughter of relief.

As the sounds of the speeding car died away, people began to open their doors and step out on the street. The sight of all the bodies sprawled around sent fear through them. Some of the men sent their women and children back into the house.

At the same time, on the west side, Lieutenant Gazier, with two police cars behind him, pulled up in front of the Rulers' clubhouse, the Roost. A young kid jumped down the steps as soon as he saw the police piling out of the cars. The teenagers standing at the bottom of the stairs, smoking reefer, fled through the opened door of the club as the kids pushed down among them yelling, "Raid!"

One young girl standing on the sidewalk was too slow to grasp the situation. She turned and ran down the steps with two policemen on her heels. Just as she reached the bottom step, the heavy door of the club-house slammed shut and she heard the sickening sound of a bolt being shoved in place.

Inside the clubhouse, young girls and boys were leaving in an orderly manner, following the orders of Shortman. His woman, Doris, small and dark-skinned with shrewd brown eyes, came to join him.

"Don't you think we ought to make it, daddy?" she asked. "The man is goin' kick the door off the hinges in another minute."

As the last of the kids hurried out the back door and window, he grabbed her arm and led her through the door. "Damn, daddy, you mean the man ain't hep to this back door action?"

"I guess not, baby," he replied hurrying her along. "They ain't busted nobody going out this way yet."

From the front of the Roost came a mighty crash as the police caved in the front door. Gazier rushed into the empty club with two patrolmen beside him. He stopped and glanced around in astonishment. "What the hell?" he said.

A young, well-dressed detective pointed to an open door leading to the rear. "Bring me that young tramp we picked up," Gazier ordered.

A big, red-faced officer half dragged, half carried a young Spanish girl forward. The closer she got the louder her Spanish cries became.

"Oh hell," Gazier said disgustedly. "Put her in my car and I'll take her downtown." Turning to another plainclothesman he said, "Tom, you and the boys check this place out and see if you can find any drugs or weapons." He turned and walked outside to his car, ignoring the girl sitting in the backseat between two officers.

A uniformed officer came hurrying out. "Sir," he began, "they had ropes in the alley to get over that large fence that made it a dead end. In fact, they even had a couple of broken-down stepladders. It looks like they been planning on a bust coming their way."

Gazier grunted and started up the car. He turned on the siren and sped towards police headquarters.

Captain Mahoney and Lieutenant Morales walked out of the interrogation room and stepped into the captain's office.

"Well, Mahoney," Morales said, "looks like that kid has knocked around with the law before this."

"He has," Mahoney answered. "But as soon as I get him out of the jurisdiction of the juvenile authorities, we'll get some of that smartness out of him."

"Well, I'll be damned!" Morales said hotly. "Just listen to this! Larry Drualle, age sixteen, arrested twenty-two times, found guilty on six misdemeanors, beat four felonies, given probation twice." Morales slammed the folder down on the desk. "No damn

wonder these kids go out and commit every crime in
the book. The killing part about all this is that the only
thing we can pin on this kid right now, if he sticks to
his story, is car theft."

"Car theft, hell," Mahoney roared. "We got that
punk in there, the one with the leather jacket on, by
his goddamn balls, Morales, and I'm going to make
him confess to being at that goddamned rumble."

A fat officer with captain's bars on his shoulders
stepped into the office. He removed a handkerchief
from his pocket and wiped the sweat from his brow.
"That kid," he began, "still sticks to his story about
dropping his girlfriend off up on the Heights before
he was picked up."

Captain Mahoney asked sharply, "Did he give you
the girl's name?"

"No, not yet. He still says he doesn't want to involve
the girl because of her parents."

"Yeah, I'll bet," Mahoney mumbled.

"Captain Harris, do you believe Drualle is lying?"
Morales asked slowly.

"Of course he's lying, but what can I do about it?"
Harris replied, then hesitated for a moment to stuff
his handkerchief back into his pocket. "That's one of
the reasons I rushed over here, Pat. I want you and
your boys to go easy on this kid. I guess you know
he's not but sixteen, so that makes him a juvenile
untouchable."

Mahoney swore angrily. "Untouchable or not,
Harris, we got that punk this time, and I'm going to
see to it that he gets his just rewards."

Morales picked up the kid's record from the desk and pointed the folder at the fat officer. "Captain Harris, do you know that any adult with such a lengthy police record would still be doing time instead of being allowed to run the streets?"

"Not only do I know it," Harris said, turning on Morales angrily, "but the kids are acutely aware of what can and cannot be done to discipline them. This is the first time *you've* come in contact with Larry, but it's not mine. I've been having problems with him ever since he turned the ripe age of eleven."

Morales slammed the folder down on the desk. "If he's been in your hair that long, why in the hell do you come in here telling us to take it easy on this kid?"

"Morales is right, Harris," Mahoney said. "Even if the kid was only ten years old, I would try to nail his hide to the door. This is nothing but a murder case, and that punk kid is up to his neck in it."

"With that kid's statement, we can blow the lid off of this thing," Morales said quietly.

"That's the damn truth, if you never tell it again," Harris replied. He removed the handkerchief from his pocket and nervously began to wipe his face. "You say you're going to blow the lid off this case—you're going to blow the lid off this town, Mahoney, if you don't take it easy."

"Well, that just might happen then, because I'm going to bust this case, and I'm not going to baby no damn punk while doing it," Mahoney replied sharply.

Harris turned to Morales. "I've been following the

incidents that have happened in the last few weeks, Morales, rather closely, and I believe I have something that might help you guys."

"My boys have been working night and day on these killings, Harris," Mahoney said impatiently, "but if you've got something you think we might want to know, I'll be glad to hear it."

"I'll start from the beginning, Pat, so you and Morales will be able to understand just what makes me think along these lines." Harris lit a cigarette and sat on the edge of the desk before continuing. "It's not Larry you really want. He's just one of the young suckers being used. The man you want I met about ten years ago. He was just big enough to see the top of his head over my desk when they brought Melvin Walker, nicknamed 'Prince' by the kids on the block, into my office. I was working my way up through the ranks at that time and they had me in charge of all the kids who plague this department. You know, the aggressively delinquent, the goddamn ones nobody can seem to do anything with."

The name Melvin Walker had rung a bell with Morales. "Captain Harris," he asked, "was Prince potentially violent, assaultive, or in need of special mental treatment at that time?"

"No," Harris replied. "That's the surprising thing about him. I knew he was capable of violence, but even then he had the ability to influence older boys. Prince had a very high IQ. He was what I call an operator—the leader who involves weak and dull boys in vice."

Mahoney asked impatiently, "Isn't there another approach to this problem instead of waiting until my department gets up to its neck in wholesale murder?"

"Don't worry, Mahoney," Harris replied, the sarcasm in his voice obvious. "I'm not going to start telling you about our shortage of young bureau officers, or the need for beds in our too few youth homes, or about the trouble we run into with mentally ill children."

Mahoney tossed his hands in the air in mock alarm. "Okay, okay," he roared, "just stick to Prince, that's enough for right now!"

"Well, I'll make this as brief as possible," Harris went on. "Since Prince's release a few weeks ago, it's appalling to see how much influence he has over the rest of the gangs in this city. I don't know how many boys Prince has following him, but from what I can get out of some of the kids, I would estimate he has at least four hundred or more kids in his organization.

There was a sudden knock, and a tall blond officer entered. He crossed the room and handed Captain Mahoney a folded piece of paper. "What the hell is the matter now?" Mahoney said as he unfolded the paper. His face turned a deathly white as he read the note. With a violent motion, he grabbed the phone just as it rang. He listened quietly, then slumped down in his chair and let the note slip from his hand.

Morales leaned forward and picked up the message. After a quick glance at the note, he reached over and took the receiver out of Mahoney's fingers. "Hello, hello," the sergeant yelled on the other end of the line.

"Yes?" Morales inquired swiftly.

"Here's Lieutenant Gazier now," the sergeant said. "He knows the full details."

"Put him on the line then!" Morales barked. "Gazier, what's the truth in this goddamn report?"

"It's the truth," Gazier answered, his voice shaking with anger. "It's all true, I was upstairs when the report came in. Mahoney's son and his partner were both killed, along with the witness they were directed to pick up. Oh yeah," he added, as if an afterthought, "they killed the witness's wife, too."

Morales remained silent for a few seconds. When he spoke, his voice was icy cold. "I'm taking Pat home, Gazier, so while I'm gone I want you to have a pickup put out for every dope addict, prostitute, and stool pigeon in this city. I want so much heat put on this city, Gazier, that when they see a cop coming they'll drop their heads in fear. If you put it on them right, somebody somewhere will talk, quick."

After hanging up, Morales spoke to the officer who had brought the note. "You take that kid downstairs and have him moved from precinct to precinct."

"For how long?" the officer asked.

"For just as long as it takes to keep him from making bond," Morales answered sharply.

"Just a minute, Lieutenant," Captain Harris said. "Don't you think you're overstepping your authority slightly?"

"No, Captain, I don't. Two officers were killed tonight, and I mean to have an arrest made on the killer as soon as possible. And I mean to see that kid as soon as I get through taking Captain Mahoney home."

A little while later Morales drove Mahoney across town to his home in the suburbs. Morales glanced over at Mahoney sitting slumped in his seat. A wave of anger ran through him, as pity for his old friend jammed in his throat. It had just been a little over a year ago that Mahoney's wife passed away; since then, he had been staying with his son and his son's bride of six months. After driving for half an hour, he turned onto a clean block with red brick houses on both sides of the street. He remembered how it had been only a few months ago on his way to the captain's house to be best man at his son's wedding. Now it was all in the past.

"Pat," he said softly, "I'll go in the house and break the news to your daughter-in-law."

"Do that for me, Jim," Pat answered, before his voice broke.

8

DARKNESS WAS JUST beginning to fall as the car weaved its way through the evening traffic. Prince rolled his window up in the rear. "It feels like winter the way that wind is shootin' through the goddamn car."

Ruby, driving, pushed a button and all the windows in the Cadillac shot up. The woman next to her on the front seat glanced out the window nervously.

"I still think you should call it off, Prince," Chinaman stated firmly beside him. "The police been raiding every goddamn place they can think of trying to find you."

"That's tough shit, baby," Prince replied as he stared

out the window. "We can't stay in hidin' forever just 'cause the fuckin' man got a hard on. They done busted everybody they can get their hands on, so it won't make no difference if they take us down. Our lawyer will be out front tonight, so if something do go down, he'll be right on the case."

"Ain't no such thing as if something should go down," Ruby said loudly. "When they see you and Chinaman up on that stage tonight, there's goin' be some arrests made."

Chinaman's girlfriend, Blanca Rodrigues, spoke up for the first time. "What else can they do but show up?" Her dark eyes flashed as she glared over the seat at her man. "All the Chicanos in the city will be here tonight to listen to what Chinaman has to say. It's too late now to think of not showing up."

Prince grinned at the attractive young Mexican. He wished silently that he had a hundred more dedicated women in the new organization like Blanca. "You see what I been telling you, Chinaman? With your woman's brains and your nerve, this thing can't miss." Prince laughed lightly, then continued. "What she says makes sense. If I don't show up tonight, you think I'll ever be able to get the crowd back again that we have waitin' on us?"

"Do you really think this thing you're going to try and work out of, Prince, is really worth it? It ain't no doubt about us going to jail sometime tonight," Chinaman asked.

"You better goddamn well know it, man. You can see what's happening in the streets now. Every time one of the Rulers hits the streets, they get their ass tossed in jail. So what we got to do is go legit. That way we can get the heat off our backs, and help out our people." Prince smiled in the darkness of the car. It amused him to speak of what he was going to do for others, when he knew his only concern was filling his own pocket.

"Man, I ain't never talked in front of a lot of people before," Chinaman said nervously. "I hope when I get out on that fuckin' stage I don't blow it."

"Don't let it worry you, baby," Prince replied smoothly. "I ain't never talked in front of nobody either, but I'm going to take care of business tonight."

Ruby pulled up and parked. It was impossible to get in front of the hall they had rented since it was swarming with teenagers and young adults.

"Mon, look at the crowd!" Chinaman exclaimed excitedly. "You don't think there'll be any trouble, do you, Prince?"

Prince studied the crowd. "Naw, baby. We got all the mean studs workin' the doors. There better not be any shit."

"We better go in the alley way, Daddy," Ruby said as they climbed out of the car. "If the man is waiting on you, at least you'll be able to get your speech across before the bust goes down."

Danny opened the stage door for them. "Man, I didn't think you'd show up. Police are all over the place. I been hiding back here so they wouldn't puke me off."

Prince walked over to the curtain and peeped out.

"Baby, the place is packed. I didn't think ya'll would pull that many people here."

Ruby smiled and looked out at the house. "Honey, when you got as many people spreading the word as we got, it can't be no other way. Dot furnished free babysitters for whatever women needed them, so we got all the A.D.C. mothers in the neighborhood, besides their boyfriends."

"Don't forget the free entertainment after the speeches," Blanca said.

The emcee came backstage and spoke to Prince. "Whenever you're ready, baby, we can get this thing started."

Prince nodded, then smoothed out his midnight-blue silk suit. He reached up nervously to pat his high natural. Ruby walked up and put her arms through his. Behind him, Chinaman and Blanca did the same thing. As the announcer began to introduce them over the loudspeaker, he could feel his stomach tighten. Butterflies began to buzz inside his stomach, but he told himself this was the big step and walked out on the stage with his woman to the sound of loud applause.

Ruby released his arm as they reached center stage and walked over to the chairs that were placed behind the microphone. Chinaman led his woman over to the seats, too.

Prince held the microphone in his hand and stared out at the crowd. For a moment he didn't have the slightest idea of what he would say, then the words began to flow.

"Brothers," he began, raising his hands high. The gesture was met with loud acclaim. "I've asked you to meet me here and listen to what I've got to say because it's a deep need for it." He stopped and surveyed the crowd. He could see his men and women working the aisles and this gave him the confidence he had been lacking. "All of you know without me telling you about it how the police have been running through our neighborhoods cracking heads lately. Not that they didn't do it before, but for the past two weeks they done got beside themselves."

Officer Morales held Gazier's arm. "Not yet," he cautioned. "I want to hear just what our smart little boy has to say."

Prince waited until the scattering of applause died down. "For some reason," he continued, "the white man thinks all blacks are crazy or something. He must if he thinks we're going to keep acceptin' this bullshit." He waited until a few mutters of anger quieted down. "For some reason, whitey likes to tell black folks about what their problems is, but they can't never see what the fuck their own hangup is all about. Now dig this," he said, raising his hands for silence. "Whitey is always talkin' about how our trouble comes from having our women rule our homes. Can you dig that shit? While the truth of the goddamn thing is that the white suburban families are matriarchal, ruled by the goddamn woman even though the man is in the home every fuckin' day."

The young brothers in the audience were on their feet, stomping and screaming. Again Morales had to restrain his partner from rushing towards the stage.

"With your help out there, brothers and sisters," Prince continued, "we can work towards the elimination of inferior education in our neighborhood schools, put an end to discrimination in some of these lilywhite bars and clubs that dot our inner city."

Again he raised his hands for silence. "The time has come when we have to stop lookin' for help from whitey. How you can sincerely believe that a white man, born and raised in a society diseased with institutionalized racism, can ever bring himself to really help someone of the black race is beyond me." He stopped briefly, then shouted, "We got to get off our knees. All that goddamn praying ain't where it's at, and singing 'We Will Overcome' ain't about nothin' either. Damn all that singin' and prayin', what we need is some businesses for us to operate."

The crowd was on its feet again, moved by the agitators sprinkled through the building.

With the patience of a good showman, Prince waited until the murmur had quieted before continuing. "After this is over, some of the kids are going to pass through the crowd signing up members for our organization. As most of you know, we call ourselves F.N.L.M., which means Freedom Now Liberation Movement. Now, if some of you out there are worried about us puttin' the bite to you, forget it, don't cost but twenty-five cents to join, and I might add," he added for emphasis, "if you think of yourself as a black brother, you'll join."

Again, his agitators started a round of applause.

"If some of you are worried about what you'd have to do, don't worry. We are not demanding the supreme price that some of our black brothers are unselfishly giving in the fight for justice in this racist country. No, we ask nothing like what the Panthers' members experience, so there's no danger involved. No more than what the average black man has to experience in everyday life. Sometimes you may be called upon to help picket government people who won't get their goddamn foot off our necks, plus some of the black politicians who seem to think all they need to do for us is to get their goddamn pictures in the fuckin' paper."

He stopped long enough to regain his breath. "This bullshit practice of comparing black and white statistics without taking into account difference in opportunities emanating from the reality of white institutional racism, by our administrators, the ones we put in office, is going to come to a flying halt." He smiled slightly and thanked his lucky stars for the many political arguments he had had in prison. "I for one am sick of whitey accepting the black man as an equal only when it relates to crime statistics." He raised his voice and shouted, "Fuck that shit! We want and we can get equality now. Not next year or the year after, but now."

This time the crowd came to its feet screaming without help from the agitators. Ruby stared at Prince's broad back; there was a look of surprise in her eyes.

"I want you to remember one thing, friends," Prince said quietly, so that many in the audience had to lean forward to catch his words. "This goes for all you mellow Chicanos out there, too, who whitey likes to display as a grinning Tio Taco on TV and in the movies. Just dig this and judge for yourself if I'm fakin'. When you went to school and they had you packed in on top of each other, did they ever tell you anything about any black heroes or Mexican ones? Hell no! Every one of you out there remembers what went down in them schoolrooms, so why should we allow our young brothers and sisters or, for some of you young parents out there, your kids to run head on into an academic death just because they got a bunch of antagonistic honkies teaching in our school system? We ain't got to stand still for that shit, not in this day and age. When the kids come home and pull your coat about some of that bullshit some of them teachers work out of, tell us. By the time we get through raising hell around the school, it won't be no room left for no funny-actin' teacher. We done passed the stage when we hope to get respect from whitey. We know how he feels about us, so what the fuck, whitey is just foolin' himself if he thinks the feeling ain't returned. In fact, I personally know a lot of brothers who hold whitey in such contempt that they're ready to get down out in the streets with him if it's necessary. If it's complete genocide for the black man, it don't make them no difference."

He hesitated for a minute, waiting for the clapping to finish. "I ain't got nothing else to really say, but I'd like for as many of you out there to join with us, so that we black brothers and sisters can work togeth-

er to stamp out this vicious racism that surrounds us."
Prince nodded his head and slowly backed towards
the chairs as the crowd erupted in loud applause.

Chinaman patted Prince on the back and grabbed
his hand. "Mon," he said, excited, "I didn't know you
could speak like that."

The emcee announced Dorothy Washington, and
Roman's woman Dot came onto the stage. She spoke
for ten minutes on the role the women should play in
the ghetto. She emphasized unity among them, playing up the possibilities of their roles in the future. She
stepped down to loud applause, while Prince stared at
her in wonder. She had spoken sharply and intelli-
gently. At times she had made acerbic remarks about
the loud manner of many of the young men in the
audience but had capped it off nicely so that no one
got angry.

The emcee then announced Chinaman, to loud clapping from the Latin part of the crowd. He addressed
them as "brothers of color," bringing applause from
everyone.

Chinaman, sweat running down his tan cheeks,
gained confidence from the applause. His words
lashed out with a sincerity that a close observer would
have missed in Prince's rambling speech.

His closing words brought the crowd to their feet.
"Unite, men of color," he screamed, *"unite!"* As he
stepped back from the microphone the crowd went
into a frenzy. They stamped, shouted, and screamed
at the tops of their voices.

From the wings of the theater, Morales led a group

of police on the stage. They snatched Chinaman and put handcuffs on him. Prince held out his hands towards the officers. At sight of the police, the crowd went wild. Men rushed the stage, cursing loudly. Seeing the beginning of a riot, Prince forced his way towards the microphone.

He shouted, "Brothers, be cool! This ain't nothin'! Ya'll just be cool and enjoy the dance." He lowered his voice as he noticed some of the crowd taking his advice. "You know how these things work, don't you? I'll be back before the dance is over, if you will just be cool."

"That's what you think," Gazier growled in his ear as he pulled him away from the microphone.

Roman, sitting in the crowd, ducked down in his seat, unnoticed by anyone except his woman. Dot glanced at him curiously. This was a new Roman to her. In the past, he had never been afraid of the police. If she could have read his mind, she would have been pleased at her man's actions. Roman was thinking of the future and he didn't have any intention of being under the police axe when it started to fall. He believed in his heart that Prince was responsible for the death of the two police officers. If that was the case, he reasoned, the police would never let up until they made an arrest.

The arresting officers pushed Prince and Chinaman into the alley where a police car was waiting. "Get in, you black sons of bitches," Gazier growled, kicking both men as they scrambled into the rear of the car.

"You peckerwood bastard," Ruby screamed in his

face, as she attempted to climb in the car with her man.

One of the men pulled her out of the car, scratching and kicking. "Goddamnit, keep it up, girl, and we'll take your ass right on down with them," he yelled. She kicked him on the leg and his palm shot up and he slapped her twice across the face.

A loud roar came from a group of kids as they raced down the alley. Some of them stopped behind garbage cans and began to throw wine bottles and whatever else they could get their hands on.

"Get this car out of here," Morales ordered from the top of the stairs. "We'll follow as soon as possible."

"Get a car, get a car!" Ruby screamed frantically at the kids near the end of the alley. "Oh my God," she moaned, "they goin' kill my man. I just know it, they goin' kill him!"

Morales turned and raced back through the dance hall, followed closely by other policemen. The place was in bedlam. The back of the theater was packed with kids trying to find out what had happened. There was an ugly murmur from the crowd at the sight of the policemen, but they allowed the officers to pass.

Blanca gripped the microphone and yelled into it. "Let them go!" she screamed. "It won't help nobody if you fight the law!" She was joined on the stage by Ruby, her hair disarranged from the scuffle. The women alternated at the microphone, begging the crowd to remain cool.

Dot made her way to the stage. She grabbed the microphone and stared insolently at the crowd. She put her hands on her hips and stood wide-legged. Her voice lashed out.

"It ain't about that," she screamed. "It ain't about that bullshit ya workin' out of." People in the audience stopped and stared up at her.

"You think jumpin' on the man now will help Prince and Chinaman?" she asked, sarcasm dripping from her words. "If you really want to help, let's all go down to the police station and picket the goddamn place."

The gang members in the audience took up the cry. Soon there was a rush for the exits as group after group of kids got together for rides.

Morales waited in the lobby until he had heard her last words. "That ain't good for us," he said to his men and rushed them towards the front door. The sidewalk was jammed with kids. They had to push their way through the sea of black faces to reach their police cars. When they reached theirs, they found the windows knocked out. The crowd scattered at their approach.

"Don't worry about it now," Morales told his infuriated officers. "We've got more important things to worry about. Let's get moving; we've got to get back to the station before those kids get there."

Even as the detectives piled into the car, other police cars were pulling away, packed with arrested teenagers. As they made their way through the crowded street, other police cars began to arrive on the scene.

At about the same time, Gazier's driver pulled up in the basement of the precinct station. "All right you

two, get the hell out of there," he growled at Prince
and Chinaman.

Both men struggled awkwardly to climb out of the
car. The handcuffs were now behind their backs. As
Prince climbed out of the car, Gazier struck him in
the face. He sprawled out on the concrete floor full-
length. One of the other officers kicked him in the
side.

"Get up, nigger," the policeman yelled at him.
"Where's all your fancy talk now, nigger?" He kicked
him again as Prince struggled to his feet.

Chinaman received the same kind of treatment as
he got out of the car. The policemen followed them
up the stairs into the station, beating them across the
shoulders with their nightsticks. The beating stopped
when they came in sight of the desk sergeant.

Both men were quickly fingerprinted, then they
were made to leave all their personal belongings at
the desk. Each time an officer wanted one of them,
they were roughly handled. The only time the handcuffs had been removed was during the fingerprint-
ing.

"What about these cuffs?" Prince asked. "We ain't
done a goddamn thing, so it ain't no need to treat us
as though we just robbed a fuckin' bank."

"Just keep your mouth quiet," the desk sergeant
warned. "Unless you want something that will really
give you something to bitch about."

"I want you to see that that tall black boy gets a
chance to enjoy our penthouse while he's here,"
Gazier remarked offhandedly. "Yes sirree, I think

that's just what our little smart nigger needs. A taste of the hole will really bring him to an awakening."

The thin, rednecked turnkey smiled and glanced towards the desk sergeant for confirmation. The sergeant had the last word on where prisoners would be locked up.

The sergeant nodded his head in agreement with the order. "You take that old Jones boy out of the hole and tell him for me, if he starts some more shit back in the bullpen I'll personally come back there and kick all the black off his ass."

Chinaman glanced quickly at Prince. Deep down inside he was thankful as hell that it wasn't him being put in the hole. He knew that there was room for only one person in the hole at a time, so he would miss that part of the ride.

The policemen standing around the lobby stared at the two men coldly as they were led past. Most of the officers knew only that these were the men arrested for trying to start an organization that would fight for Negro rights. Many of them were angered by the thought of men they considered their inferiors trying to be equal.

After following the turnkey down a narrow corridor, the two prisoners stopped and waited patiently as he unlocked a large steel door.

"You find you an empty cell and lock up," the turnkey ordered. "I'll come back a little later and remove those cuffs if you don't make no noise." He slammed the door behind Chinaman.

Prince stared around curiously as they went down

some steps and entered the basement. The smell of musty clothes and unflushed toilets filled his nostrils as they stopped in front of a small steel door.

The turnkey opened the door and stepped back. An elderly Negro with gray hair and an alcoholic's grin came out. "Thank you, cap'n," he said with a toothless grin.

"We lettin' you out now, boy, but you start that goddamn hollering again, I'll bring you back down here and throw the fuckin' key away. You understand me, boy?"

The old man nodded his head. Saliva ran out of his mouth, and the left side of his face was covered with stale vomit. His clothes had the odor of urine; it appeared as if someone had used him as a receptacle for body waste.

The turnkey held his nose. "You go stand on the goddamn steps, boy, and don't leave. I'll take you back up when I finish here." He turned to Prince. "Boy, you get them clothes off, hear?"

Prince held up his handcuffed hands. "How the fuck you expect me to do it, peckerwood? I know you don't think I'm Houdini!"

The guard removed his blackjack from his back pocket. "You listen, nigger, and listen good. You don't need your goddamn hands loose to wiggle out of them pants. Now, I want to see your black ass shining, quick like, you understand?"

Prince stared at him bitterly. There was an urge to hurt, to kill, inside of him, but he knew it was useless to rebel. He forced a smile as he removed the pants. "It's your turn now, Whitey, so make the most of it," he said with all the pride a half-naked man can muster.

"Get the hell in there," the guard snarled, pushing Prince inside the filthy cell. "Don't you be worrying too much, boy, about when your turn is coming. We been handlin' niggers for a lot of years now, so don't you begin to think we don't know how to keep you in your goddamn place."

"You dirty white peckerwood bastard," Prince cursed through the small bars in the door of the cell.

The turnkey only laughed and started towards the stairway. "You remember them names, boy, when you start yelling your black head off for me to come and remove them cuffs, hear?" His laughter drifted back down the stairs.

Prince turned and examined his temporary home. It was just barely long enough for him to lie down in. He paced it off. After six steps, he had to turn around. If it hadn't been for the handcuffs, he could have stretched out his arms and touched both walls at the same time. There was a hole in the corner of the cell that was used for a toilet. Beside it sat a wooden bucket, half full of body waste, giving off a smell so offensive that Prince almost puked. The bed he was supposed to sleep on consisted of eight long iron rails held up by smaller pieces of steel. He sat on the edge of the steel bed, as far away from the obnoxious smells as he could get. It wasn't the first time, Prince thought coldly, that they had tried to break him with this kid shit.

Upstairs, the desk sergeant spoke to Gazier. "Your partner just called in. He says to get prepared for some pickets. It seems that those punks you brought in have a lot of friends worryin' about them."

Gazier sneered and turned to the red-faced, hefty officer who had displayed so much cruelty to the prisoners. "Come on, Fred, let's do some ridin'. Maybe we can be lucky and find some more of these mean-ass Rulers."

Both men laughed and left the station.

9

SHORTMAN PARKED IN front of a small, unpaint-ed, two-family flat. "Donnie," he said to the husky, light-skinned man next to him, "can you reach that wrench on the backseat?"

The young man reached over and picked up the wrench. He climbed out of the car and met Shortman on the sidewalk. Both men were extremely well dressed. Earlier in the evening they had attended the meeting at the auditorium where Prince had been arrested; now they were worried about the conse-quences. Both men were known to the police as mem-bers of the Rulers.

"You know, Shortman," Donnie began, "it's kind of lucky Prince assigned us to this whiskey thing, man.

We ain't up on none of that bullshit that been goin' down, so even if we do get picked up, ain't nothin' the man can hold us on."

They continued up the walk and onto the porch of the unpainted house. The screen door was latched, but they could see people sitting inside in the dark. The sound of loud music filled the air. From where they stood, they could see someone dancing in the living room.

Shortman knocked harder on the screen. "Come on, goddamn it," he yelled through the open doorway.

A girl who looked no older than a teenybopper came to the door. She stared out at Shortman and Donnie, then opened the door quickly.

"Hi there, Shortman. Earl, Earl, here's the big fellows, man," she yelled over her shoulder.

Someone cut on a light as the two men came in the room. The house was scantily furnished. There were two couches along the wall, while the dining room was empty except for a portable record player sitting on the floor. Beside it was a stack of 45 records and two empty album covers. Two young girls were dancing together, or rather practicing dance steps, in the dining room.

Earl came hurrying into the room. "Hey man, I didn't expect you. I been upstairs taking care of business." He was tall and thin and looked to be still in his teens. His voice was shrill.

Shortman nodded in his direction and continued towards the stairway, Donnie following closely. Earl and his partner waited until the two older men had passed, then fell in behind them. They went up the stairs single file. As soon as they reached the top, the first thing that hit them was the heat. Donnie blinked, dense smoke in his eyes. Both men continued until they reached the front room of the upstairs apartment. Sitting in the middle of the room was a whiskey still made out of two fifty-gallon barrels welded together. From the top of it a copper pipe ran across the room to the cooler. The specially made gas range under the cooker was blazing; fire leaped out and around it, climbing up halfway on the outside of the connected barrels.

Shortman coughed. "Goddamn thing puts out enough smoke to kill a motherfucker," he cursed and made his way towards one of the bedrooms. Donnie and the other two boys followed him closely.

Inside the bedroom, barrels were lined up against the walls all around the room. The drums each contained cracked corn mixed with wheat rye, plus fifty pounds of sugar.

Shortman stuck his finger down in one drum and sucked the stuff off the tip. "It's bitter. Maybe you better run this batch off tomorrow, Earl." He didn't wait for a reply. He walked out and entered the bedroom next to the first one. Again he tasted the fermenting enzyme. He removed a large paddle and dipped down into the barrel. He stirred the corn and rye and sugar up until he was sure it was well mixed.

"You been stirring this shit up regularly, Earl?" He tasted the juice again. "Damn, this bastard is still sweet. Stir them up one more time tomorrow, Earl, then leave them alone. You should be cookin' this batch off some time this weekend."

Donnie stepped over and tasted the stuff. "I like this shit just like it is," he said to an empty room, Shortman and the two boys having walked out. He followed them to the whiskey still and watched closely as Shortman took a small glass and tasted the harsh liquid as it came out of the cooler.

"Goddamn, this is some strong shit!" Shortman exclaimed, almost blowing smoke from his mouth.

"How many gallons you think you goin' run off tonight?" Donnie asked, watching his partner cough with amusement.

"I don't know." Earl hesitated. "Somewhere between fourteen or sixteen, I hope. This is the second run today, Donnie. Blue picked up fifteen gallons this afternoon, so I figure our output for today to be somewhere in the neighborhood of thirty."

"That ain't too bad," Donnie answered quietly. He removed his bankroll and peeled off six tens. "That should be enough money for you to take care of your young girls with." He held the money out towards Earl.

Earl sneered. "Don't no bitch get no money out of me."

Shortman laughed and led the way back downstairs. They sat around for a few minutes talking shit, then Shortman stood up. "I got to be running, Donnie," he said as soon as Donnie had finished dancing with one of the girls. "What you goin' do, man, stay here with that jailbait or pull up?"

"Huh, I don't see no jailbait," the teenybopper said from the dance floor. She pushed out her chest, trying to make her tits seem larger.

Shortman laughed and started for the door. "Tell me if it has any hair on it," he said and went out.

The young girl cursed. Donnie grinned and beckoned her with his finger. She came over and sat down in his lap. He put his hand under her short skirt and felt around.

"Is it hairy enough for you?" she asked, staring into his brownish-green eyes.

"Don't let the hair part worry you, honey," he replied slowly, pulling her down on the couch.

She stared up at him. "Donnie, do you know you got green eyes?" she asked huskily. She spread her legs slightly as he let himself down on her.

"In a few minutes, baby, you won't care what color they are," he said, then added, "Can you dig it?"

She smiled slightly in the dim room, then pressed her young, firm body against him. "You goin' make me your woman?" she asked naively.

Once outside, Shortman took his time about leaving. He started the car up and drove slowly away. For a minute he was tempted to go back and try out one of the teenyboppers. Young girls didn't have much fascination for him, though, so he changed his mind and went on. He decided to run by the Roost and see if there was some strange cunt hanging around. He pressed down on the gas pedal and started back across town for the west side.

Gazier and his partner passed the Roost again. It was deserted, so they continued on. The kids were getting leery of the place, so they stayed away in droves. Both officers had just about given up hope of finding one of the big fish when Shortman drove past.

"There goes one of the black bastards now," Gazier yelled. His partner made a sharp U-turn, running up and over the curb in his haste to catch the other car.

Shortman spotted the police car at the same time they saw him. He pressed down on the gas pedal as he saw them make their U-turn. His small Ford leaped away from the larger car for a minute, but he wasn't fooled. Shortman realized it was just a matter of time before the police car caught up with him. He searched the deserted street desperately for a place to park so he could run. Not finding a good place, he raced for the Roost. If he could make the front door, it would be a sanctuary.

"That bastard's looking for some place to jump out and run," the driver said harshly to his lieutenant.

Gazier laughed coldly. "I hope that black sonofabitch does run." He removed his pistol from his shoulder holster.

His partner, Fred, smiled. "You goin' pop the bastard?" he asked with unwarranted glee. Both men laughed as though there was something amusing about killing a black man.

Shortman watched the car in the mirror as it gained on him. He slammed on the brakes and pulled to the curb in front of the Roost. Before the car had completely come to a stop, he was out of it and running for the basement stairway, not knowing that one of the officers was already aiming his pistol at his back. He hadn't reached the steps when the first shot hit him. He felt a heavy blow between his shoulder blades and stumbled. Before he could regain his stride, another blow smashed into him and he fell to his knees. The sound of shots rang in his ears. He attempted to struggle to his feet, using the building in front of him for support. He turned to glare at his pursuers. As he feebly attempted to get to his feet, he realized that he was going to die.

Shortman stared at the approaching white men out of fading eyes. "You killed me," he murmured and fell over on his face.

Slowly the neighborhood came to life. Before the officers reached the body, people were starting to come towards the scene of the crime. In a matter of minutes, the street was packed with angry bystanders. Many of them had witnessed the murder from their doorsteps.

"All right, break this shit up. You ain't at no goddamn movie," Gazier barked at the crowd. He moved through the people as though herding cows. They slowly backed up at his approach. He made his way to the car and called in, reporting the incident as an act of a criminal trying to escape.

In less than five minutes, more police cars began to arrive on the scene. The police went to work dispersing the crowd. When a few people tried to explain that they were witnesses, the police ran them off.

One of the officers cursed at a stubborn woman,

"We don't need no fuckin' nigger witnesses. We got two officers who saw everything that happened."

The crowd began to back up away from the police. There was an ugly murmur running through the group, but cool heads prevailed. In dingy cold-water flats, crowded apartments, well-furnished rooms, black people were busy. Already the news was spreading to every black area in the city. It was the hottest news in the ghetto. Another black man had been shot down by the police in cold blood. Black people everywhere gritted their teeth angrily at cruising police cars. Before the night would pass, six different police cars would be fired on by infuriated black men who had never even heard of Shortman.

As soon as the news reached them, Preacher and Roman got busy. Roman moved with the experience of a professional executive. He got on the phone and stayed there for an hour, ordering his gang members to get off the streets.

Preacher, on the other hand, moved with the anger of an aroused militant. His gang moved into the streets, burning and looting with a passion. Before the night ended, ten members of his personal organization were arrested.

When the news reached Ruby in front of the police station, she quickly got in touch with Dot and Blanca. They discussed the matter for a few minutes, then moved through the crowd preaching calmness and fortitude. They began slowly to send people home, breaking up the crowd of pickets.

Inside the police station, Morales paced up and

down angrily. "That's just about all we needed," he muttered. "They couldn't have picked a better time to kill someone. Here we are being picketed by over a hundred people, and those ignorant bastards go out and kill one of the fuckin' leaders of the crowd."

"Hey, Lieutenant," one of the officers called from the window. "Looks like they're breaking up out there."

Morales glanced out the window. "Well, I don't know why, but I'm sure in the hell glad to see them go home."

"You think maybe they haven't heard the news yet, Lieutenant?" a young officer asked politely.

"No, no, that wouldn't be the reason. I'd be willing to bet they know about the shooting. That kind of thing has a way of traveling through the black communities like wildfire. Whoever's in command out there must be trying to keep down trouble. I'm glad they have some kind of common sense."

Watching the crowd break up in silence, he noticed Prince's lawyer talking to Ruby and idly wondered what they were talking about. The lawyer was probably telling her not to worry. There was no doubt in anyone's mind about whether or not they could hold Prince. As soon as the courts opened in the morning, they would have to release him. That trumped-up murder charge they had pulled him in on would never stand up in front of a judge. But it gave them a chance to put the pressure on Prince's ass.

Lieutenant Gazier and Fred came through the back of the station and stopped at the desk. Both men were grinning. The other white officers standing around the station patted them on the back as though they were heroes, cracking jokes with them. Two colored policemen turned away, shamefaced, and pretended they didn't hear what was going on.

Morales walked up to his partner. "What happened out there, Gazier? We heard about it over the radio but nothing really concrete on the shoot-out."

Gazier stared at his partner for a minute. "Me and Fred was just cruising around, you know, when we got this call about some black male stickin' up a grocery store and escaping in a dark-colored Ford. Well, about this time this guy speeds past us, so we took it for granted that this was the holdup man. When we turned around, the bastard speeded up. We didn't know who was in the car, but when he stopped in front of that clubhouse, I had an idea he was one of the members. You know them bastards are capable of doing anything. Well anyway, when the guy jumps out and starts to run, I yelled halt, but he didn't slow down one bit, so I shot over his head the first time. Then when he didn't slow down, I let him have it."

"If it happened like that," Morales began, "we shouldn't have any trouble."

"What the hell do you mean, if it happened like that? I just told you how it happened," Gazier snarled.

"We been getting angry calls from people who said they saw it different," Morales said coldly.

"What you mean by that, Morales? You got me and Fred's word on it. What you goin' do, take a bunch of black bastards' word over your fellow officers'?"

He glared at his partner.

Morales made a gesture of impatience and walked away. "It's not up to me," he said over his shoulder. "We'll leave it up to the captain to handle."

Across town, Donnie walked out of the bedroom with his shorts on. His brow was pulled tight with worry. It was hard for his mind to accept the fact that Shortman was dead. The man had just left the house, and now he was lying in the morgue. It didn't matter that he had been given Shortman's former position. He enjoyed the prospect of being the big wheel now, but it carried a lot of responsibility he didn't really want. He had told the kids in the house about Shortman's death, and they were subdued from the shock. Donnie could feel the significance of it. He had a feeling that this was a turning point in his life and that he would now become one of the major actors on the stage. But he hoped not. He preferred the background. His shrewdness told him this was the best place.

Donnie's teenybopper came out of the bedroom behind him. She was wearing a half-slip with nothing on top but her bra. Her eyes followed him as he paced up and down. Something inside of her wanted to reach out and take him in her arms and console him with a woman's love, but she managed to stifle the emotion. He would resent it, she realized. She leaned against the wall and watched him patiently until he came over and took her hand and led her back into the bedroom.

Donnie knew with certainty that his promotion

sealed his doom. He was caught in a box. There was no way out. He had seven brothers and sisters at home who were dependent on him. He had to make big money to survive. Between him and his mother, the house was run. His younger brother was preparing for college, so he knew he needed the promotion. He made up his mind to make as much money as possible before the end came. Maybe that way there would be enough money to hold his people until one of the younger ones could help.

From where Prince sat in his cell, there was no way to tell when morning came. He waited patiently until a trusty showed up and pushed a hard roll under his door.

The trusty pushed his face against the bars and whispered, "Hey, Prince, that you in there?"

Prince got up and peeped through the small bars. "Yeah, man, it's me. What's the deal?"

"Your partner Chinaman told me to tell you that Shortman got hit. He says the cops killed him last night." The trusty's voice was low, just carrying through the bars.

Prince was stunned. "What, man, you sure he knows what he's talkin' about?"

"Yeah, man, I'm sure. That's all the rollers are talking about upstairs. Seems like this stud Shortman got blasted running from the scene of a holdup."

"That's bullshit," Prince cursed, then asked, "Who shot him, man? Can you get the name of the pig that shot him?"

"That ain't no problem, baby. It was Lieutenant Gazier, man."

Prince returned to his seat, not even bothering to answer. His heart was filled with rage. It couldn't be anything but a frame-up. Shortman never carried a gun, and the last thing he would be involved in was a holdup. He swore angrily and started to pace his tiny cell. Even the offensive odor was beyond him now. He waited impatiently for the footsteps of the turnkey.

10

AFTER LEAVING the interrogation room, Prince stopped at the desk and picked up his personal belongings. The idle officers stared at him coldly. He returned their glares look for look. His lawyer came in with Chinaman. Both men remained silent until after Chinaman had picked up his stuff and they had left the station.

"I'm sorry about you guys having to put up with that crap all night, but that damn murder charge stopped me from being able to spring you on a writ or bond," the young lawyer explained.

The sound of a horn blowing caused Prince to look up. Ruby was sitting at the curb behind the steering wheel of one of their cars. "I understand, man," Prince replied, "but regardless of us, what's the deal on Little Larry? I want him out, man, as soon as possible."

"Don't worry, everything's under control." The lawyer's voice was smooth and convincing. "As soon as Larry comes up for his examination, we'll have that damn case thrown out. They're trying to be clever by using those murder charges, but it won't work. If they don't come up with any more evidence than what they had before, the judge will have to dismiss the case."

"See that it is," Prince replied coldly and walked off. As he neared the car, Ruby flashed her magnificent teeth in a lovely smile.

Blanca got out of the passenger side and smiled at Chinaman. "Hi, honey," she said as he got in. Her voice was soft and filled with love.

As the car pulled away from the curb, the women started to tell the news, but they were cut off. "We already know about it," Chinaman said.

"Preacher and his bunch went on a rampage last night," Ruby said slowly, feeling out her man's reactions.

"Yeah, I'll bet that helped a lot," Prince said, not even attempting to hide the sarcasm. "It ain't about that," he continued. "We can't beat the man in the streets fightin'. Whitey got all the guns and tanks in the world. What this thing is all about is cash. If we get enough of that green stuff, we'll be able to handle shit like this."

Both women felt disappointed because neither man had commented on the picket they had thrown around the station. Both of them remained silent, listening to the men.

"You know, I was thinkin', man," Chinaman began, "last night while I was locked up I kicked the idea around, Prince, and I believe I'm going to come down strong on all the pimps and hustlers in our neighborhood. You know, man, we got damn near as many Mexican pimps as you got black pimps in your neighborhoods."

Prince glanced up sharply. "Yeah, man," Chinaman continued, "I figure if we put the arm on some of these guys who keep talking about doing something but try and make a whore out of every broad that comes their way, we could show our neighborhood that we're really trying to do something."

Prince hushed Ruby when she started to say something. He wanted to listen to Chinaman.

"After the way them cats at the auditorium went for our speeches last night, Prince, it's only right that we really try and do something for our people. Man, this organization crap can really turn out to be a big thing."

"Yeah, man," Prince replied suddenly. "I'll give it some thought, but you hold on, Chinaman, don't put no pressure on them guys yet. We got to think this thing out. Ruby, head for the hideout, baby. I can take a bath and change clothes out there. We better talk to them studs out there, too, 'cause some of them might be a little worried over this shootin'."

Prince leaned back against the seat and closed his eyes. His instincts warned him that Chinaman could become a problem. He knew just what had happened.

The guy had gotten a taste of power last night; he couldn't see it any other way. Dedication to a cause was beyond Prince's imagination. Everybody had to think of number one, he believed. It never entered his mind that Chinaman really believed they could do something constructive for the people in the ghettos. As far as Prince was concerned, there had always been ghettos, and there would always be ghettos. The people who lived there either learned how to get out or died in the small confines of their prison. It was cut and dried. He was well aware that he knew how to get out. All it took was money. There were two kinds of people in the world: the haves and the have-nots. If you were hungry, if you needed clothes, if your rent was overdue—take it. It was better to be a taker than one of those who got took!

When they got to the hideout, there were three black sedans and two Cadillacs parked in the private driveway. The house was one of the old mansions on Chicago Boulevard, kept at one time by a millionaire of the auto industry. The place still held a magnetic glory.

"Man, oh man!" Chinaman exclaimed as their car pulled around to the side of the house and stopped beside a fifty-foot swimming pool. "How did you manage to swing a place like this, Prince?" he asked excitedly.

Prince grinned. "I went through my lawyer. For five hundred dollars extra fee, he'd find some way to sell his mother."

The car came to a halt and was immediately sur-

rounded by a crowd of boys and girls. They had heard
about Prince's arrest, and at the sight of their leader,
they screamed their happiness.

"Prince," a young girl wearing shorts called. "If this
is what you and Ruby call a hideout, I'd hate to see
what kind of pad you and her stay in."

"Don't worry," Prince yelled back good-naturedly.
"You and your man won't be left out of the goodies."

Kids began to stick their heads out of windows as
news of Prince's arrival came to them. A large group
of kids came running out of the house yelling at the
newcomers.

Prince shouted over the uproar, "Chinaman, find
Preacher, then ya'll get all the boys together someplace. We got some important matters to kick around."
He spoke lower to Ruby. "Baby, you see to it that all
the broads are taken inside the house until we get
some matters taken care of."

He watched her as she rounded up the girls with
Blanca's help. After they had been herded into the
house, Prince waited until Chinaman returned with
Preacher. They had rounded up most of the boys. In
front of Prince there was a sea of faces, all of them
young and dangerous.

Prince raised his hand for silence. "All of you are
aware of what happened last night to Shortman, so we
won't even go into that. It ain't no new thing to us.
We been hep to what the white man calls *justice*." His
voice went up on the word. "*Justice* means just one
thing: *just us*. That's the only way whitey looks at it—
just-us, and he wants us to accept justice for just-us.

Well, we ain't going for it. We know what he means, so we can get down. Leave the bullshit for the squares who don't know no different."

He waved down their yelling impatiently. "There have been some changes made since quite a few of you came out here, so I've made it a point to send enough girls out to keep you from gettin' bored." He smiled as they grinned. "We may be out here for a while, so I want all of you to understand where we stand."

Prince stepped back to brush some imaginary dust off his silk suit. There were no wrinkles in his clothes to reveal that he had spent the night in jail. "Every one of us out here is going to have to do his share," he said, "if we want to come out of this on top." He stared out over the crowd, waiting for the murmuring to die down. "If we don't stick together now, a week from today every one of us will be in jail."

As a mutter of discontent broke out, Prince raised his hand for silence. "There's not a man out here who's not involved in this trouble up to his goddamn neck, so just shut your mouths and listen. I went to the trouble of having everybody I could reach brought out here, so there ain't no one left to put the finger on anyone."

"What about Larry?" Preacher asked suddenly. "He could put some of us on the spot."

As the sun beat down on them, Prince stared at Preacher's dark face. Preacher's eyes were hard, bleak, unreadable.

"Don't worry about Larry," Prince snapped. His

eyes flashed sparks as he stared at the crowd of men around him. He was like a lean and hungry lion, aware of the responsibility of keeping his pride in line. From growing pressure, his reflexes had sharpened. Though he ruled over vicious creatures, he was by far the most vicious. His voice lashed out at the men. "I'll have Larry out of the county jail before next week, if he don't talk. If he starts to run his goddamn mouth, I'll have his mammy and every goddamn baby in her house killed." He hesitated for a moment, then added, "And that goes for any of you that might get diarrhea of the mouth."

His words carried a dangerous meaning that was not lost on anyone. All the men knew it was no idle threat.

"Actually," Prince said into the silence, "we don't really have anything to worry about. Just 'cause the papers have been playing up that second-degree murder charge, that really don't mean shit. I got an iron in the fire, so when I pull it out, Larry will be out on the street on bond, fighting a case of joy-riding."

The crowd broke into loud laughter. Chinaman stepped up and waved for silence. "They goin' have Shortman's funeral sometime this week, but most of you won't be there. Prince done already told me who to take, so if you ain't in the bunch, don't get no attitude. It's just playing safe, that's all. Ain't no reason to let the man pick ya up just 'cause someone got hit. It's sad, but it don't change the game. We're playing for big stuff, so the dues goin' be high at times. There's one thing you ain't got to worry about, though, we goin' send him off in style, so won't nobody be able to say we ain't lookin' out for our people. There will be enough of our people there so that everyone will know Shortman wasn't no loser."

The crowd gave Chinaman a roar as Prince took his arm and led him towards the house. "That's my main man," Prince said softly out of the side of his mouth as the men went up the winding path to the rear of the house. Prince waved at some girls lying in sunchairs on the recreation porch. As they passed the kitchen, he waved at another bunch. They walked into the study where four more young, beautiful girls were hanging around listening to records.

"Beat it!" Chinaman ordered sharply. "What the hell do you think this is, a ballroom?"

"What the hell goes on around here?" a young girl with a short natural asked. "First you run us from the pool, now from the house. What is this—some form of new concentration camp?"

"I don't care if you go play with yourselves, just get the fuck out of here," Chinaman replied.

Two of the girls yelled something smart over their shoulders as they went out the door. "Wait a minute," Prince called.

They stopped and waited in the doorway. "One of you find Ruby for me and send her in here," Prince ordered, then closed the door on them. He sprawled out on the couch and stretched. "Goddamn, I'm tired. I think I'll take a quick nap, Chinaman. I didn't get no sleep in that funky hole last night. Man, that's a funky place if I've ever smelled one. Ain't nothing like that in the penitentiary."

There was a sudden knock on the door and Ruby walked in. "What's up, baby?" she asked slowly as she crossed the room.

"I want you to make a run for me, Ruby." Prince lit a cigarette before continuing. "We goin' need some more weed and coke, so take one of the cars and run across town and pick some up from Billy. Get enough to hold us out here for a while, too."

She started to get up from the couch, then stopped. "Baby, I been thinkin'. Since we started this new organization, we ought to make somebody else the minister of finance instead of Roman."

Prince waited so long before replying that she began to think that he hadn't heard her. "Why?" The question caught her by surprise. "You don't think he's been stealing anything, do you?"

"It's not that, Prince," she replied. "I don't know if he's rippin' us off or not. The thing is, he has too much say-so about the money. The way everything is set up, he's just about the only one next to his woman who knows what's happening with our bankroll." Ruby hesitated, then added, "Our income, counting the whiskey and dope money alone, is somewhere around fifty thousand a week. That's a lot of money, Prince, even though I'm counting just the gross. With our overhead, we ain't clearing five thousand dollars a week."

Prince stretched and got up. He walked over to the desk and opened a drawer with a key. His finger ran down a page quickly. "At this moment, we got eight hundred people on our payroll, Ruby. That's a lot of kids." He held his hand up before she could speak. "I know they don't get that much. Some of them, though, make more than you realize. The kids we got cookin' the goddamn whiskey make anywhere from two hundred to four hundred dollars a week. The pushers that work for us even come higher."

Prince examined the small notebook he had taken from the drawer. "I'll go along with your judgment, though, Ruby. If you think we're giving Roman and his woman too much play with our cash, I'll tighten up. But who in the fuck can I put in charge of the new bookwork and money problems? This new organization is going to be one sharp pain in the ass for me. I just don't have the time to spend on it."

"Put Blanca in charge of it," Ruby replied quickly. "She's good with figures, plus she done been through high school. I'll put a couple of other girls on the case with her, and they can watch each other." She smiled at Chinaman, taking the sting out of her words, but he wasn't fooled. He knew she meant just what she said.

"What about Dot, Ruby? You think you might be able to put one of those young bulldykers you tight with on the case and find out if Roman is playing sticky fingers with our bread?"

Ruby shook her head. "It wouldn't do no good. Dot is colder, than any jasper we could put on the case. No, that ain't the answer. It ain't no weak spot there. In fact," she added, "we'd have a better chance playing on Roman than we would fuckin' with Dot. We ain't goin' take down nothing messin' with her."

Prince put the notebook back in the desk drawer and locked it. "I'm going to take a nap, Ruby, while you're gone. When you get back, wake me up. Oh yeah," he added as though it had slipped his mind, "stop by Shortman's mother's house and let them know we're paying all the expenses. She can keep the insurance money, if there was any."

When Ruby left, Prince made his way upstairs and took a quick bath, washing the jail smell out of his skin. He stretched out on the bed and instantly fell asleep. It was later in the afternoon when Chinaman came up to the luxurious bedroom and knocked softly at the door. At the sound of Prince's voice, he entered.

"Ruby just pulled up," he informed Prince. A young girl came in behind him with a tray. Prince removed a piece of chicken from it, walked over to the window and pulled back the drapes. He glanced out of the window as Chinaman walked out of the door.

Ruby was just stepping out of a snow-white Cadillac. The car gleamed like crystal in the strong rays of the afternoon sun. Ruby was dressed immaculately, wearing a tight white miniskirt with matching blouse and a wide black belt and black heels. Not a speck of dust was visible on her or the car. Both appeared to have been wrapped in cellophane, then released from it and placed down in the driveway. She seemed totally unaware of the impression her figure was making as she leaned into the backseat and removed a suitcase. The young men watched her voluptuous body with male lust. Out of the twenty or more young girls already there, none of them could compare with Ruby. She started to walk up the driveway, her long smooth legs displayed to perfection.

She stopped and slammed the suitcase down. "Damn it!" she swore. "One of you gaping sons of bitches come and carry this goddamn thing."

Hawk, a short, husky, brown-skinned young man in his early twenties, rushed over and picked up the suitcase. He followed her into the house. When she reached the study, Ruby stopped and took the suitcase from him.

"Thank you, darling," she said lightly and waited until he had retraced his steps before opening the door leading into the study.

"Prince will be down shortly," Chinaman stated as he watched her set the suitcase on an end table. Ruby sat down and made herself comfortable. They didn't have long to wait. Prince opened the door and stepped in. His glance went to the suitcase, then back to her face. He noticed her change of clothes and smiled.

"What's the deal, baby, you trying to give the other girls a little competition?"

Ruby smiled back at him. "I was only trying to bring my small existence to your attention, Prince. It seems that you forget what my main function is sometimes." The tone of her voice changed suddenly. "I couldn't get all you wanted, Prince. All I could shake loose from him was ten pounds of reefer and six pieces of cocaine."

"Six pieces of girl!" Prince exclaimed angrily. "Goddamn, Ruby, it should have been more coke than that left. Billy ain't supposed to sell but so much of that shit. The rest, we got special customers to take it off his hands."

"I thought so too, daddy, but this is just one of our problems."

"What else is wrong?" he asked grimly.

"Well, for one thing, we're having trouble with our heroin contacts."

"What's wrong, we been having too many killings?" he asked wearily.

Chinaman got up and walked over to the portable bar, fixed two drinks, and brought them back to the people on the couch.

"No, that's not the trouble, Prince," Ruby said slowly. "Our connect says he doesn't like his drop-off men getting their hands dirty dealing with dopefiends. He said he just ain't going for it, honey. I called him before I came back out here."

Prince frowned angrily. "What dopefiends?" Prince asked harshly. "The only person his drop-off men come in contact with is Billy-boy."

"Don't you remember, daddy, I told you about Billy. That's your dopefiend right enough. Billy-boy, or girl, is a full-fledged addict."

Prince walked back over to the bar and fixed two more drinks. "Are you certain, woman?"

"It ain't no doubt about it, Prince. I also stopped by Tess's pimp's apartment, baby, and got the real deal from her."

"I'm up on Tess being a user," Prince said slowly, "but Billy doesn't deal with any dopefiends, and besides that, Ruby, you know as well as I do he don't mess with no women, period."

She shrugged her shoulders. "Billy-boy likes the meat, daddy. Tess's pimp is a dopefiend from the old school, so he plays up to Billy on occasion so that he can get both of their blows free." Ruby set her glass down and stared at Prince closely. "I know we can't stand too much more bloodshed, daddy, but the fag is shootin' ten to fifteen things every time he goes to the cooker, and that's at least six times a day."

Prince whistled. "He sure ain't chippin' then. That's a goddamn oil-burner. If he's running fifteen caps a shot," Prince said, "that will just about do it. We can't afford to just cut him loose; he knows too much." He hesitated briefly. "He done just about signed his own death warrant."

Prince stood up and began to pace the floor. His mind raced over the new problem quickly, found a solution and settled on it. He stopped behind the bar and pushed some whiskey aside from the wall rack. He pressed a button and a panel in the wall slid back. "Ruby," he said, speaking over his shoulder, "you call the connect back and have him send the next two kilos over to our place, 'cause Billy won't be around. Get some girls lined up who can deliver the drugs for us. Get about four, that should do just fine. Have two of them pick up the money, while the other two drop off the drugs."

Prince paused for a moment, allowing his eyes to run over the assorted group of guns and knives inside the hollow wall panel. It was a small arsenal with enough guns to supply at least twenty men. "I think, baby, if we do it this way, the girls won't have to worry about gettin' busted for sales. Possession maybe, but not sales."

Ruby walked around the bar and kissed him on the neck. "You take care of the inlet and outlet, Ruby, and I'll take care of Billy-boy," he said coldly.

"Uh-mmmm, daddy," she said coyly, pulling a ten-inch carving knife from its perch. "Let me take care of Billy-boy—please?"

"I don't know, Ruby," he answered softly. "There's no room for mistakes this late in the game."

"Don't worry, daddy," she whispered huskily. "There will be no mistakes."

11

DONNIE EXPLORED the flat with his brownish-green eyes. He twisted his lips in a sneer of disgust at the sight of the frayed curtains that hung over the living room windows. The wooden floor had grimy linoleum covering it, and there were crushed cigarettes all over it. A black couch occupied one wall, and opposite it was what could have passed for a deep-cushioned chair, with spotted and greasy upholstery. He tapped his foot impatiently as he waited for Fran, Shortman's woman. The sight of the littered flat angered him. He wondered how Shortman had put up with living in such filth. With a much larger family to take care of, his mother would never allow her house to become anywhere near this filthy.

"Just a minute," Fran called from the bedroom. "I'm just about ready." Her voice was loud in the small apartment.

"I guess you know they ain't about to hold up the funeral for you, don't you?" he asked sarcastically. If there was anything he disliked, it was a trifling woman. He glanced at his watch again. He had called last night and told her what time he'd pick her up. If it wasn't for Prince, he thought, he'd walk out. Actually, he didn't give a damn if she went to the funeral or not. He hadn't liked the idea when Chinaman called and told him what he had to do.

Finally, Fran came out of the bedroom. He cursed under his breath at the sight of her. She was wearing a tight black minidress. With her large breasts pushing through the top, the dress seemed vulgar. She grinned at him, revealing yellow teeth. He stared at her too-large nose, mannish-looking natural, and wondered again what Shortman had seen in her. Besides her voluptuous body, he couldn't find anything in her favor. She had a body, though, and she was well aware of it.

She made her hips sway as she started towards him. "You ready, honey?" she asked sweetly.

"Am I ready?" he repeated and bit back a sharp retort. "Yeah, baby, I'm ready," he said and took her arm. She swayed towards him, brushing against him provocatively. Just for the hell of it, when they walked out of the door, he let his hand search over her body. She stopped in the doorway, giving him plenty of time to finish his feel.

"Damn," she cursed. "I wish we had a little more time. We might be able to reach some kind of mutual understanding." She laughed loudly. "Maybe after the funeral, huh, Donnie?" She rubbed his hand in such a way that it was impossible to miss her meaning.

Not in your lifetime, bitch, he thought coldly. The last thing in the world he wanted was a trifling woman. "You done forgot all about Shortman, baby, mighty quick," he said shortly. She missed the sharpness in his voice.

"Me and Shortman was cool, Donnie, when he was living, but ain't nothing a dead man can do for me. Don't forget, man, I got two kids to take care of."

"I thought you was gettin' A.D.C., Fran," he said slowly.

"Shit, man, you know A.D.C. ain't no money. How you expect me to really live off that little shit, huh?"

"I guess you didn't live off your check before you met Shortman?" he asked. This time there was no missing the anger in his voice.

She tossed him a skeptical glance. "You know as well as I do, Donnie, that those babies belonged to Shortman."

He made a gesture of impatience. "Shortman, hell. Fran, I knew you when you was fuckin' before Shortman ever came into your life. You may have told him them kids was his, but baby, you'd have to do a hell of a lot better than that to make me believe it."

Fran stopped and put her hands on her hips. "I don't

give a fuck if you believe it or not. I'm gettin' money from A.D.C. in his name, so what you think is your goddamn business." She started towards the car, then stopped. "If you don't want to take me to the funeral, I can get there without your help, you know."

"I'll take you," he said hurriedly. "You ain't got to get your ass up on your shoulders, though."

She turned with the lean motion of a sinewy leopardess and stood before him quivering. "I don't know who or what the fuck you think you are, nigger, but I don't have to take no shit off you, you understand that?"

He stared at her angrily, but there was an indication that her rage was mounting. He cautioned himself to be cool. It wouldn't do at all if he was to knock her on her ass. For a moment he let the picture of her sprawled out on the ground flash through his mind; then just as quickly he put it out of his thoughts. He ignored her and walked over to the black Cadillac he had been loaned for the occasion. He opened the door and held it for her, not really caring if she got in or not.

"That's better," she snapped as she switched her hips past him and got in the car. He watched her as she sat down, legs wide open, skirt pulled up around her large thighs.

"You might as well pull your skirt down," he said coldly. "I ain't interested in what you got to offer." He slammed the door before he could hear her loud reply. Her words still reached him, though, as he went around the car. "Black bastard!"

He climbed in and started the motor up in silence, not allowing himself the pleasure of replying to her angry outburst. They drove on in silence until they reached the church. Cars were lined up and down the street. Donnie could tell it was going to be a large funeral. He pulled up as close to the front of the church as he could get, then double-parked beside another Cadillac. He followed her into the church and found a seat in the rear. He watched her switch her way to the front. People were packed inside, and some teenagers were standing at the rear.

He listened to the preacher with one ear while his mind traveled over other things. A lot of responsibility had fallen on his shoulders since Shortman's passing. It would be quite a while before he could go home and sleep peacefully at night.

As soon as the choir started to sing "He's on the Way Back Home," loud crying broke out in the church. People began to file out and go up the aisle to view the casket. He made his way slowly up the aisle, and when he reached the front, he had to hold back a grin. Fran was in the front with the family crying louder than anyone else in the church. The bitch should have been in Hollywood, he thought coldly as he walked past the body. He glanced down and looked away. Death always gave him a feeling of being very small. At the sight of it, he had a feeling it wouldn't be long before he would be lying in his own casket.

Soon after he returned to his seat, people started filing out of the church towards the waiting cars. Fran stopped at his seat and whispered, "I'm going out to the cemetery with the family."

He stared at her coldly. "Good!" he exclaimed and watched her walk away mad. He got up and made his way out of the church. People were still milling around outside. There were large groups of kids everywhere. Most of them were scheming to get out of going out to the cemetery. As he glanced around, he noticed he was just about the only male Ruler around. There were quite a few of the girls around. He noticed Dot and Blanca moving from crowd to crowd. After a while, he realized what they were doing. When one of the women would leave a group of teenagers, the kids would slowly move towards one of the funeral cars and get in. The car would then get in line for the trip to the cemetery.

Ruby slid up beside him. "Donnie, you better get away from here as soon as possible. I just saw two detectives on the other side of the church. I don't know if they'll bother you or not, but it's best not to take any chances."

He nodded and slipped away from her. He moved through the crowd of people quickly and made his way to the car. Glancing over his shoulder, he saw the detectives looking his way. He pushed through some women rudely and almost ran towards the car. The detectives started in his direction, but they were too late. He started up the car and drove on the opposite side of the street. The man directing the funeral cars as they lined up tried to wave him down, but the only thing he got for his trouble was being almost run down. People stared after the car curiously.

Once Donnie got clear of the funeral traffic, he slowed down. He drove slowly, making sure he didn't break a traffic law. His first stop was to return the Cadillac and pick up his own car, a late-model Ford. He relaxed a little more after he had gotten out of the Cadillac. He wondered why black men who hustled bought Cadillacs. As far as he was concerned, a Caddie brought too much heat to a black driver. It was an open invitation for the police to stop you.

After making his rounds of the whiskey stills, he began to check out the corn joints that bought his whiskey. The owners of the joints were all patronizing towards him. When he reached his last whiskey joint, he bought a bottle of beer and sat down and relaxed. The sound of the jukebox blaring loudly didn't disturb him. He settled back comfortably and enjoyed the sight of the drunks clowning. He watched the women, most of them in their forties or early fifties, trying to dance. They twisted and belly-bumped with loud squeals.

One woman in a bright red dress kept glancing in his direction. She finally made her mind up and came towards him. When he refused to dance, she stood in front of him and rolled her stomach. The house man came over and chased her away. When the record ended, Donnie sent drinks over to her and the two women she was with. He walked over and started the jukebox back up. The women rushed back to the middle of the floor.

A little later, two men entered, one of them wearing work clothes, the other carrying a shopping bag.

From the top of the bag, a greasy pants-leg could be seen hanging out. He called one of the women dancers over and an argument developed. Their voices began to rise in anger. The house man rushed over, but he couldn't seem to quiet the man down.

Finally, the heavyset man walked out to the middle of the floor and grabbed the woman with the red dress. He held her arm tightly and yelled, "Whose dress is that you got on, Pearl?" His voice was slightly slurred from drinking. "Whose dress is that, goddamnit?"

"Let me go, man; Mabel let me wear it," she shouted as she tried to break loose.

"Mabel, hell," the man shouted back. "Mabel ain't got no dress. That's mine. I bought it for her ass. She ain't bought a goddamn thing, so get your funky ass out of it now. Right now!" he screamed.

She stared at him as though he was losing his mind. He shook her hard, then released her. "Woman, either you take that goddamn dress off now or I'll take it off for you." The longer he talked, the more furious he became.

"You ain't got no cause to take on like that, Bill," she said, filling her voice with a cordiality that fooled no one.

"Ain't goin' ask your ass no more, woman, get your funky butt out of my woman's dress. If you want one like it, bitch, buy one, but that one there ain't for your use." He snatched her again and shook her harshly. Her teeth were rattling before he sat her back down on the floor. He shoved the shopping bag he had been carrying into her arms. "You can put these on, woman, if you want to. But you got to get your ass out of my dress, now. Right now!" he yelled.

"Just a minute, Bill. Can't I go in the bedroom or something?" she asked, now thoroughly frightened. She grabbed the bag out of his hands and clutched it to her.

He stared after her with murder in his eyes as she rushed towards one of the bedrooms. In a few minutes she returned, the old pair of coveralls falling off her like a blanket. She held the dress out towards him timidly.

The drunks sitting around the house started to laugh at the sight of her. It started slowly, then built up to a roar of wild, unfeeling laughter. The woman dropped the dress on the floor and ran back towards the kitchen. Tears of humiliation ran down her cheeks.

Donnie got up from his chair, stared around angrily at the drunks, then started for the front door. He made it a point to walk across the middle of the room and step on the dress as the heavyset man picked it up. There was a tearing sound as his foot hit the hem of the dress at the same time the owner tried to retrieve it from the floor. The owner glared up at the hot-eyed young man but just as quickly decided to forget about the open insult. He wasn't afraid of the young man in front of him, but he had lived in the ghetto too long to think you could fight one teenager without worrying about his friends. He knew he could always buy another dress for his woman, but getting a new ass would be a problem. He dropped his eyes to the floor. Some instinct warned him that Donnie was searching for trouble. His whole being cried out to meet it, but a small voice in the back of his mind told him that it wasn't like it used to be. The kids nowadays didn't fight anymore, they believed in killing.

Donnie stopped and stared at the man insolently. He didn't bother to apologize. There was a savage eagerness about him that was not lost on the people watching. The house man held his breath, praying his house wouldn't be ruined by a fight.

When there was no answer to his silent challenge, he whirled on his heel and continued towards the door. He cursed himself quietly as a soft-hearted bastard. The sight of the woman being humiliated had brought a lump to his throat. He realized it was foolish of him. He told himself the woman wasn't worth it. But the sight of her pitiful figure in the coveralls made him instantly want to stand beside her and stop the hurting laughter. He opened the door and walked out on the porch. It had always been like this, he thought. The sight of a baby bird hurt could bring tears to the corners of his eyes. There was no doubt about it, you big baby, he told himself, you're just too soft. He started down the steps towards his car. Another thought ran through his mind, causing him to shudder. To think that he had allowed Roman to talk him into stealing whiskey money from Prince filled him with dread. It was just a matter of time, he reasoned, just a matter of time.

12

WEAVING THE INCONSPICUOUS black Ford in and out of the evening traffic, Ruby drove past the city's new shopping center without giving it a glance. Any other evening she would have stopped and gone into one of the exclusive fur shops to steal something if the opportunity presented itself. As soon as she started to turn off of Woodward Avenue, a red light caught her. She waited impatiently until the light changed, then made a left turn on Davison heading for the west side. She caught the expressway and followed it out towards the suburbs. Finally she parked in front of a luxurious apartment building and hurried into the lobby. A short, fat white woman came out of

the elevator with her French poodle on a chain. Both
of them were adorned in mink, the poodle sporting a
miniature jacket, the woman a stole.

Ruby could feel her feet sinking into the carpet as
she walked over to the elevator and asked the operator to take her to the tenth floor. After stepping off
the elevator, Ruby glanced up and down the corridor.
Finding it empty, she removed her red wig and stuck
it in her purse.

A young man answered her first knock on the door,
then stepped back and allowed her to enter. "My,
Ruby-do," he said in a high, feminine voice, "you
could have called to let me know you were coming,
couldn't you?" He stopped talking, put one hand on
a hip and started to tap one of the high-heeled shoes
he wore. "How do you like this outfit, Ruby-do?" he
asked.

With a contemptuous twist, he pivoted around on
his heels and modeled the tight, light green toreador
pants he wore. The pants were set off by a dark-green
sheer nylon blouse that matched his women's shoes.
His hair was long and bleached red, with a large wave
falling down over his forehead. Where his eyebrows
had once been, Billy now had midnight-black eye-
shadow; it went well with his light tan complexion.

Ruby walked over to the bedroom and pushed the
door open. Finding the room empty, she walked back
towards the well-equipped small kitchen. "Billy-boy,"
she called, "it's a wonder you ain't got kicked out of
the joint by now."

"Darling, I don't have the least idea what you are

trying to hint around about. You know as well as I do that I don't do anything wrong, honey."

"Don't fool yourself," Ruby answered over her shoulder as she walked into the bedroom. Billy followed her, stopped at the door, and stood back on his heels like a woman.

"If you are referring to what I think, Ruby, I'll have you know that I'm just as much woman as you are, honey—and maybe I might be just a little more."

Ruby laughed harshly. "I'll bet you are," she replied as she pulled out a dresser drawer.

"Ruby, just what are you supposed to be looking for in my dresser, dear?" His voice had become a bit firmer, more masculine. Now there were no more superfluous gestures as he watched her closely.

"Where do you keep the stuff at, Billy? I want a little blow, if you don't mind."

He seemed to relax a little. "Why do you do this to me, Ruby? You know you took everything I had the last time you were here."

She closed the bottom drawer and walked over to the double-doored closet. The large gold-rimmed mirror revealed her flaring black skirt and tight-fitting white blouse. She opened the large door and gasped in amazement. Beautiful gowns, in the latest fashions, hung from every rack.

Billy reached over her shoulder and pushed the sliding doors closed. The larger mirrors built into the closet doors revealed the anger in Ruby's eyes.

Billy smiled disarmingly. "Here, Ruby," he said. "Here's some cocaine for you." He gave her a small package wrapped in tinfoil.

"Thanks," she replied, taking the dope and walking over to the dresser. She removed a ten-dollar bill from her bra, rolled it up, and made a quill out of it. She opened the package, slowly bent down towards it with the quill in one nostril, and snorted deeply. With a deep sigh, she reached across the top of the dresser and picked up a cigarette lighter. Next, she picked up the empty paper that had held the drug and set it on fire, then dropped it into the nearest ashtray.

"Billy-boy," she called, her voice husky. "I've never had a fag make love to me." She put one hand on her hip and turned in his direction. "Wouldn't you just love to be the first one?"

"Ruby darling, you are the most! Really darling, I never expected that coke to react on you that way, dear. I know it makes some people freakish, but not that freakish, darling. My sweet Jesus, no!" He burst out laughing.

Ruby moved over to the door. In one smooth motion she hit the light switch and closed the bedroom door. Billy's eyes widened with revulsion as he watched her remove her loose-fitting skirt.

"Don't come near me!" he screamed in mock alarm as Ruby moved in his direction. The sound of the evening traffic in the street below was the only noise in the room. Billy jumped across the bed and made a rush towards the door. He was already thinking about how he would tell his friends Ruby tried to rape him. He grinned to himself in the dark. The thought of their faces when he related his ordeal filled him with joy.

Ruby, almost naked from the waist down, stepped aside and let him pass. Quickly she removed the ten-inch knife from under her slip where it had been strapped to her thigh. She leaped upon Billy's back with the lithe motion of a leopardess.

Billy frantically fumbled open the bedroom door and stumbled out into the living room as Ruby clung to his back. Her face twisted hideously as she put one of her small hands over his mouth and stabbed him viciously in the side. Instantly, astonishment and pain wiped the sneering smile from his face. With a manly jerk, he swung her from his back and staggered over to fall across the baby grand piano.

He managed to turn around just as Ruby leaped towards him. The scream that started in his throat died as bursts of pain exploded in his stomach. In desperation he shoved her away and staggered back across the room, falling on top of the white marble coffee table. The long blade did its work again. He felt the intolerable pain in his back; it caused him to fall off the table and clutch at the couch as he slid to the floor.

Ruby used her foot to turn him over on his back. As his eyes fluttered open and he stared up at her in horror, she reached down and stabbed him again and again in the chest and stomach.

The interior of the beautiful living room was ruined. Blood streamed from the tan couch. The coffee table was covered with pools of blood. The cream-colored carpeting was spattered with dark stains. Ruby watched as convulsions shook Billy's body for a moment before he lay perfectly still. She stood over the body and laughed while blood from Billy-boy's wounds ran down her naked legs. Her breasts rose and fell with her excited breathing.

Ruby sat down suddenly and forced herself to become calm. After awhile she was able to hold down the trembling in her legs. She stared around the apartment, detached. It was as though what had happened had transpired in a dream. She felt as though she had only been an observer. She got up and went into the bathroom. After taking a shower, she entered the bedroom and picked out a two-piece outfit that must have cost over a hundred dollars. Then she tried on a pair of heels, but the shoes were too large, so she carefully cleaned off her own and put them back on.

Later, after making sure she wasn't leaving anything, she put her wig on. She glanced at herself one more time in the mirror. As she reached the door, the telephone rang. She waited a second, then opened the door and peeped out. Finding the corridor empty, she slipped out into the hallway and took the stairs down to the back exit.

At the same time across town, Donnie paced up and down in the small quarters of his motel room. For the tenth time he reached for the phone, only to turn away in fear. At last he found the courage to pick the receiver up and dialed a number.

"Hello." He spoke quickly, fearful of what the call might do to his personal health. "Let me speak to Prince, please?" He waited, frightened by his own behavior.

"Prince, Prince," he could hear the unknown voice calling in the distance. Suddenly the extension was picked up and he heard the voice he had been dreading. All the rehearsals he had been going through failed him now.

"Prince," he stammered, "this is Donnie. I don't know how to begin telling you, man, but Roman got me giving him a kickback on all the whiskey money I pick up." He blurted out the story, not allowing Prince to ask any questions. "The paperwork I turn in to Fatdaddy is all wrong, Prince."

He listened to the silence from the other end of the line. Again he wondered if it had all been a frame. If so, he had done the right thing. Prince would already know that he was keeping back some of the money every day.

Suddenly Prince's voice came over the line, sharp and harsh. "How much?"

Donnie didn't hesitate. "We pick up close to thirty gallons of whiskey from each joint, Prince, every day. After disposing of it, we hold back at least five gallons from each house."

Prince did some quick calculation. They owned over twenty joints; five gallons of whiskey from each one was running into big money. At ten dollars a gallon, he was losing somewhere around a thousand dollars a day. "How long has this shit been going on?" he asked sharply.

"Ever since I took over Shortman's job, Prince. He hit on me the second day after Shortman died."

There was a quick knock on the library door and

Ruby came in. Prince glanced at her quickly, noticing the strange glitter in her eyes. He put his hand over the telephone receiver. "Did everything go all right?"

She nodded her head, then dropped onto the couch, crossing her legs. "Everything is mellow on my end, Daddy," she replied, her voice husky.

More from habit than anything else, his eyes roamed over her thighs; then he forced his attention away from her and spoke into the receiver. "How much money did you make, Donnie, since this shit has been going on?"

Again there was no hesitation. "I got fifteen thousand dollars out of it, Prince, but I ain't spent a penny of the money. I been saving all of it until I had time to tell you about it. I didn't really know if it was something you was trying to test me on or what."

Prince listened to the voice and fought back his anger. It filled him with rage even to think that one of his men was stealing from him. He knew he paid them more money than any of them had ever made in their lives. The real problem was Roman, he reasoned coldly. Without Roman, Donnie would have never found the nerve to take from him.

"Fifteen thousand dollars!" Prince exclaimed angrily into the phone. "Well, I'll be goddamned! I didn't think this shit had gone that far. That's thirty thousand dollars we should have had here to work with. I want you to stay right where you're at until I call you back, Donnie. I'm going to get to the bottom of this shit today. Ruby," he yelled, "take this phone and get his phone number." He dropped the receiver onto the couch beside her.

Prince began to pace the room, his mind working swiftly. There had been too much bloodshed already; he couldn't retaliate the way he wanted to. There was murder in his heart, but common sense told him to move slowly.

Ruby wrote down the phone number, then hung up. She watched her man pace up and down. The phone rang, and she picked it up and listened quietly. Prince glanced at her once or twice but kept pacing. She hung up and glanced at him worriedly.

"What now?" he asked as he sat down on the couch.

"That was Blanca, baby. She says our dope connect dropped off two kilos, then told her there wouldn't be any more dope coming. Seems as though they don't like dealing with women now."

Prince leaned back and stretched out on the couch. He kicked off his shoes and put his feet in her lap. "This thing we got going is bigger than I thought it was, Ruby. We ain't got enough smart people up front helpin' us. It's just too goddamn much for the few we got who are qualified to help us." He rubbed his hands over his eyes, then continued. "We got troubles, baby. If I was smart, I'd take the little bit of money we got stashed away and pull out before this thing gets out of hand."

She removed his feet from her lap and stretched out on the couch beside him. Prince pressed against the back of the couch so she would fit in his arms more comfortably.

"Blanca also said to tell you, daddy, that everything

was set for the picket line Friday. You ain't changed
your mind about having us picket that A&P market,
have you?"

"No, baby. We got to get those goddamn guns as
soon as possible. Everything is ready for Friday, I
made sure of that myself." He brushed the hair out of
her face lightly, then continued. "When you call
Donnie back, tell him to start turning his whiskey
money in to Fatdaddy. Also, tell him I want ten thousand dollars of that money he took from Roman. The
other five grand he can keep for puttin' me up on what
was going down."

"You haven't even asked me about Billy-boy," she
said as she cuddled in his arms, her breath hot on his
neck.

"You said everything was taken care of, didn't
you?" he asked slowly, letting his hands roam over
her soft young body.

Her breathing became heavy as his hands continued
to explore. He twisted his head away as she tried to
arouse him by darting her tongue in and out of his
ear.

He laughed and held her back from his neck. "Be
good now, woman. I got business for you to take care
of." As she started to wiggle in his arms, he continued. "I want you to get in touch with Preacher and
have him set up a meeting with Roman. I don't want
this business handled over no phone, baby. It's too
important. Tell Preacher to have Roman meet him at
some gas station on the outskirts of town tonight.
When they get together, tell Preacher to tell him I want

him to take over the dope business. He's got to get a connect somewhere, so by the time he gets it set up I'll have something else for his ass." He added as an afterthought, "Oh yeah, baby. Tell him to tell Roman that he ain't handling the whiskey business no more. It's completely out of his hands. All I want him to do is get the dope connect."

While he had been talking, Ruby had slowly unbuttoned his shirt. Now, she pressed her face to his chest. He could feel her hot mouth searching, then her nimble tongue began to work around his nipple. Slowly, he could feel himself beginning to respond. Her head began to sink lower and lower, her tongue constantly exploring, her teeth nibbling, until he knew there was no avoiding the pleasurable sensations she was stimulating. Her fingers fumbled with his pants. As he felt the buttons being opened, he asked, "Did you lock the door when you came in?"

"Fuck the door, and the lock, too!" she exclaimed.

13

IT SEEMED AS THOUGH he had just gone to bed when Dot shook his shoulder. Roman rolled over and sat up. He rubbed the sleep out of his eyes and stared at her curiously.

"It's time to get up, baby," she said lightly. She grabbed his shoulder and gave him a hard shake. "Come on, baby. You know Prince is going to be waiting for us to show up. Besides," she added, "our plane leaves at five o'clock."

Roman reached over and picked up a pack of cigarettes from the table beside the bed. "I still don't like it," he grumbled.

"Well, I do," Dot replied quickly. "I'd rather be in

Chicago than here today. When that shit hops off at that A&P market, no telling who the police will end up bustin'. If we ain't nowhere in sight or reach, we ain't got no problem." She stared at him for a minute, then turned on her heel and walked towards the bathroom, stepping out of her housedress on the way. In a few minutes, the sound of the shower running came to Roman's ears, so he pushed back the covers and sat up on the edge of the bed.

"Leave the water running when you get through," he yelled. He stood up and stretched, then walked over to the window and pushed back the drapes. The sky was still covered with stars. He stared out for a moment, then the cigarette he held burned his finger, and he cursed and dropped it on the carpet; as he bent slowly to retrieve it, his mind returned to the thought of what lay ahead. Ever since the whiskey business had been taken out of his hands, he had been wondering and waiting. If he could only have reached Donnie, it would have relieved his mind, but every time he called, it seemed as though Donnie had just left or would be back shortly.

"The water feels wonderful, baby," Dot said as she came out of the bathroom nude. She walked over to the dresser and removed two towels. She tossed one to Roman, then began to dry herself.

Her nudity didn't even arouse his interest. Any other time he would have paid attention because her body was very stimulating, but now his mind was occupied with his problems.

"You better hurry, Roman. We got to stop and pick

that money up from Prince before going to the airport." Her voice carried the sound of a woman who
was sure of herself, who knew just how far to go with
her man. She carefully selected her traveling outfit
from the closet. She was fully dressed and sitting in
front of the mirror fixing her hair when Roman came
out of the shower.

"You better get a hurry on, baby. We ain't got all
night." She pulled off a red wig, then slipped on a
black one and straightened it on her head.

Roman glanced around at her. "You really got your
nose open over this trip, ain't you, Dot?"

Dot didn't even bother to answer. She knew what
he said was true. This was the first time in her life
she had ever left Detroit, let alone flown on a plane.
She was looking forward to the trip more than he realized. It was not just the idea of going to Chicago; it
was the joy of being able to travel, being able to see
something besides the slums that were over ninety
percent of her life. If she had anything to do with their
future plans, she thought coldly, it wouldn't be the last
time they traveled.

"Why don't you wear a suit, honey, instead of that
sports outfit?" she asked. "You look better in that dark
silk one, baby."

He continued to put on the checkered sportcoat.
"Don't worry about it, woman. We ain't going to no
goddamn fashion show. Besides," he added, "I want
to be comfortable."

Before they left, Roman glanced quickly around the
apartment. "You're worse than some old woman, man.

We ain't goin' be gone but a couple of days at the most, Roman, so ain't no sense you acting as though we were leaving for good."

"It ain't about that, Dot," he snapped. "I got this funny feeling, woman, as though something is wrong. I don't know just what the real deal is, but I got a hunch something is boogie about this whole funky affair."

"*Shit*," she replied, drawing the word out. "Whatever happens while we're gone, daddy, ain't goin' hurt us. We ain't got no money here, so if something should happen to the pad while we're away, we ain't goin' lose nothing we ain't able to replace. Besides," she continued, "ain't no nigger in this city crazy enough to break into your apartment, man." She hit the light switch, flooding the room with darkness.

In the Twenty Grand Motel on the west side, Prince glanced at his watch irritably. He realized that he would have to bring this impromptu meeting to an end before Roman arrived. "As I've already told you guys, ain't nothing to worry about. Chinaman is going to be there with three carloads of men. You, Preacher, all you got to do is make sure one of your lieutenants arrives on the spot at the proper time. I've already made preparations, so there won't be any problem about transportation. There'll be three cars at your disposal for your people." He glanced quickly at Ruby to confirm his words.

She picked up a tablet from the bed where she was stretched out. "That's right, Preacher. We got one

Ford, plus two '64 Buicks waiting to pick you up at
the warehouse." She pointed a pencil at Danny.
"There's two cars there for you, too, honey," she said,
raising a hand to stifle a sigh.

Prince flashed them his self-contained smile. "That
makes eight carloads of activists we are sending out
today. There ain't no way for nothing to go wrong."
His voice began to rise. "If each one of you instructs
your men properly, ain't nothing going wrong. At
three forty-five today each and every one of those men
will instigate trouble somewhere in that crowd. When
the police move against the instigators, they won't be
pickin' people. The first blacks that don't get out of
their way quick enough will get their heads cracked.
In a crowd that large, them niggers ain't goin' stand
for it. They goin' start to fight back. That's the time
your boys will make their move and get away. It's as
simple as that." He chopped down with his hand to
emphasize his words. "It's gettin' late. Preacher. You
and Fatdaddy hold up a moment; the rest of you get
on home and get some rest. We got a busy day ahead
of us." He waited patiently until Ruby closed the door
behind the other men.

Prince glanced at his watch, then nodded to Ruby.
She picked up the phone and had the desk put through
a call for her. He waited until she hung up. "No
answer," she replied to his questioning glance.

He removed a key from his pocket. "Here, Fatdaddy.
Get some real cool help, then go over to Roman's
place. I want you to search it real good. Bring back
all the paperwork you find. Anything that looks like

figures or addresses. You know what I mean. Anything you think the police might be interested in, bring it to me. Oh yeah," he added, "if you come across any money, pick that up, too." Before Fatdaddy could speak, he continued. "Don't worry about Roman or his woman. They won't be there." He tossed the key to Fatdaddy. Ruby got up and walked to the door. Fatdaddy glanced at each of them, then took the hint. Ruby held the door open, then waited until he was in his car before slamming and locking it.

Preacher grinned. "I hope you don't give me the fool's rush when I get ready to leave." They both laughed at his remark, then Prince opened a package of cocaine and held it out towards Preacher.

"You know, Prince, I got the biggest goddamn responsibility in this shit jumpin' off tomorrow, or rather, today." He snorted a nose full of coke, then held out the package to Prince. Prince gave it to Ruby as she sat down on the bed beside him.

"I know, Preacher, but I ain't got nobody else I can trust with such a job. As you know, man, Chinaman's got his fool-ass head in the clouds over this picketing bullshit." Prince made a disgusted sound. "Can you beat that, man! The guy is really sincere. He thinks we are really working towards helping some of these nuts. Man, I don't give a fuck what happens out there, as long as we get ours."

Preacher reached for the cocaine. "Yeah, baby, I can dig that, but this is big potatoes, man. If we rip off that bank like you got it planned, the feds are going to be all over this motherfuckin' city before God gets the news."

"Ain't no ifs about it, Preacher; the thing is going down today, whether you lead them niggers or not."

Preacher threw up his hands. "Wait a minute, man! You know I'm going to take care of it; it's just that I was kickin' the thing around a little, that's all. You know how the old saying goes," he said, then added, "telephone, telegraph, or tell a nigger. Those are the three quickest ways in the world for people to learn your business. You know that, Prince, as well as I do."

Prince laughed coldly, then reached for the cocaine. After taking a big snort, he said, "All the men on this job with you, Preacher, are handpicked. It ain't no game for no lame, man. I got the very best, baby. I got the strongest brothers you could ever want to work with you on this. If you should have to hold court in the streets with the cops, you couldn't ask for any better help. Each one is a killer."

"And you already know you ain't goin' have no trouble out of the police, Preacher," Ruby said, speaking in her softest voice. She flashed her magnificent teeth at him.

He smiled in return. "I don't need that soft con, Ruby," he said. "Your man is doing a good enough job of that already without your help." They all laughed good-naturedly. It was as though they were planning a weekend picnic rather than a bold daylight robbery.

"Okay," Preacher said loudly as he got to his feet. "I been sold on this thing ever since you brought the idea up, Prince. It's just that the day done arrived, and

I know I got to get off the pot or shit."

Prince walked him towards the door. "I'll stop by the crib today and talk to the other guys as well as you, Preacher. Ya'll can look for me around two o'clock. Don't worry about nothing, baby, this thing is in the bag." He held the door open and stood in the doorway until Preacher drove out of the motel parking lot. Then he stepped back into his suite.

Ruby stared up at him from the bed. "So far, so good," she said calmly. They understood each other better than they realized. Each in his own way needed the other, mentally as well as sexually. If either had any qualms about what could happen later on that day, they were well concealed.

"You ain't made that call to Chicago yet," Ruby reminded him quietly.

"It's too early, honey. I think it will be better if I wait until we get outside somewhere and make it from a pay phone."

She smiled. "You really got a thing about phone calls, ain't you, Prince?"

"Ain't no sense taking unnecessary chances, Ruby. Whoever they got on the switchboard might like to eavesdrop on calls, and at this time of morning a long-distance call would probably be right up the operator's alley. No baby, I think it will be a hell of a lot wiser to stop at a pay phone after we drop Roman and Dot off at the airport."

"I wish they would hurry up and get here," she said. "I'm gettin' sleepy as hell." She started impatiently for the kitchenette, but a knock at the door stopped her in her tracks.

She rushed to the door, but before opening it she glanced carefully between the large drapes that covered the picture windows.

"It's them," she said over her shoulder as she opened the door. Roman and Dot came in quickly, and Ruby shut the door behind them.

Prince snorted some of the coke and held the dwindling pile of dope out towards Roman. He started to reach for it, but Dot's voice froze him. "Roman," she said loudly, "don't you know you'll get sick on the plane if you snort that shit?" He hesitated briefly, but before he could make up his mind, Ruby had taken the cocaine and snorted the rest of it.

"When mama speaks, you listen, boy," Ruby chided him harshly. The undercurrent of contempt in her voice didn't escape Dot's notice. She bristled but decided not to say anything, although her eyes glittered with hate.

Prince reached under his pillow and pulled out a long envelope. He tossed it over to Roman. "There's ten thousand dollars in there, Roman. Be sure to take good care of it."

Roman managed a smile. He glanced down at the unsealed envelope, then started to stick it in his jacket pocket.

"Count it, man. I don't want no shit from you when you get back about it being short." Prince got up and glanced at his watch. "You better slip on a sweater, Ruby. This time of year it's kind of chilly in the mornings."

They waited until Roman had finished counting the money before leaving. Ruby got up under the steering wheel. "It'll be better, man, if we drop you at the airport. That way the car won't be tied up out there until you get back," Prince said quietly.

Roman didn't bother to comment as he held back the seat of the Cadillac for Dot to get in. She climbed in, stiff with unconcealed anger. "How the hell are we supposed to get back from the airport when we return from Chicago?" she snapped as she sat down.

Ruby laughed coldly. "You're supposed to be coming back from there on the train, aren't you, darling?"

Roman broke in, attempting to change the subject before sparks started to fly. "You know, Prince, I'm kind of glad to be gettin' the fuck away from here today. When that shit jumps off, it's going to raise plenty hell for some people."

"Maybe," Prince replied shortly.

"I done tried, but I just can't see no reason for rippin' off that gun shop, man. What do we need with all those guns? It ain't goin' do nothing but bring more heat down on us." The baffled note in Roman's voice revealed that he was really upset by Prince's plan.

Ruby drove in silence, and when she hit the expressway she put her foot on the gas. At this hour in the morning there was very little traffic. She caught the outside lane and stayed there, passing everything in sight.

"We aren't really in that much of a hurry, dear," Dot said coldly, her words dripping with sarcasm. "We really have plenty of time, you know."

Prince smiled self-consciously. It was rare that these two women could come together without one of them trying to hit a tender nerve that the other couldn't conceal. "I have to disagree with you, Roman," he began. "It's very important that we have enough guns to go around. In this day and age, any organization like ours has to have plenty guns or the police will kill you like a dog every time they catch you in the streets."

"I can dig where you're coming from, Prince, but our thing ain't about that, man. We are supposed to be going for the buck—hard, green cash. It ain't about open conflict with the police."

Prince snorted. "You can't help but have conflict with the man, baby. No matter how hard we try, we goin' run into trouble with the police. So the best thing in the world for us is to have some shit to return an eye for an eye. Dig this, man, we can't allow the man to shoot down our people whenever they feel like it, like they did Shortman."

Roman cut in. "Some police got shot down first, Prince, before anything happened to our people."

"Damn that!" Prince exclaimed. "It ain't our problem to worry about every pig that gets shot down in the streets. That's their job, baby. That's what the city hires them for. What I'm trying to get across to you is that, from now on, every time they retaliate on one of our people, we goin' sock it right back to them." Prince tossed him a skeptical glance, then continued. "What you don't understand, Roman, is that whitey don't understand but one thing—violence. Brutality is his way of life, baby, so he don't respect nothing but violent measures. If you don't show him that, he goin' keep his foot right in your backside."

Roman shook his head, baffled. He could feel that this day spelled big trouble. It was just a matter of time now, the way Prince was going. It couldn't possibly last. He began to wonder if Prince could be insane. It was possible, he thought. All this killing lately had to be the work of a deranged mind. No sane person could order wholesale murder without any qualms. He glanced at Ruby and wondered if she had any idea of just how mad her man was becoming.

Suddenly, Ruby left the freeway and pulled in towards the airport. They parked quite a way back from the main entrance and walked the rest of the way. Ruby and Prince followed closely behind Roman and Dot.

"You sure everything is set up, right, Roman?" Prince asked quietly.

"Oh yeah, baby. We called before we left and everything is ready. That young dago I been dealing with is really into something," Roman said. "He's really big time, Prince, and I mean big time."

Prince smiled slightly but did not bother to answer They continued in silence until Ruby spoke up.

"This really is a big thrill for you, ain't it, Dot? An old country girl like you gettin' a chance to ride on the white man's big iron bird. Girl, I'll bet you ain't goin' know how to act once you get back from that old big city you goin' to." Ruby laughed loudly as Dot stared over her shoulder. There was no concealing the mounting rage in her eyes. Roman put his arm around his woman's shoulder and felt it unyielding, a sure sign of anger. He knew if Ruby kept baiting Dot, there would be an explosion he didn't want to see.

Prince watched the two women and laughed. He pulled Ruby's arm. "That's enough, baby," he said lightly. "We don't need no floor show out here between you two."

Roman stayed at the rail with them until Dot bought the tickets, then they waited together silently until the loudspeaker informed them that their plane was loading on Ramp Six.

"You wait here and watch them go aboard," Prince instructed Ruby, then made his way to the telephone. He dialed a long-distance number, and when the receiver was picked up at the other end, he asked for room 48. He waited patiently until the night clerk put his call through, then he said four words, "They're on the way," and hung up.

As he went back to rejoin Ruby, she met him halfway. "Our little pigeons are on their way, daddy." She put her arm in his and they walked from the airport arm in arm.

Roman settled back in his plane seat. His mind was working ten miles a minute. He touched the envelope containing the money. It wouldn't be any problem, he reasoned, just to keep on traveling. They had enough money to last a while, and when it was gone, all they would have to do would be to make a trip back to Detroit and slip down to the bank one afternoon and get out the twenty-five thousand they had stashed there. The gang was headed for prison, there was no doubt in his mind about that. You couldn't toss bricks at the prison walls day in and day out and hope not to get caught. There would be no better opportunity than now, he reasoned, to step right away from it all before he was caught up in the madness.

"Dot," he began, "how would you like to just keep on going?" She stared at him surprised. "I mean," he continued, "when we reach Chicago, we just catch another plane out for the West Coast."

"What about the dope, honey?" she asked.

"Fuck the dope," he replied harshly. "Let's just get the hell on away from it all. Just keep on going. We got ten grand right here, and we can always come back and get the rest of our money."

The airplane hit an air pocket, causing her to clutch at her seat. "Roman, don't talk crazy. We ain't got no clothes with us or nothing. When Prince finds out we done pulled up with the ten thousand, he goin' go over to our place and take everything out that ain't nailed down."

"So what?" Roman asked sharply. "We ain't got nothing there we can't replace, have we?"

"Sure, you can replace it," she replied sharply, "but just look at how much it's going to cost. Don't forget, I left two mink stoles there that I damn sure want. Just stop and think for a minute, honey, please. If we run off with the ten grand, it's going to take that much money just to replace the stuff we left behind. All your suits, plus them alligator and lizard shoes of yours, baby. No, we can't do it like that; we got too much to lose."

She had a point, he bitterly agreed. He had a wardrobe any man would envy, and it had taken him a long time to get it. For the first time in his life he had enough clothes so he never had to worry about what to wear. Too many years of having only one pair of shoes, one pair of pants, sometimes not even one dress suit to wear, came back to his mind. You don't forget hardship overnight.

"You're right," he said suddenly. "It's too much to just up and leave."

Dot smiled slightly. "All we got to do, Roman, is plan. When we return, you're going to have all the responsibility of the dope money. Why take off with ten grand when, with a little patience, we might be able to string for another twenty-five or fifty grand if things hop off right." She laughed at her own cleverness. How stupid men were, she thought. Roman, Prince, all of them. Any woman, except that foolish Ruby, she reasoned, could get anything she wanted out of a man if she used her wits.

The pilot announced the landing. Everyone began to fasten their seatbelts. Dot sat back in her seat, proud of the fact that she knew what her future would be. It wasn't everyone who could control their destiny as well as she planned on controlling hers and Roman's. He was a lucky man, she thought, to have her standing beside him. He was so easy to lead. At times she wondered how he had managed to rise so high in Prince's organization. There was a man, she thought. If she could only move Ruby out of the way, it would be nice taking her place. She frowned slightly. What Roman feared was a possibility. Things couldn't last the way they were going, so maybe it wasn't such a good idea wishing she were Prince's woman. When the castle fell, everyone close was sure to fall with it.

The plane came down on the runway, took two bounces and landed for good. People were already unbuttoning their seatbelts. It took about fifteen minutes to get clear of the airfield and run down a cab.

Dawn was breaking out over the city as they leaned back against the seat of the cab. Dot rolled up the window to escape a cold blast of the September wind. As the cab left the freeway, she stared out the window in disgust.

"It looks just like one great big slum to me," she remarked as they entered Chicago. "I don't think I'd like this city. Just look at that!" she exclaimed, pointing out the window at some dirty tenement buildings.

The cab driver glanced at Dot in his rearview mirror. The little black bitch, he cursed under his breath. He turned into the driveway of a motel.

"This is good enough," Roman said to the driver, as he glanced out at the name of the motel. The Desert Inn was large and modern with a swimming pool. At this time of day, there was no one about. Roman glanced at his watch after paying the cab driver. It wasn't even six o'clock yet. He shook his head in wonder. They had left Detroit at four-thirty; now here they were at the end of their journey in less than an hour and a half.

The female nightclerk glanced out the window at

them as they walked up the pathway. She watched them from her desk until they stopped in front of number 16. When the door opened and they went in, she returned to the paperback book in front of her.

Tony stepped back to allow them to enter. He smiled at Dot, then closed the door behind them. "How was the trip?" he asked politely.

Roman's eyes scanned the room; the half-open bathroom door caught his attention at once. "Is it all right if I use your toilet?" he asked casually. Ten thousand dollars was a nice piece of money, so he wasn't taking any chances, even though he had done a little business with Tony in Detroit.

Tony walked over to the dresser and opened one of the drawers. "I'm afraid not," he said coldly, then whirled around, a long-barreled thirty-eight in his hand. Dot managed a light scream before he hit her across the face with the gun.

Roman started to make a move in their direction, but a sharp blow in his back caused him to wheel around. Racehorse stood behind him grinning, the pistol in his hand aimed right at Roman's chest.

"What the hell is going on?" Roman demanded with as much authority as he could manage. "You guys must be out of your minds if you think Prince will stand still for me being stuck up."

Both men laughed. "Don't worry about Prince," Racehorse snarled. "We'll take care of him when the time comes." He ordered, "Set that goddamn money out, now."

Roman fumbled with his inside pocket, shaking

uncontrollably. He managed to pull the long envelope from his pocket. "Here, take the money, man, just don't hurt us."

Tony laughed and pushed Dot towards the bed. "Say, man, take a gander at them big hips on her, will you?" he said as she sprawled out on the bed. "You think we ought to take a little time and find out what she's got that keeps our boy here so happy?" He laughed, glanced at Roman's face, then started to laugh louder. When he managed to stop, he said, "Take a look at him, will you. The guy's more worried about us bustin' out his woman than he is over the ten grand."

Racehorse grinned, then made an impatient gesture. "Get your ass on the bed beside your woman, boy. Don't nobody want none of that stuff."

"Speak for yourself!" Tony exclaimed, then grinned when Roman glared at him. "We better tie the boy up first. He might try to be a hero or something." Tony opened up the dresser and pulled out some rope. They tied Roman tightly to the bed, his arms above his head, his feet together, with the rope tied to the springs under the bed. Racehorse tied the ropes, making sure Roman couldn't move an inch.

"Please, please, just tie me up," Dot begged as Tony ran his hands over her breasts. He stuck one down inside her blouse, fumbled around and removed it as she squirmed and moaned.

Racehorse watched him unconcerned as he removed some more rope from the drawer. "You having fun with that dark meat, Tony? She don't move me at all,"

he said in a matter-of-fact voice. He tossed Tony the
rope. Tony tied Dot's hands first, then, before tying
her feet, he ran his hand inside the top of her pants.
When she started to cry, he slapped her viciously.

"Stop that goddamn whining, bitch," he ordered,
pushing his hand deeper in her pants. "Sonofabitching
pants is tight as hell," he said. Roman struggled with
his ropes, but they wouldn't give.

Racehorse laughed, pulled the envelope out of his
pocket and counted the money. He laid five thousand
dollars on the dresser, then glanced at Tony. "You really want to knock some of that off, man?" he asked
abruptly.

Dot began to kick her legs wildly as Tony's fingers
found what he had been searching for. He played with
her for a while, then removed his hand. "Naw, man,
I don't think so. It felt kind of big to me. Help me tie
her legs down, baby. I don't want this bitch to kick
me in the face." They worked quickly to subdue her,
and after tying her firmly to the bed, Racehorse began
to wipe the room clean of fingerprints.

Tony gagged Roman and Dot, making sure that no
matter how much they struggled, they couldn't dis-
lodge the knots from their mouths. He took his share
of the money from the dresser, then spoke to his partner. "You better take off, buddy. I'll take care of the
rest of the business here." He slipped on a pair of
gloves.

"Mellow, baby, I dig that," Racehorse replied and
turned back to the bed. With one swift motion, he
ripped Dot's pants down. "I don't know, Mellow, it

might be all right. It's good and goddamn hairy," he said and walked towards the door laughing.

When the door closed behind him, Tony walked over and peeped out the blinds. He watched Racehorse walk down the driveway and start up the street. "You know, honey," he said to Dot, "I didn't really want no audience, you know what I mean?" He laughed brutally.

Roman's eyes followed him closely. He swore to himself that he would remember every goddamn thing about Tony, and one day he would settle the score. He still didn't realize that he would never get the opportunity.

Tony sat down on the bed beside Dot. He ran his fingers up between her legs. She couldn't kick now, so she just lay as still as possible. He stared down at her, then ripped her blouse off. He stared at the dark nipples. He took one in his fingers and squeezed it tightly, playing with it until it became hard.

"Hey, man," he yelled. "Look at your woman, she's gettin' hot as hell over here. But she ain't nowhere near as hot as she's going to be before it's all over." He tossed back his head and roared at his own joke.

Dot stared up at him; she wanted to spit in his face, but the gag prevented it. She was as helpless as a baby. She closed her eyes as she felt his fingers begin to play with her again. Hurry up, she pleaded silently. Just hurry and get it over with. She would give Roman plenty hell about this when it was over.

Tony got up suddenly from the bed, tired of playing. Dot tried to watch him out of the corner of her eye, but he went into the bathroom. She closed her eyes for a second, then felt something cold splash on her. Her nose told her what it was immediately. It was gas. She opened her eyes and stared frantically at Tony. He was slowly but carefully soaking the bed with gas. She tried to open her legs, to tell him it was all right, do whatever he wanted to, but just please turn her loose.

Tony didn't even bother to look at her. He was an expert; he had a job to do, and he didn't leave anything to chance. He removed a straight razor from his jacket pocket. He grabbed Roman's head, twisted it sideways, then made a quick slice with the razor. Blood shot across the room.

Dot could feel herself gagging. She felt tears running down her cheeks as her eyes grew wide with terror. This couldn't be happening, not to her, she told herself, but there was no avoiding the truth. She felt Tony's hand on her head and tried to plead with him with her eyes.

He glanced down at her once, then make a quick slice with the razor. He slowly checked his clothing for bloodstains, then lit a match and dropped it on the bed. There was a loud swoosh, and the bed went up in flames.

He opened the door and slipped out, not bothering to glance back. He knew beyond a shadow of a doubt that it was a job well done.

14

THE AFTERNOON SUN had come out and the autumn day was beginning to take on the glow of Indian summer. People were out on the sidewalks standing around and gossiping, anything to keep them out of the stuffy, smelly flats they called their homes.

Ruby drove slowly down the crowded street, watching for the kids darting in and out of traffic. She had to stop and wait until a boy chased a beat-up football across the street. Prince glanced up from a paperback novel he had been reading. He watched the boy pick up the ball, almost under the wheels of the Cadillac, then run back and join the crowd of boys who had been watching from the curb. They waited until the cars drove past, then reentered the street to continue their game.

Ruby pulled over and parked beside the curb. "You want me to wait, or would you rather I come back for you later on?"

Prince glanced up and down the street. "There's a drugstore down there, baby. You can walk down there and get you a pop or something while you wait on me. It shouldn't take me too long to finish up here, so make sure you hurry up back." He climbed out of the car, then waited until Ruby had got out, too, before continuing on his way.

Prince stopped on the second floor of the apartment house. His knock was quickly answered by someone peeping through a small hole in the door. Quickly the door opened and Prince stepped into the room. Men were lying all around the apartment, each with a weapon under his armpit in a shoulder holster.

Preacher shut the door. "What's happening, baby?" he yelled. "I was beginning to wonder if you was going to show up."

Prince smiled at the remark. "I started not to show up, man, but the thought of all that cash being left alone if I didn't forced me to get off my ass and come on over." He examined the other men. "Hawk, you look like you might be a little nervous." Prince grinned, taking the sting out of his words. "And you, too, Bossgame," he said.

Bossgame grinned in return. He was tall, with a golden brown complexion. His extreme thinness had once earned him the nickname of "the Shadow," but his success at playing on people had caused his associates to call him "Bossgame."

"What about Eddie, Prince? You don't think he's a monument of pure nerve, do you?"

"I ain't shittin' on myself!" Eddie exclaimed loudly, his words bringing a roar of laughter from the men. Eddie was the youngest man in the room, just eighteen, but he had spent six years in reform schools, so he was considered reliable.

Prince stared at the young, brown-skinned man. Out of all the men in the room, Eddie was his main concern. He didn't want him to do anything that would bring more heat down on them than was necessary. Eddie was a good man, he believed, but he might do something that was uncalled for. He glanced over at the two brothers, Ronald and Donald. He wasn't worried about them. They were seasoned stickup men. Both had been to prison, so it wouldn't be anything new if they got busted. They were both nervous, since they were used to working only with each other. If it hadn't been for Prince, neither man would have been there, but since he was jeopardizing his own freedom, they had decided to go along.

Prince wasn't fooling himself. He knew if something went wrong, he was as vulnerable as the rest of them, even though he wouldn't be on the scene. "Preacher," he said suddenly, "I want you to use Eddie as the getaway driver." He wasn't going to take a chance on having blood spilled without cause. He could see the effect his words had on the other men. They seemed to relax a bit.

"Fuck that shit, Prince," Eddie said angrily. "I ain't no goddamn driver and you know it. I ain't never drove no fuckin' car in my life."

"Listen, punk," Prince said coldly as he grabbed the smaller man by the shoulders, "I got too much riding on this job to have some trigger-happy punk spoil it. I know it wouldn't take much for you to shoot somebody, so I ain't takin' no chances. If you don't like the idea of keepin' the motor running until they come out, you're out of the job. It's as simple as that. Either you go for it or you don't."

"Why me, Prince?" Eddie cried. "I can handle any part of this job as good as any of these guys, man." He was brokenhearted at being left out of the heavy part of the stickup.

"That's the reason right there," Prince said. "Any of these other guys would be glad to be sitting in the car and getting the same split, but you, you're looking forward to the job with just too goddamn much joy, Eddie. I can't take the chance, man. If trouble should come up, you just might shoot before you thought about it, baby."

"Shit!" Eddie cursed loudly and kicked the couch. A large rat ran out from under the couch, saw the men in the middle of the floor, hesitated, then scurried along the edge of the wall until he disappeared behind a large chair.

Prince stared with horror at the spot where the rat had disappeared. Ever since an incident in his early childhood, the sight of a rat paralyzed him with fear. He remembered how he had awakened one night when he was a child to find a large, red-eyed rodent on his bed. The rat had bitten him through the sheet on his leg. His screams had brought his grandmother hurrying into the room. Now, the fear was there again, his heart pounding like a sledgehammer, sweat soaking his shirt.

"Put that gun up," Preacher ordered sharply. Eddie had his pistol out and was trying to get a shot under the chair.

Donald came out of the kitchen carrying a broom. "Pull the chair out, I'll kill the bastard," he yelled, waving the broom.

Ronald, a younger replica of his brother, came out of the kitchen carrying a heavy skillet and a large steel pot. His cold black eyes glistened eagerly as he pranced around the chair, waiting for the rat to attempt his escape. Donald grinned as he held his broom ready.

Prince scrambled on top of a wooden chair, unconcerned about what the other men might think. They all knew that the only thing in life he feared was rats.

"Hey, man, I see you takin' care of business," Hawk yelled from atop the back of the couch. He flashed a friendly grin at Prince. "It ain't that I'm afraid of rats," he said. "It's just that I don't believe in taking any unnecessary chances. Let the big game hunters run that sonofabitch down."

Eddie was bent over double laughing. Now and then he would manage to point his finger in the direction of the two men on top of the chair and couch.

Prince gritted his teeth, fighting back his anger.

"Fuck all this laughing. If ya goin' kill the goddamn thing, get it over with."

The rat made the decision for them. He darted out from behind the chair. Ronald had been watching for just this chance. He threw the skillet and caught the rat across the back. Before the rat could regain his balance, Donald was on him, beating him with the broom.

"Let me at him," Ronald yelled, brandishing the pot. He tried to dance around his brother so he could get in a good blow.

"The bastard's back is broke," Donald said, stepping back from the rat. Ronald picked up the skillet and quickly finished the job.

"Wrap that rat up in some newspaper and toss it out the back window," Preacher ordered. "You wash that fuckin' skillet off good, Ronald. No telling what kind of goddamn germs you done picked up on it."

Prince climbed down off his chair. He rolled a stick of reefer from the package Preacher tossed him, then waited until things returned to normal. When the two brothers returned from disposing of their burden, Prince tossed them a stick of reefer apiece. He waited until they had settled down, then began. "After I leave, Preacher will tell each one of you what position you'll handle on the job. What I want to get across to each of you is the importance of the disguises you will wear." He gestured towards the two brothers. "I want both of you to shave off those heavy mustaches you wear." He raised his hand for silence when they started to protest. "What's more important, wearing a goddamn mustache or getting away from a robbery with plenty of cash and no witnesses that can identify you?" Prince waited until they nodded their heads in agreement. "Okay then, after you shave your mustaches off, Preacher will give you some shit that will make you jet black." He stared at the two light brown-skinned men. "You shouldn't have any problem gettin' away with it. Once white folks see a black man, they won't think of anything else."

"What about me?" Hawk asked curiously. "Ain't no way to make me white, is there?" He grinned. "If I get any more darker, man, I'll be able to pass for an ink spot."

"We got a old man's wig with gray hair in it for you, Hawk. That plus a beard should help you get past the people." Prince grinned at Preacher. "Brother Preacher is going to pass as a lady, with a pretty red wig." He smiled as the men made a few lewd remarks.

"You goin' need any help puttin' your panties on, Preacher?" Hawk asked, then laughed uproariously at his own wit. Preacher just grinned at them, then walked Prince to the door.

"Make sure you're on the case at three forty-five, Preacher," Prince instructed him. "Everything is going to go off like clockwork. When you finish and change cars, head towards the hideout. I'll get in touch with you out there."

When Prince reached the car, it was surrounded by teenage boys. Ruby had the window down and was giving them a tongue-lashing. One or two of the boys recognized Prince and stepped back out of his way.

Ruby moved from the passenger side of the seat to behind the steering wheel as Prince got in.

"I see you got a lot of admiring young boys on this block," he said. "Maybe I better start watching you from now on whenever we come this way."

She laughed lightly as she started the car. "Them kids are something else." Ruby glanced at her watch. "Where to from here, daddy?"

"Time's gettin' real short, woman. I think we better go somewhere and establish us an airtight alibi, because after this shit jumps off we're going to be very important people in the police department's eyesight."

"It seems as though you might just have a point there, honey. Where do you suggest we go?"

Prince studied the problem for a minute. "I believe the best place in the world for us right now, baby, is down to the police station with our lawyer. Maybe we might even be able to spring Little Larry while we're killing time."

In Hamtramck, the Polish shoppers were staring around in wonder. Their neighborhood was being invaded by Negroes of every size and shape. Carload after carload of young blacks parked, and the men and women inside jumped out to surround the A&P supermarket. Traffic was congested because of the curious drivers slowing down to look at the pickets. Police cars arrived but had to park back from the crowd because there was no space for them to get closer. The clerks in the market glanced nervously out the window at the milling crowd.

Chinaman and Blanca moved through the crowd, keeping down any unnecessary disturbance. As soon as they left a spot, though, it was filled with agitators. The agitators moved through the crowd building up tension. Wherever they found police, they concentrated on that spot. The police, already short-tempered, were easily aroused to anger. Shouts of "white pigs" filled the air. The police moved through the crowd roughly, pushing people aside, swinging their clubs at any who hesitated. The only thing that held them in check was their small number. They waited impatiently for reinforcements to come from neighboring precincts.

The signal came from one of the agitators: *"Now! Now! Now!"* The shout filled the air. The few policemen caught in the midst of the crowd were turned on with a fury they had never seen before. It was beyond their understanding to find themselves faced with black people who were fighting back. They were so accustomed to cracking heads without fear of being turned on that, now that it was happening, they were frozen with fear. It was a different matter when you swung your club at a head to find that head trying to take the club from you. The people in the crowd who had no knowledge of what was happening only saw that the police were trying to break up their peaceful demonstration. When they saw a black woman fall under the feet of two white policemen, they moved in a body towards the officers. As more police began to arrive, the agitators began to throw rocks. The rocks broke windows, angered the police, and turned the street into a riot. The fighting was now going on up and down the street. Black officers and white stood shoulder to shoulder trying to turn the tide. Store windows were broken, fire bombs were tossed indiscriminately. The street became a nightmare of chaos as people tried to escape from the police retaliation.

Chinaman kept his arm around Blanca as he fought his way out of the crowd. He pushed her into a small dress shop. The woman proprietor stared at them as though they were animals. He glanced back over his shoulder at the riot and shivered. He couldn't understand what had happened. All he could think of was that it was the policemen's fault. His anger almost overcame his reason as he turned around and stared at the woman. "I ain't goin' ask you but once, woman," he snapped. "Which is the quickest way out of here? I'm talking about the back way, too."

She stared at him with fear. Before she could answer, the door opened and two more black men came in, pushing their women in front of them. One of the women was holding a hankie to her bleeding nose.

"We ain't got time for games, bitch!" Chinaman yelled at the woman. She trembled at the sound of his voice, and managed to point towards the rear of the store.

"What about a key? Do we need a key to get out?" Chinaman asked. Before the woman could answer, one of the men snatched her arm and pushed her towards the rear. When they reached the back door, one of the men rushed past her and opened the lock himself.

The door opened onto the alley. As the small group stepped out, a police car rushed past. The group broke and ran up the next nearest alley. The only thing they could think about was escape. Behind them the street was filled with struggling figures. Black men tried to build a protecting wall around their women as they fought their way down the street. Time and time again police broke through the wall of men who fought courageously with fists and feet against pistols and billy clubs.

Fatdaddy and his group finished loading up the guns in the panel truck. When he returned for his last trip into the gun shop, he examined the ropes that the owner was tied with. He loosened them slightly so the man wouldn't have much difficulty getting free. His wife's bonds were still tight, but Fatdaddy ignored them, surrendering to his greed and tapping the cash register on the way out of the store.

Before the small truck had gotten out of the neighborhood, the proprietor of the gun shop had gotten loose and made a hurried call to the police station before even bothering to untie his wife.

The desk sergeant took the call and immediately went into action. Since all of his cars were at the riot, he had to make an emergency call for cars to take care of the robbery. His call was answered immediately by four cars that were needed in the riot.

When Preacher and his men reached the bank two miles from the gun shop, there wasn't a police car within a mile of the bank. They entered it quickly. Before the people inside knew what was happening, they were covered by the men with the guns. The bank guard had been caught completely off guard. Hawk removed his gun and ordered him to stand still.

Donald and Ronald moved behind the cage windows and took all the cash from the cash drawers. Preacher pushed the bank manager towards the half-opened vault. In less than three minutes he was back carrying an army duffel bag half full of money. Hawk climbed on top of a counter and ripped out the movie camera that had been working all the while they were in the bank. Each man wore a pair of thin gloves and dark sunglasses. Preacher caught the camera as Hawk tossed it down, stuffed it inside the bag on top of the money without ever taking his eyes off the customers. With the help of Donald, Preacher made the customers lie down beside the cashiers. The guard was clubbed to his knees by Hawk as the men prepared to leave. Ronald had already left for the car when the rest of the men followed, walking quickly from the bank, not running, afraid they might draw attention if anyone should see them. Eddie was sitting under the wheel when they reached the car.

The men jumped in, Preacher taking the front seat beside the driver. He took off the wig he had been wearing and kicked off the women's shoes as the car leaped away from the curb.

"Take it easy," he cautioned Eddie. "We got everything going in our favor, so just be cool. It couldn't have been no sweeter if Prince had been in charge," he gloated happily.

The other men began to relax now that the ordeal was over. The tension was beginning to disappear. Ronald and Donald began to wipe the makeup off their faces, while Hawk came out of his wig and beard. Ronald took another wipe at his face with the wet rag Eddie had given him.

"Am I got most of this shit off?" he asked loudly.

"Don't worry about it," Preacher said. "In another block we're going to start changing cars, so you'll have plenty of time to take all your war paint off."

"Man, oh man," Eddie exclaimed excitedly. "Is all that cash really unmarked?"

"We ain't got nothing but the smaller bills. All that big shit we would have had trouble gettin' rid of we left alone," Preacher answered.

"Ronald," he added a moment later, "that Buick up there, that's the first car you guys change in." He glanced over his shoulder. "Hawk, you stay with me. The rest of you take that piece and head for the hideout. We'll be there in a few minutes, as soon as we reach the other car."

15

THE OFFICE OF CAPTAIN Mahoney was a scene of bedlam. The detectives were in an uproar. Reports on what had happened that afternoon were still coming in.

"Damn it, Morales," Lieutenant Gazier swore. "If we release that punk, this whole city will blow up in our faces."

Lieutenant Morales ignored his partner and spoke to the other two men in the office. "Gentlemen, I have to disagree with you. I believe that the killing of that homosexual last week is definitely tied up with the other killings that have plagued the city lately."

"Lieutenant Morales," one of the Federal men

began. "You have misunderstood us. We will definitely give you all the cooperation we possibly can, but under the circumstances, my partner and I will have to concentrate on the apprehension of the men who held up that bank today." He glanced at his partner, then continued. "I for one can't see offhand how this would tie in with the rest of your problems. It's possible, true, but I just don't believe that any young group in the city would, or could, control what happened out there today."

Captain Mahoney stood up behind his desk, a piece of paper in his hand. "I don't know, Morales, if you are correct or not, but from my report, Roman was followed to the airport this morning, where he and his woman boarded a plane for Chicago." He held up his hand so he wouldn't be interrupted. "The same man that followed him out there followed Prince and his woman back to the city. Now, in regards to Prince, he was downstairs all afternoon working on the release of Larry with his lawyer. So whatever happened this afternoon, he had an airtight alibi. Since Roman was probably still in Chicago, he has an airtight alibi, too. Now, as far as I'm concerned, that's the two big men in this gang, and it's just a little beyond my imagination to believe they wouldn't be needed on an operation like the one that went off today."

Morales tilted his chair back. "Well, there is one thing you can't ignore. That's facts. Just plain, ordinary facts. First, what most of you fail to realize is that the organization that caused that riot is the brainchild of no other than our boy, Prince. Now, the rest of this crap that happened, you can take from there. The gun shop was hit at just the right time. When the only available police cars in the vicinity answered the call, the bank was hit."

He stared around at the listening officers. "Timing, not luck, gentlemen. We didn't have a car within eight blocks of that place during the holdup. Now, do you really want me to believe that what happened was just luck?"

The taller of the two Federal men cleared his throat. "You have a good point there, Lieutenant. Of course we will work as closely as possible with you on this, but our main concern is the bank robbery Did you have any definite plan of action?"

"Yes," Morales answered. "I have a plan, but it will take a little while to put it to work. As you know, we were holding that kid, Little Larry, on second degree, but they put so much pressure on us from upstairs that we had to release him this afternoon."

Lieutenant Gazier swore. "How the hell do they expect us to break these killings up if they turn loose every punk we pick up? What the hell goes on around here anyway, Morales? Everybody knows about that punk being released but me. Am I working on the case or what?"

"I was planning on telling you," Morales assured him, "but Mr. York and his partner came in before I had a chance to bring you up to date. Mr. York," Morales went on, "if you and Mr. Fulmer will bear with me for a few days, I think I'll have something definite to go on. I've sent off pictures to Chicago of

Roman, so they'll be watching for him when he leaves. I have a hunch he's over there trying to make a buy on some heroin. I didn't have any mug shots of his woman, but we sent along a fairly good description."

The phone rang. Captain Mahoney picked it up and listened quietly. "Before you guys ruin my day," he said after hanging up, "have a cigar." He smiled at Morales. "She has had a five-pound boy. A little too soon, of course, but the doctor says, for a premature baby, he's damn healthy."

"That's just great, Pat," Morales replied, then added for the sake of the other men, "That's his daughter-in-law. Don't you guys go getting the wrong impression about this old buzzard. He's too damn old to get one up, let alone get a baby." The officers grinned.

The captain cut off their congratulations. "Now, let's hear about this plan you boys were talking about."

Morales glanced around the room. "First of all," he began slowly, "we must acknowledge the fact that we are dealing with young men who possess the cunning of professional criminals and the morals of alley cats."

"Morales," Gazier remarked acidly, "what we need is some common facts. That's all, simple facts."

Captain Mahoney spoke sharply. "Gazier, you keep your big mouth shut or get the hell out of this office." He stared the younger officer down, then said politely, "Please continue, Lieutenant."

Ignoring the interruption, Morales nodded towards the captain. "Gentlemen, we are not just dealing with a gang of young hoodlums. This group of individuals is highly organized and the core of their unity is murder. Now, what we must try and understand is their motivation for wholesale murder. They are not committing murder just for the joy of it."

He stopped and waited until his words had sunk in. "This trouble has gone far beyond what the average delinquency would be. This trouble that we have today is our problem. I don't want to preach, but we must face the truth. We must do something about the slums. There is no doubt in my mind, gentlemen, that if we don't, this problem will keep coming back again and again. The overcrowded tenements, playgrounds, and poolrooms breed violence, crime, and prostitution. I know this seems to be getting away from the point, gentlemen, but bear with me a minute."

He hesitated briefly, then launched into a subject dear to him. "The playgrounds that are overcrowded are the cause of kids joining gangs. They join a gang so they can utilize the playgrounds without fear of another gang kicking the hell out of them. And now we come to the big problem. The slums. The ghettos are the place where corruption is born. Mexicans, Negros, Italians, and other minority groups are stuck down in these cesspools with no way out. These ethnic groups have to join together for protection, thus the beginnings of organized crime. If some of these people could only live where they can afford to live, their children would grow up in an environment that would push them towards something constructive in life instead of towards something detrimental."

"All that may be true, Lieutenant," Captain

Mahoney said, "but do you think that has any bearing on this case?"

Morales smiled slowly. "Gentlemen, I apologize to you for getting carried away. I'll try to stick to the facts from now on. Out of all the neighborhoods I visit, there's not much being said except that the leaders of the gangs have gone into hiding somewhere. Since Little Larry has been released, I honestly believe this will give the gang leaders courage, and they will crawl out of their holes. Another thing I've learned from the informers is that there is a slight drug shortage. That's one of the reasons Roman went to Chicago, to make a buy. If that's so, we may have a case against him when the Chicago police pick him up."

Federal agent York spoke up. "If you think they're trying to transport drugs, we can step into the picture, Lieutenant. We'll notify our office in Chicago to be on the lookout for this couple, too."

"Good," Morales said. "Now, even though I don't have much of a plan, if the captain will give us the okay, we can put it into operation."

"If it sounds good, Morales, you know you can get the green light," Mahoney replied.

"I want you to call the heat off, Captain," Morales said. "I want these punks to start feeling secure."

"I'll give these punks a feeling of security all right," Mahoney answered hotly "I'll run them into their rat holes and keep so much heat on them that their smell will draw us to them."

"That's just the point," Morales replied. "When you

run a rat into his hole, you seldom see him again unless you know where his hole is. At present, we don't have the slightest idea where our killer rats are hiding."

"Do you really believe that taking the heat off will do any good?" Mahoney asked quietly.

"I do," Morales answered quickly. "I believe once those punks come out of hiding, they'll try and take the lid off this town. And we'll be waiting to put it right back on—this time for keeps."

The phone rang shrilly. Captain Mahoney reached across his desk and picked up the receiver. Morales, accustomed to his superior's behavior, knew at once from his face that something was wrong. "Well, Morales," the captain said as he hung up, "looks as though that picture you sent to Chicago got some results."

The other detectives looked up expectantly.

"It seems that, from the picture you sent over, Morales, they were able to identify the body of a male black man who was burned up this morning in a motel. The woman with him was not identified. We can only assume it was Roman's girlfriend."

"How?" Morales asked in a shocked voice. "How the hell can they be sure, if the bodies were burned?"

"The night clerk. She saw them when they entered the motel room that was later set afire. She says she didn't see them leave, so it's a good chance it really was our boy and his girl that got burned up." The captain hesitated briefly. "There's no doubt in their minds about this fire. It was cold-blooded murder. Parts of a rope and other evidence clearly reveal that the couple were tied down to the bed and set on fire."

The detectives shook their heads over the brutality of the crime. They were used to violence, but this was an extreme case.

Agent York spoke up. "Captain, we will have our people help you as much as possible on this. If you don't mind, I'll put a call through from here and get them on this right away." He waited until Mahoney nodded, then picked up the telephone.

Captain Mahoney turned to Morales. "How long do you think it will take to bust this case if we take the heat off?"

"I can't give you anything but a guess," Morales replied slowly. "If we get any breaks, though, I believe we can start pulling punks in off the streets, with good cases against them, in less than three weeks."

"All right, then," Mahoney answered, "you got your three weeks before I put the heat back on. But if I have to put it back on, hell will be cooler than what it's going to be around here."

Earlier in the afternoon, across the street, Little Larry had gotten a surprise. He was lying on his cot in the county jail when the turnkey called his name. He had been told, "Bag and baggage." A little later, Larry found himself outside the jail, still not believing it was all true. A shrill voice called him from across the street. Glancing up, he saw the attorney, Antares Noetzold, threading his way through the passing cars. In a moment the lawyer had joined him on the sidewalk.

"Here, Larry," he said, pushing a piece of paper into his hand. "Take a cab to this corner and wait. Someone will pick you up as soon as possible." Before Larry could nod his head, the lawyer had pushed him into a waiting cab and closed the door.

Larry quickly read the note. "Drop me off at Mich and the Boulevard," he directed the cab driver. In less than ten minutes he was at his destination. Larry pushed a dollar across the seat and got out, ignoring his change. Before the cab could turn the corner, a new snow-white Cadillac pulled out of an alley and stopped in front of him.

Frenchie, sitting behind the steering wheel, had her long black hair combed to one side; it fell provocatively across her left shoulder. Larry glanced at her thin, pretty face before examining her body. "I'm really getting the royal treatment," he said to himself. He was well aware of Frenchie, but he wondered if she had ever realized he even existed. She was one of the big girls in the club; she never messed around with anyone who wasn't one of the big boys. She had a soft, dark-bronze complexion and thin but well-proportioned legs. She had the look of the models in *Ebony* or *Black America*, that detached, expensive look.

"Well, Larry, are you going to get in or stay out there staring?" Her voice was husky, its undertone sophisticated yet sexually arousing.

Larry opened the car door and slid in beside her. "How did you know who I was?"

"Well, honey," she began, "I don't think there's another person in this city wearing one of those Ruler outfits right now."

Larry glanced down at his uniform. "You mean to say the fuzz done put on so much heat that the fellows are scared to wear their outfits?"

"Heat ain't the word, baby," she replied. "The fuzz have gone stone mad."

"That's bullshit," Larry retorted. "It ain't so goddamn hot that Prince couldn't spring me, and them fuckin' pigs were really trying to stick a big one in me."

Frenchie shrugged her shoulders and fell silent. She turned a corner and passed the railroad depot, then entered the beginning of the west side slums. "Prince told me to make sure you get seen before I take you out to the hideout, Larry."

"What am I, some kind of freak that has to be displayed before the public?"

"It's not that, baby," Frenchie said, amused. "It's just that you being released today will give some of the boys a shot in the arm. You must realize, Larry, that since you've been under wraps, a lot of people have been worried. Now, when they see you again, it will give them that lift they need, so that when it comes time to sew this city up, they'll be right there on the case."

"After you get through sporting me off, Frenchie, then what?"

"I'll take you to the hideout, baby, and everything you see out there will be yours."

Larry let his eyes run over her legs. "Baby," he began, "do you really mean everything I see?"

She pulled the armrest up and put her arm over the back of the seat. Larry moved over and sat close to her. She picked up one of his hands and dropped it on her thigh. "Everything you see, honey, including me, if you're qualified to handle it," she said huskily.

Within two hours Frenchie and Larry had completed their job. Larry had been seen in poolrooms, whorehouses, after-hours joints, even though it was too early for them to be crowded; wherever the underworld hung out, they went there. When they reached the driveway leading to the hideout, Larry stared out the window in fascination. When Frenchie pulled up in front of the house, he let out a shout.

"Damn," he exclaimed. "Is this what you been calling the hideout?" He couldn't conceal his astonishment. To a boy who had never lived anywhere but a cold-water flat, the sight of the old mansion was like stepping into another world.

Frenchie laughed. "This is it, honey."

Larry stared at the couples sprawled on the lawn and by the swimming pool. Before he could make up his mind to get out of the car, Prince and Ruby were at the door.

"Hi, baby," Ruby called. "Welcome to our summer resort."

"Yeah," Larry replied grinning. "I guess you do come out here to relax when it gets too hot in the city."

The kids gathering around the car broke out in laughter when they heard Larry's retort. Prince grabbed Larry's arm as he got out of the car, and they went up the path arm in arm.

"Damn, Prince," he said quietly. "I don't know how you worked it, but it sure was beautiful."

"Don't worry about it, Larry. Anybody who works for me should know I'm in his corner all the way. Whenever they're as cool as you, they know they ain't got nothing to worry about." He added, "As long as they keep their mouths closed like you did."

Larry replied quickly, "That's your least worry, Prince, when it comes to me, even if I get a bite out of it."

"I ain't worried about you, kid," Prince answered, slapping him on the back. "No, baby boy, I sure ain't worried. Just keep on carrying yourself like that, Larry."

Before Larry could answer, a shout of welcome went up for him from a group on the recreation porch. Preacher, sitting on the couch beside Hawk, beckoned for them to join him. In front of him was a small table full of reefer; it was being rolled into cigarettes by Hawk.

"Here, baby, have a joint," Preacher said loudly, holding out a cigarette towards him.

"Thanks, baby, this is just what I been dreaming about all the time I was locked up. Man, oh man, what I would have paid for some good ol' weed this time last week!"

Ruby and Frenchie went on into the house. Prince

took Larry's arm and led him towards the library.
Larry blew smoke from the reefer over his shoulder
and started to cough from the strong smoke. Prince
slapped him on the back until he caught his breath.

Prince had just enough time to reach the library and
pour two drinks before the women returned, each carrying a try full of cocaine.

Larry gasped. "Man, is that cocaine on those trays?"

Fatdaddy came in behind the girls carrying two
album covers. Preacher was right behind him with a
newspaper full of reefer. They put all the stuff down
on a small end-table. Prince took the trays from Ruby
and Frenchie. He removed a small index card from
his pocket and began to make separate lines of cocaine
on the album covers. Then he took two one hundred
dollar bills from his pocket and gave them to the girls,
and they rolled the bills for quills. Ruby inserted one
end of her bill into her nose, leaned over, and put the
other end against one of the lines of powder on the
LP cover. She inhaled and the powder began to disappear into her nose. She handed the quill to Larry,
while Frenchie inhaled some dope with her quill.

Teenagers began to line up for their snort, and as
soon as they had taken their turns, Preacher gave each
of them a joint he had made from the pile of reefer.
Gradually the pile of drugs began to disappear.
Someone turned up the stereo, and the sound of modern jazz leaped from the ceiling and walls in a crescen-
do of intoxication and desire. One couple in the middle of the room swayed in each other's arms while
other couples began to move to the music. Slowly, a

few of the girls began to undress. The room became living sound. The drug was taking effect quickly. Any sensual delight the couples wanted to indulge in was permitted. There was no one to restrict their behavior.

Two young hoodlums standing began to laugh hysterically from the effects of the reefer. "Man, dig the tits on that bitch," one of them said, pointing a finger at a naked couple.

The other youth raised his voice to ridicule the girl's extremely small breasts. "If one of them didn't have long hair, I wouldn't know which one had the dick," he yelled. The girl, with an impudent shake of her head, raised the middle finger of her right hand to show them she had heard. Her boyfriend glared over her shoulder.

Another couple, too high to care, had moved the balls off the pool table in the corner and were beginning their own private affair as if they were in a feather bed. Yet another couple, seeking a little privacy, had crawled under the table to copulate. Larry and Frenchie, wrapped in each other's arms, lay on the floor with their backs against the couch.

Prince glanced at the squirming bodies all over the floor. "Preacher, you and Hawk round up Donald and Ronald. I'll meet you upstairs in my bedroom." He stared around until he found Eddie, then moved over and tapped the younger man on the leg. "Come on, Eddie. We got some business to finish. *Now!*" he ordered sharply as Eddie turned back to his girl. "You can catch up with her later on." Prince turned his back and walked away as Eddie climbed to his feet and zipped up his pants.

As Ruby followed the small group of men from the room, Eddie stopped to take his anger out on her. "I didn't hear him tell you to come along," he said quietly so that no one but her heard his words.

Ruby stopped and glared at him. "You didn't hear him say that I couldn't, either, did you?" she asked sharply, closing the door behind them. Preacher, the two brothers in tow, joined the small crowd going up the stairs.

"Ruby," Prince said as they entered the bedroom, "fix the boys something to drink. We'll probably be here for a while, so they might as well be comfortable."

She stopped and switched on the light, then opened up the drapes. She hesitated a moment to admire the beauty of the early evening. It was just dusk-dark, the sky was still starless.

The king-size bed had a huge hump in the middle of it. Prince pulled back the covers and the hump became a pile of money. "We got ninety-five thousand dollars there," Prince said loudly. He waited, sure of everyone's attention. "Not bad for an afternoon of work, was it?" He grinned at his men. "In each small pile, there's ten thousand dollars. Each of you take one." It was an order. He stepped back from the bed and waited until each man had picked up his bundle.

Eddie was the first to complain. "Goddamn, Prince," he began, "you mean to say that's all we're going to get? We did all the work, now you goin' take all the money."

Prince met his stare without batting an eye. "I ain't taking all the money, fool," he replied sharply. "But since some of you will be bitchin', it's best I explain." His sharp eyes covered all the men in the room. They met his gaze without turning away.

"First of all," Prince explained, "there was more people than just you involved. All the people in the riot belonged to us. I've got to make bond on at least fifty people, plus pay the men who ripped off the gun shop. They didn't make nowhere near the kind of money you guys did. In fact, they didn't make any money at all, yet they stuck up the joint so we would have guns whenever we needed them." He waited until his words had sunk in, then continued. "That should be enough for all of you, but if it ain't, I ain't got but one more thing to say. If you still don't like the way the money was split, kiss my black ass!" Ruby, bringing the drinks, stopped and laughed harshly.

"My, my, my, just listen to daddy. What ya done done, Preacher? It ain't too often I hear my old man inviting you muleheaded bastards to do such things." She set down the tray of drinks, and from under it pulled out a pistol. Without pointing it at anyone in particular, she made her point clear. "I don't understand why any of you are complaining. You got more money than you've ever seen, yet you want more." She gave the pistol to Prince.

He stuck the gun in his belt. "All that money on the bed is spent, except what you guys made out of it.

The rest is going back into this organization. Lawyer fees, bond money put up for later on…. I ain't goin' make a slug out of it, yet I planned the whole fuckin' thing."

"We hadn't thought about it thataway," Preacher answered, speaking for the group. "At least, I hadn't." The two brothers nodded their heads, while Eddie managed sullenly to show that he was in agreement.

"I ain't said nothing about the split from the bell, Prince," Hawk stated. "However you handle it, man, is cool with me. I know you ain't goin' fuck over me for no reason at all."

Prince relaxed a bit. "I owe you an apology, Hawk, and the rest of you, too." Prince picked up a drink, then glanced at his men closely. "It's going to be kind of tight for a few of you. I know you'll probably want to get away from here and spend some of that cash, but it ain't goin' work like that. I want you to hang out here for a few weeks. We'll try and let the heat cool off. Preacher, I'll have to have you back downtown to help me take care of a little business, but the rest of you can make yourselves at home. It won't be but for a few weeks, then you can go wherever you want."

"That's cool with me," Hawk said quickly. "I ain't got no place to go. With all this ass running around out here, this is about the hippest thing going anyway."

Prince waited until all of them had agreed to stay around. "Preacher, I want to talk to you about some important business in your neighborhood. You and

Ruby stick around. The rest of you can go on back downstairs and start having big fun again. We'll be down in a little while."

He waited until the door had closed behind the last of them, then turned to Preacher. "Preacher, after this evening, I want you to get back into the city and raise the dues on all the prostitutes in your district. Instead of five dollars a night to work, they got to come up with seven. I'm going to get in touch with Chinaman and have him start putting the pressure on every Puerto Rican and white whore in his district. Our protection money has been coming in too slow. It ain't paying for itself. The cost of some of them goddamn kids we have to support is keeping me busted."

Preacher listened to him quietly, not surprised. "We been having a little problem with the Black Cougars in our neighborhood, Prince. They been trying to stop the prostitutes from working out on the streets. It's a rumor out they're going to start trying to close down the dope houses in all the black neighborhoods."

Prince laughed. "If things get any worse, they won't have to close them down. I'll do it for them. I ain't been able to keep half of our dope houses supplied."

"What about that nigger, Fox?" Ruby asked curiously. "I thought he was supposed to raise so much hell when he got out of prison. He's home now, and he sure ain't keeping my girls up with enough dope to take care of no city."

Prince shook his head. "It ain't his fault, honey. The man ain't never had any reason to handle so much stuff before. You know, we buy a lot of poison in the run of one week. He's trying to fix up a new connection now that might be able to handle our problem."

"What about these Black Cougars, man? You ain't worried about them closing up none of our joints?" Preacher asked stubbornly.

Prince made his familiar gesture of impatience: his hand cut down with a swift, chopping motion. His eyes glittered dangerously. "Nobody, and I mean nobody," he said coldly, "is going to close down our places, unless it's the man, and then we're going to open up another one around the corner."

16

THE OUTER OFFICE of the storefront headquarters of the Black Cougars was decorated with posters of black revolutionaries. A large poster of Chairman Mao adorned the wall just over the entrance of the inner office. Inside, three dedicated young black men watched Chinaman as he paced back and forth. Blanca sat on the couch by herself, watching her man closely. What had just been revealed to him would have far-reaching repercussions.

"Sonofobitching dirty-bastard," Chinaman cursed. "You mean all those people were just used so that Prince could rip off them joints?" He asked the question of no one in particular. It was the rambling of a man who has been hurt by someone close. He was hurt, yet he still searched for an excuse for his friend. His eyes were full of unconcealed pain.

"Don't take it too bad," a tall black man stated. "You're not the only one who was played on. Everybody out there marching that day was used. It just hurts you more because you realize that you were put on Front Street."

Chinaman stared up at the six-foot-six giant. "I don't want to believe it's true even now. It's not bothering me that I was the one out on Front Street. What really hurts is that so many of the kids out there believed in us. They put their faith in me—me—then ended up being crossed." He dropped his head, looked away for a moment, then turned back. "Mr. Yates, do you think there's any way for me to regain the confidence of those people?"

The huge, dark-skinned Mr. Yates smiled reassuringly, with a tenderness surprising for a man his size. "Most of the people who were caught up in that madness don't realize it was all planned. The only reason we know about it is that one of our men happened to be in the crowd of agitators. He likes it when it's hot, so he went along just to get in a few licks at the pigs."

"I wouldn't have minded being up on that myself," one of the other Cougar members said. "It's not every day that we get a chance to knock a few heads without worrying about reprisals."

"I'll go along with that one hundred percent, brother," added the third Cougar present in the room.

"You see?" Yates asked, pointing at the others.

"Both of my devoted brothers are ready to go on the warpath. Any other time, Mr. Davis and Mr. Williams would both be preaching patience."

Both men laughed good-naturedly. Yates continued. "You have nothing to worry about on that point, Chinaman. In fact, we would like to see you continue with the work you began. From what our source has told us about you, plus what we have been able to learn for ourselves, we believe you're completely dedicated to working for the freedom of all men of color." He waited until Chinaman had nodded in agreement, then spoke softly. "If you are really sincere, Chinaman, there's no reason why you can't pull your people into our organization. I don't think anyone could find any reason not to like the idea of us combining. After all, brother, our organization is nationwide."

Chinaman shivered visibly. "Ain't no sense in me foolin' you, brother. Prince ain't goin' like the idea at all." His eyes searched out Blanca on the couch. He could tell that the idea of trying to put Prince out of the organization had shaken her up, too.

Mr. Yates had noticed their shock. "We realize that Prince could be a problem for you, but we have taken it on ourselves to handle this responsibility. If you will give us your word on this matter, we will take it from there." He hesitated briefly, then walked over and opened the door to the outer office. He glanced out and beckoned to the young woman sitting on the bench.

Ruby threw down the magazine she had been try-

ing to read for the past ten minutes. She twisted
around on the bench and stared angrily at the young
man sitting behind the scarred desk. She wished
Prince had accompanied her to this meeting. When
the huge black man beckoned to her, she was already
highly irritated. She marched into the inner office,
swinging her pocketbook by the strap.

When Chinaman looked up and saw Ruby come
storming in, he had to sit down on the couch to stop
his legs from trembling. The other men stared at her
in open admiration. Mr. Yates bit his lip. He had heard
about how beautiful she was, but this was the first
time he had ever seen her.

Ruby stared at Chinaman and Blanca with anger.
"Does Prince know you're here?" she asked sharply.
She didn't bother to wait for an answer. She stared up
into the face of Mr. Yates. "Prince was busy," she said
coldly. "He said to tell you, if you had anything to
say, to send the message by me."

"I would have rather taken up my business with
Prince," Yates began. "In fact, I don't know if we can
really get anything handled without him being here."

"Either you take it up with me or you don't take it
up at all," Ruby said flatly.

Davis spoke up, stung by her words. "Tell the sister what the real deal is, Bobbie," he said, speaking
to Yates.

Bobbie Yates hesitated, then beckoned towards
Chinaman and his woman. "We have just been
enlightening these people on how your man used them
to start that riot so his men could take off that bank

and gun shop."

Ruby tried not to reveal her surprise. As far as she knew, no one knew about the robbery except the people who were up on it. "So you say," she replied slowly. "You don't really have anything to prove that."

Bobbie shrugged his huge shoulders. "It doesn't take proof in this case, sister. We are up on what happened, and so is the brother and his lady."

Regaining his composure, Chinaman spoke up. "We realize we been played on, Ruby, so it ain't no reason for you to try and deny it. As of today, we're pulling out of everything Prince has a hand in, plus taking as many members of the new club as we can pull. After we get through pulling their coats to what went down, there won't be enough people left for you to waste your time on."

Anger blazed in Ruby's eyes. She spoke without thinking. "What you better realize, Chinaman, and you too, Blanca, is that Roman and his woman were found in a motel in Chicago burned to death."

Her words had an immediate effect on Blanca. Her eyes grew large and she clutched frantically at Chinaman's arm. She put her face against his chest and muttered over and over again, "I told you, I told you, I told you."

Chinaman held her in his arms and glared at Ruby. "Bitch!" he began. Bobbie Yates cut him off. His eyes were flashing dangerously as he whirled on Ruby.

"Sister," he began, "we would like to avoid trouble if at all possible, but we won't go out of our way to step around it. Now, what I want you to do is to inform

Prince that Chinaman and his lady are both completely under my personal responsibility. If anything should happen to the brother and sister, I'd use every resource at my disposal to correct the wrong."

Ruby snorted. "Your name ain't Jesus by any chance, is it?" she asked sarcastically. "If I were you, I'd remember your ass ain't made out of stone, either."

Yates stared down at her with a deep hurt in his eyes. At first the sister had filled him with pride. To see such a lovely black woman come marching into the room with her head back and eyes flashing had made him smile. But after a while, he realized that she embodied something unspeakably evil and vile. Suddenly he knew that he was facing the most dangerous woman he had ever met.

"Sister," he said slowly, "I'm aware something could happen to me any day. If not from your group of people, the white pigs might decide to get rid of me. But that is not important." His voice rose, filled with pride. "For every one of us black brothers that falls, you will find three more ready to take his place." He waved his hand at the two men standing behind him. "If I should fall, these two would quickly take over. If they should fall, we have others. As soon as you leave, I'm calling our headquarters in Los Angeles, sister, and tell them just what's happening out here. Our organization is nationwide—in every large city and many smaller ones. So it's more than just me or my few members you'll have to deal with if something happens to this couple."

He waited until he was sure she understood, then

added, "I hope you explain this to Prince, and while you're at it, tell him he has more to worry about than Chinaman. We are starting a program of wiping out all the dope in black neighborhoods. I'd rather Prince would just quit backing the dope in our ghettos, but if he doesn't, we will personally put his dealers out of commission."

Ruby threw him a withering look. "I'd say your best bet was to get on that phone and call those other people, because if you start stepping on Prince's toes, I'm sure he won't waste any time getting you off." She turned on her heel and stalked out of the room.

"Well," Chinaman began, "it's all left up to Prince. I don't know how he'll take this, but I'm sure he'll give it a hell of a lot more thought than what Ruby would. She's ready now to start fighting in the streets."

When Ruby arrived back at the Twenty Grand Motel, Prince was just getting out of bed. He listened quietly as she told him what had happened, then went into the bathroom and took a quick shower. She tapped her foot impatiently, then got up and went in the bathroom.

"Honey," she began, trying to use as much patience as possible, "what we goin' to do about Chinaman and that little bitch of his, huh?"

Prince cut the water off and stepped out of the shower. Ruby grabbed a towel and dried off his back. "Nothing," he replied sharply. He took the towel out of her hands and finished drying off. "I don't know if you know anything about the Black Cougars or not, but I do."

"I know this much about them," she snapped, "they said you wasn't nothing but a white man's nigger. They said you was worse than a black plague to our people, that's what they said!"

Prince forced a laugh. Her words had hurt him deeply, but his face revealed nothing. "Just because I'm out for the almighty dollar, that don't make me no white man's nigger, and you know that as well as I do. They can say whatever the fuck they want to, it don't mean nothing."

Ruby nodded. "I know, honey," she said with the intuition that she had hurt her man. "But what about our dope houses? They said they was going to close up all our places. You ain't goin' stand still for that, are you?"

"Ruby, just stop and think for a minute, baby. The police ain't able to close up our dope houses, so what makes you think the Cougars might be able to do it? They don't have half the people the police got, so why worry? All we got to do is wait and keep gettin' money, that's all. This little shit you're worried about will blow over sooner or later."

"Okay, daddy, if you say so. I still don't like it, though. I'd feel better if we sent some people down there and cracked some heads. That way they would know we ain't laying down for no fuckin', you can bet on that."

Prince smiled at her. "Don't let it worry you, baby. Just remember, the last thing we need is an out-and-out war with some of our own people. So what if we blowed that organization? If Chinaman wants to spend his time trying to help out the have-nots, that's up to him. You just keep on remembering that it's only two kind of people in this world, Ruby, that's all. The have-nots and those that have." He waved his arm around at the suite they lived in. "We pay more rent in a day for this place, baby, than some people make all week. It speaks for itself. You don't see no god-damn roaches running all over the walls, do you? Let the Cougars and Chinaman work out of the love-your-brother shit. We goin' continue to work out of love-that-green-stuff, baby, can you dig it?"

She smiled at his words, and some of the worry left her face. Slowly, she moved into his arms, enjoying the feel of his muscles tightening around her. As he kissed her on the neck and shoulders, she squirmed in his arms, then pressed her body tightly against his, feeling his manhood pushing against her thigh. They fell over on the king-size bed and lost their anxiety in each other's arms.

17

THE WINTER WIND had run most of the night people off the streets and into the bars and after-hours spots, poolrooms and greasy spoon restaurants. The neon lights beckoned them to the dim-lit places of entertainment that were their very existence. Many had been victimized, but still they returned, night after night, in search of fugitive pleasures. The dopefiends, whores, muggers, and other parasites who earned their income off of them moved with them through the shadows.

Frankie, a tall, brown-skinned lesbian, walked from one end of the Silver Dollar Bar to the other, cursing fluently. "I'm not going to pay no goddamn protection dues so that my whores can work," she yelled in her masculine voice.

A short, slim Negro spoke up from the bar. "You must not have seen what happened to Chico's girls, did you?" he asked, glad of a chance to put this arrogant dyke on the spot.

"That's because they had a punk for a man," Frankie replied harshly. "You didn't see it happen to any of my girls, did you?"

A fat prostitute sitting in the rear of the bar remarked drily, "It might be because you've been paying your dues these past few weeks just like the rest of us."

"You're telling a goddamn lie," Frankie said, glaring at the girl. "If I was you, bitch, I'd think twice before telling that goddamn lie again!" She stared at the other people in the bar. "I ain't paying a damn penny and ain't planning on paying one either."

Fatdaddy, Apeman, and Brute entered the bar on the last of the conversation. Before Frankie had got all the words out of her mouth, Apeman had grabbed her by her shoulders and swung her around. He slapped her twice across the mouth.

"Bitch," he yelled, "just 'cause you look like a man, don't be trying to fill a man's shoes, because you may find yourself in more damn trouble than you know how to handle."

With the speed born of long experience, Frankie pulled a knife and lunged at Apeman. The move was so swift that it caught Apeman unprepared. He threw up his arms as Fatdaddy moved in, catching Frankie's right arm in mid-air. He grabbed her other arm and twisted it behind her back until she had to stand on her tiptoes. The knife dropped slowly from her fist.

He slammed her to the floor, and Brute stepped in and kicked her in the stomach. As she lay squirming, Apeman leaned down and snatched back her head, twisting his fingers around in her hair.

"Have you got the money for them six whores you got workin', Frankie?" he asked harshly, then slapped her across the face.

Frankie managed to prop herself up on one of her elbows. She stared at Apeman. "You dirty black sonofabitch!" she screamed. "I'll see that you pay for this." She spit straight into his face.

Apeman stood up and wiped the spit from his face with the back of his hand. Then he drew back his foot and kicked her in the side.

Before he could kick her again, a heavyset Negro woman ran up with some money in her hand. "Here, man," she yelled, pushing the money towards him. "Here's twenty-eight dollars; ain't but five of us girls working tonight and whatever I'm short of you can pick up later, just leave our man alone."

Apeman slowly stuck the money into his pocket and watched Frankie trying to get to her feet. As soon as she reached her knees, he kicked her brutally on the side of the head. "Next time, bitch, don't be telling people what you're going to do. If you got any kind of sense, you won't be late with your payments, 'cause if you are, I'm goin' knock all the gribbers off your ass."

Two young boys, notebooks in their hands, moved up and down the bar collecting money from the pimps and whores, while the "fearsome threesome" watched closely.

With the help of three of her girls, Frankie made her way out of the bar. One of the girls waved down a cab. At her apartment building, Frankie paused on the steps and waited for one of the girls to open the door. After they entered the apartment, she spoke to the girls. "You bitches get in the bedroom and stay there until I tell you to come out."

She picked up the phone and dialed long distance. "I want to speak to either Black Pete or Tommie Hall," she demanded when a masculine voice answered on the other end.

"This is Tommie speaking," the voice replied.

"This is Frankie, baby. I'm having a whole lot of trouble over here in this funky city, Tommie."

"Anytime a black bitch is as dirty as you, Frankie, she's supposed to have a lot of trouble, baby."

"I'm not bullshittin', Tommie. I'm in trouble and I need your help."

"How much money have you got, Frankie?"

"I got five hundred dollars I can put my hands on in the next five minutes."

"It's goin' cost you more than that, Frankie."

"Wait a minute, Tommie, this is me, baby. You don't even know what I want you to do yet."

"It don't make any difference, honey," he said coldly. "I know what's going on over there and I don't want no part of it."

"You mean you wouldn't come over here for an old friend like me?" she asked slowly.

"As much money as we got floating around Chicago right now, baby, I don't see why you don't just pack up and bring your ladies here. It would save you some money, besides the cash you'd have to pay me if I made the trip."

"I'm not worried about saving money. All I want to know is how much are you going to charge to make a hit on a punk over here for me?"

After a long pause, he replied. "For you, baby, I'd do it for fifteen hundred."

"What!" Frankie yelled. "How in the hell are you going to charge me like that? It ain't but one guy, baby. I don't want you to hit J. Edgar Hoover. Just one small-time punk, that's all."

"Listen, Frankie, and I'm not trying to snow you. If you wasn't such a good friend, I wouldn't take the job unless it paid three grand or more."

Tommie waited for a moment, listening to the silence on the other end of the line, then continued. "Dig, baby, I told you I knew what was going on over there. Alphonso showed up here two weeks ago and gave us the rundown on what Prince is doing, and I don't want no part of that stud if I can possibly help it."

"Okay, Tommie, when will you be here?"

"What about the money, when will I get it?"

"This ain't no game I'm playing; you'll get your money as soon as the job is done."

"All right, girl, me and a couple of the boys will

drive over tonight, so have my money ready. I don't plan on being there no longer than a few hours."

Frankie held the receiver in her hands for a moment after Tommie had hung up. Then she walked over to the bedroom door and called her girls out. "All of you go back to work now. After you finish, stay with each other. I don't want none of you coming back here before this time tomorrow night, is that understood?"

"Okay, Frankie," one of the girls answered. "You sure you ain't goin' need anything before the morning?"

"Just do as I say," Frankie replied softly. After the last girl had gone out, she leaned on the door for a brief second, then walked over to the couch and stretched out, waiting patiently for the arrival of her friends.

Across town in another apartment, Prince listened quietly to his lieutenants. Preacher continued to argue his point. "I don't care what Danny says, Prince," he said loudly. "We catch pure hell trying to collect money from them whores in black bottom."

"That's bullshit," Danny snapped back. "Them whores on your turf pay off better than the welfare."

Preacher laughed, but his eyes were black chips. "You just don't understand, Danny. Last night some bulldyker tried to stab Apeman when he tried to collect."

"At least he can catch up with his whores and try and collect. Them fat bitches in my district change locations so much I don't know where to look for them most of the time." Danny spoke to Prince, seeking sympathy.

Prince walked over to the far end of the room and removed the cover from a large wall map. "Here's something that's goin' really make you holler, Danny. If you think you got troubles now...." He removed a pencil from his pocket and drew a line on the map. "You know that warehouse down by the waterfront that all those trucks pull in and out of?"

"You ain't talking about that big trucking company about a block from the waterfront, are you?" Danny asked

"That's right, Danny. Right around the corner from where Fatdaddy picks up his waterfront collections," Prince replied.

Danny stopped and stared at Prince for a moment. He seemed to be stifling an outburst. "Prince, if you're thinking what I'm thinking, it ain't goin' be nothing but trouble, man."

Prince smiled coldly. "You might be right, man. What I got on my mind is that you won't have far to send Fatdaddy to pick up the contributions from the trucking company."

"What you mean is that I won't have far to go to bury our pickup men, Prince. Stop and think on this, Prince," Danny urged desperately. "What you're talking about is going up against the Mafia. It ain't that them truckers is all that tough, Prince. It's the backing behind them. They ain't goin' stand still for no shakedown. Remember, man, we ain't goin' be shaking no truckin' company down, man, we goin' be shaking the Mafia down, and they ain't goin' for it."

He was saying what Prince had already thought about, but it didn't change his mind. He didn't believe anyone in his right mind would turn down his request. If the truckers wanted to keep their trucks rolling, they would pay up. It was impossible for them to refuse his demands and hope to stay in business. Prince walked over and picked his sports jacket up off a chair. "Don't worry about a thing," he said, appearing more confident than he actually was. "I've taken care of everything. By this time tomorrow night, we'll have one of the largest trucking companies in the city paying us protection dues."

"Have you heard from them yet?" Danny snorted.

Prince made his favorite motion of impatience. "Tomorrow night at the club, while we're paying off the other members, I'll personally show you the money that came from this big bunch of so-called gangsters." He stared at his men, unyielding, selfish, indomitable. He had chosen a path for them to follow, and they would follow, no matter what.

The next morning, Fatdaddy and Brute stood in the outer office of the trucking company waiting for the receptionist to come back and usher them in. "Damn," Brute exclaimed. "I wish we could have found Apeman."

The same thought was running through Fatdaddy's mind. He tried not to reveal his slight fear though, as he replied, "I believe the sonofabitch was in his room shacking up with some bitch."

"If he was, I'll make sure Prince racks his ass up for it," Brute answered, a bit nervously.

"I done got about just enough of this waiting shit," Fatdaddy snapped, more from fear than anger. At that instant, a small fat man came into the office. He nodded at the two young blacks, walked across the room, and entered a door marked "Private," without knocking.

"Shit!" Brute exclaimed. "If he can do that, so can we! Come on, Fatdaddy, ain't no sense in us waiting no goddamn longer!"

Fatdaddy grabbed Brute by the arm. He could feel his heart beating wildly. "Wait a minute, Brute. Maybe we ought to run over to the Roost and get a few more guys first."

Seeing his partner's fear, Brute gained courage from it. Had he mentioned getting help earlier, Brute would have quickly taken him up on it. Now, he wanted to show that he wasn't afraid.

"What the hell are you worried about, Fatdaddy? You got your pistol, besides a pair of brass knuckles, ain't you?"

Before they could decide on what to do, the inner office door opened and the secretary stepped out. She walked over to the coat rack and removed her coat. With a shake of her head, she motioned to the men to go in.

"You don't believe in being polite, do you?" Brute asked.

"Not to scum," she replied over her shoulder as she walked out the door.

"Bitch!" Brute yelled after her. They entered the inner office and stood near the door.

"Come over here," the small fat man ordered sharply. "We want to get a better look at you."

Sitting behind the desk was a tall slim man with a pencil-line mustache. As the two men moved to the middle of the room, he laughed. "Where's the other guy who's generally with you boys?" he asked in a heavy voice that was surprising from so thin a man.

The fat man pulled a notebook from his pocket. He thumbed through the pages, then pulled three pictures out. "He's asking about the big black one," he said, staring down at the pictures. "These punks call themselves 'the big three,' Ed." He laughed harshly.

Brute and Fatdaddy stared at each other in amazement. "How in the hell did you know?" Brute asked, his voice belligerent.

The man called Ed stood up from behind the desk. "There is very little we don't know about you punks," he said drily, then added, "except what brings you here to my office."

"If you know so much about us," Brute replied slowly, "you should really know what brings us here."

"Well, I don't," the man answered easily. "I don't have the slightest idea what you boys want."

"Well, you should," Brute continued. "Everybody else that runs a business in this neighborhood pays protection dues, and the time has come for you to start paying yours."

Ed sat back in his chair laughing. "I told you so, Bill. That's just what these punks came here about."

He continued to laugh until tears ran out of his eyes.

Bill didn't seem to find anything funny though. "Just how much is this organization supposed to pay, may I ask?" His words were polite, but his blue eyes had turned cold.

Fatdaddy began to feel a little more assured. He spoke up for the first time since entering the office. "As of today, you owe us one thousand dollars."

Bill lit a cigarette. "Ed, I think these punks are serious." He glanced back at the two men as though he had just seen them for the first time.

Fatdaddy leaned forward, now confident that everything would work out right. "It's like this, Ed. Every time one of your trucks turns down Eighth Avenue and comes to this building or your other one across the street, it costs you one dollar. Since Monday, over five hundred trucks have pulled in and out, and we do count both ways."

"Yeah," Ed answered slowly. "I guess you are counting both ways to come up with a figure like that."

"We figure it this way, Ed. You ain't got to pay the money. Since the truck drivers are mostly brokers, all you got to do is tell them and they'll all pay the two dollars every time they come to your warehouse." Brute grinned.

Bill walked over and picked up the phone. He dialed a number, let it ring once, then hung up. "That's just who I figured you'd want to give the screwing to," he said softly. "The truck drivers."

"Just what is it out of your fuckin' pocket?" Brute

demanded. "I don't see you driving no fuckin' truck."

Bill answered quietly, his voice revealing no anger. "No, I don't drive a truck, but I'm connected with them. My job is to protect the drivers from just this very thing. And that's what I'm going to do."

Brute pulled a set of brass knuckles from his pocket and slipped them on. "That's a pretty big job you cut out for yourself, little man," he growled. "We just might have to show you how rough it's goin' really be."

Before Brute finished speaking, he had started to move forward. Bill quickly stepped behind the desk. Ed never moved from his seat. He just leaned forward and pushed a concealed button, and the outer door burst open and four huge men rushed in. All of them carried iron pipes, swinging them freely. There was no contest. Brute fought desperately to get behind the desk to reach the men who had set him up, but it was a losing battle. As he sank to his knees beside Fatdaddy, he could hear someone yell, "Don't kill them yet!" It was Bill's voice. "We have to find out where this guy Prince lives."

Ed came from around the desk and glanced down at the two men on the floor. "I wish there was some other way of handling this. I don't like it. The last thing I wanted was for someone to end up getting killed over this crap."

"It's out of your hands now, Ed," Bill replied. "The only thing these punks understand is violence, and that's just what they're going to get—a one-way trip to hell."

18

THE MUSIC FROM INSIDE the Roost could be heard out on the sidewalk as the party inside went into full swing. A microphone had been set up and a group of girls was standing in front of it, singing the latest hit along with the record.

"Hey, Ruby," a boy yelled from across the dance floor. "What time is Prince goin' get here with the green stuff?"

Ruby, sitting at a table with a group, ignored the question until one of the young men with her addressed her directly. "What about that, Ruby, what time is Prince showing up? I got to pay my boys off this evening or they goin' worry me to death."

Her chair squeaked as she pushed it back and stood up. "Why don't you go and find you a telephone and call him if you really want your money that fast," she replied over her shoulder as she started to walk away.

The Roost had been redecorated. There were new tables and booths around the dance floor, which had been sanded and varnished until it glowed with a glossy finish. The front door had been reinforced with two long iron pipes, making it impossible to kick in the door from the outside. As the buzzer rang from the outside, the two young door guards began removing the bars, after first taking a quick peep through the slit.

Prince came in, followed by Danny and Preacher. Each man carried a black bag about the size of what a doctor would carry. Prince crossed the dance floor and went into the back room, which had been converted into an office. Ruby followed and slammed the door on the overanxious teenagers.

"Prince, what in the hell is Apeman workin' out of?" she asked.

He motioned towards the desk before answering. "Just dump the money out on top of it. Danny, you stack it up so we won't have no trouble counting it out when those kids start pouring in." He turned to Ruby. "Woman, how in the hell am I supposed to know what Apeman is working out of? I ain't seen him in three days." He hesitated, then asked, "Didn't he go with Brute and Fatdaddy to take care of that business?"

"Hell no," she replied bluntly. "I tried to reach you

on the phone but I couldn't catch up with you." She glided towards him with her swift, sinewy grace. "Brute and Fatdaddy stopped at his place to pick him up, but he wasn't there. They called and told me to tell you they were going on over by themselves."

Prince shook his head. Again he wished he had followed his right mind and left this job alone. He had believed from the first that it just might turn out to be trouble but had ignored his hunch. Oh well, he reasoned, whatever happened, he'd find a way to handle it.

Prince pulled out a pack of cigarettes and lit one, trying to conceal his slight nervousness. "It ain't nothing to worry about, baby. Apeman is more than likely gettin' him a piece of leg somewhere, and it done got too good for him to let go." He laughed loudly. Where in the fuck could that bastard be, he wondered. I'll fix his goddamn ass whenever he does show up, he promised himself angrily.

"Goddamn," Danny exclaimed. "I ain't never seen that much money in my life." He reached down and picked up some bills and let them trickle through his fingers, the way a child would do.

Preacher emptied his two bags of money. "Prince, just how much is that on the desk anyway?" he asked.

Danny laughed excitedly. "He ain't stiffin', Prince. Goddamn, that's a lot of cash for just one week's take." He hesitated, then added, "Besides, we don't even know how much you took out for other expenses."

"What I took out for myself and other people that

won't be here tonight would just above cover what you see on top of the desk now, Danny."

"Beautiful, baby, that's just beautiful. You mean to say, Prince, we don't even miss that money from them four dopehouses the Black Cougars closed down?" Preacher asked.

A flash of anger crossed Prince's face, but he quickly covered it. He smiled tightly. "That shit the damn Cougars are workin' out of ain't about nothin'. We opened them same joints back up, only in different spots. I don't see no reason for us to have no goddamn shootout with them brothers, so I just move the joints when they pressure them."

He glanced up at his men. He didn't want them to become worried about the Black Cougars, even though it was becoming a very sore spot with him. It went a lot deeper than just moving his dopehouses. The pushers were becoming frightened to such a degree that even more money was no temptation. Two of them had just quit, packed up, and left the city.

Ruby stopped stacking the money long enough to put her arms around Prince's neck. "We got this city right in the palm of our hands, baby." She kissed him gently on the cheek.

He unwound her arms from his neck. "Not quite yet, baby," he replied, "but give us a little more time and it shouldn't take too fuckin' long. Ruby, go out and tell everybody that came to collect money for their district to get in line outside the door. Make sure that no more than two come in at a time. After all that goddamn noise and shit they made before, my nerves ain't up to handling it tonight."

After the last couple to get paid off had left the
office, Prince leaned back in his chair and lit a stick
of reefer. He slowly made eight large stacks of money
out of the pile left on the desk. He gave Preacher and
Danny both a stack, then put one in his own pocket.

He glanced down at the five stacks remaining.
"Ruby, you see to it that Fatdaddy, Brute, and Apeman
get three of these, then find Donnie and give him one.
The last stack is for you, baby. Take it downtown and
get something for yourself you think I might like."

Preacher moved towards the door. "Since my old
lady's belly is too big for her to do anything, I think
I'll ease out of here and try and find me one of them
young girls that just love to be with me." He grinned
over his shoulder as he stopped before the door. "I'll
be around if you want anything, Prince."

Prince smiled at him and waved him out the door.
He knew Preacher was just about the only married
man in his gang. The rest of them just shacked up
when the mood hit them, but Preacher had been married to Dee Dee for over three years.

"I think I'll do the same thing," Danny said, waiting for Prince to okay it.

As the cigarette began to burn his finger, Prince put
the reefer out and made a cocktail out of the roach.
"Get a table near the dance floor," he said contented-
ly. "I'll be out there in a few minutes myself."

The phone rang and Ruby reached across the desk
to pick up the receiver. "Just a second," she said, holding out the receiver to Prince.

"Where are you at?" Prince asked sharply after listening for a few seconds. "It shouldn't take you more than ten minutes to get over here, Racehorse. Come through the alley and knock on the back door. I'll make sure no one sees you on this end."

Ruby whistled as Prince hung up. "Something must have really come up to make Racehorse come here," she said.

Prince grunted his answer, then settled down to wait. Something always seemed to come up just when he was hoping everything would turn out all right. He didn't have long to wait. In eight minutes, a slight knock was heard, and Prince stepped quickly to the back door. He removed a large two-by-four and unhooked three chains. The door swung open into the room and Racehorse stepped inside.

His eyes quickly scanned the room, taking in everything of importance. "Hi there, Ruby, what's been happening, girl?" he asked politely. "It's been a little while since I've seen you, baby."

She flashed him a brief smile. "I hope whatever brought you here ain't so important that I'll wish I hadn't seen you tonight."

He shook his head. "You know it's got to be bad or I'd never risk coming over here, baby. I don't dig this section of the city, no kind of way."

Prince made sure the door was locked tight before joining the conversation. "Let's make it as quick as possible, Race, I know the police have got this goddamn place watched."

Racehorse glanced nervously at the back door.

"Man, I know the fuzz would catch hell trying to kick that door down, but how the hell would I get out if they were back there trying to get in?"

Prince pointed to a rope hanging down from a hole in the ceiling on the east side of the room. "That leads to the roof. From there you can jump to the building next door. Then you just follow the rooftops. By the time you come to the end, you should be at least eight houses away from here."

Racehorse nodded. "I'll get right to the point then. Apeman done gone and got hisself killed." His words had the effect of a gunshot. There was stunned silence in the room for a brief moment.

"You sure of that?" Prince asked sharply, his mind reeling.

"There's no doubt about that part of it. The bastard's as dead as he'll ever get."

"It don't seem like anyone else in this whole city is up on this news, Racehorse. Where did you come by all this first-hand information? I know couldn't none of them white whores you stay with be up on it." Prince tried to keep his confusion from showing.

"If me and Tony hadn't been over in Chicago pickin' up those tommy guns, Prince, I might have stopped it. These cats come over from Chi the other day and as soon as they hit the city they called me up. After they couldn't reach me, baby, they went on and took care of the job they came for." Racehorse waited, watching closely. He was curious about the effect his words were having on Prince. He had realized that his message would produce some sort of impact, but he hadn't expected Prince to be shaken so hard.

Prince managed to get himself together. At first, he had thought it was the Mafia striking back because he had attempted to pressure the trucking company, but he realized that that couldn't be the reason.

"Who did it?" The question was sharp and direct. Prince stared coldly at Racehorse, waiting for an answer.

Racehorse walked over and sat on the edge of the desk. "One of the studs was my rap partner in a bit a long time ago. He took the prison sentence, Prince, just so he could cut me loose."

"That don't mean shit!" Ruby exploded. She had been trying to stay out of it, but her anger got the best of her. "The stud knew Apeman was one of Prince's men, so he shouldn't have touched him. Now he's going to have to pay for his error."

Racehorse stared at Ruby for a moment before laughing. "What's the deal here, Prince?" he asked sarcastically. "You got a bitch running your business now?"

Ruby blushed scarlet with more than anger. "Just who in the hell do you think you are, Racehorse?"

"Shut up, Ruby!" Prince ordered. His eyes glittered as he stared from one to the other. "We got enough problems without you two squabbling like kids. Racehorse, I don't understand this. You say one of my boys got killed, yet you don't want to tell me who's behind it."

"I didn't say I wasn't going to tell you who was

behind the killing, Prince. I just said I couldn't tell you who actually did the job."

Prince shrugged. "I don't like the idea of some butchers coming into my city and killing one of my boys and getting away with it, Race, but if you can put me hip to who wired them up for this, I'll let it ride for now."

Racehorse grinned. "You ever hear of a bulldyker called Frankie?" He waited until both of them shook their heads. "Well, she called the boys in from Chicago. Seems as though she don't like the idea of having to pay for her ladies to work."

Ruby walked over and removed the cigarette from behind Racehorse's fingers. She slowly lit a stick of reefer with it, then handed the reefer to Racehorse. "Here, baby," her voice was husky. "I'm sorry about that little misunderstanding we had. You know you and me are a whole lot cooler than that, Horse."

"You know how that goes, baby," Racehorse replied as he inhaled the sweet-smelling reefer. "Everybody can't be right all the time. Prince," he said, turning away from her, "let me try and straighten something out with you before we go into this thing any further."

"Come on out with it," Prince answered quietly.

Racehorse removed the burned-up joint from his mouth and made a cocktail. "Look here, baby," he began. "These guys never would have called me if they didn't have something else on their minds besides idle gossip." Prince remained silent and waited for him to continue. "The studs want you to toss them some business, Prince. That's the real reason the guys wasted the time getting in touch with me and then pulling my coat to what went down. They say things are kind of slow in Chi right now, and they seem to be catching pure hell waiting on somebody to call them with a decent contract."

Prince laughed ruthlessly. "This stud you've been talking with has plenty of nerve, Race. First he kills one of my best men, then turns around and asks for a goddamn job."

"He acts like he ain't never heard of you, Prince, or else he thinks your middle name is Pussy," Ruby snapped, her face flushed with anger.

Racehorse threw her a savage glance, then spoke to Prince. "That ain't the reason, Prince. The stud's got a good idea of how this thing can be worked out between you and him."

"Just how would he like to handle it?" Prince inquired, sarcasm dripping from his words.

"Wait a minute, baby," Racehorse said, well aware of Prince's ways. "You done went and got the wrong impression already, man. You know what kind of business the guy deals in, Prince, so you know damn well he has to be careful. Plus, he don't trust you too much, baby, 'cause of that killing."

"How the hell would he work for me if he don't have any trust?"

"The stud has an idea you might go along with using me as the middle man. That way, neither one of you would have to ever meet."

Ruby inquired sarcastically, "Won't that put a little heat on you, Racehorse?"

"You know it does," Racehorse answered easily, "but I trust this stud, and I'm also going to get me a small commission out of every job he takes care of to make up for the trouble I might have to go through."

A sharp knock on the door ended the conversation. "Who is it?" Prince asked sharply.

"This is Preacher. I got some very important news for you, Prince, or I wouldn't be bothering you."

Prince glanced at Racehorse, undecided. "Don't worry about me," Racehorse said quickly. "Me and Preacher grew up together. Let him in."

The door was opened halfway and Preacher slipped through the crack. "Well, look what the garbage truck dropped off," he said, then grinned at Racehorse. He stuck out his hand and Racehorse jumped from the edge of the desk and grabbed it.

"I hear you been coming up in the world, Preacher," he said as he pumped Preacher's hand. "They tell me you done got to be just about the biggest frog in the pond down in black bottom." He grinned. "How's your wife, man? Last thing I heard, you was on your way to becoming a daddy."

Preacher grinned. "Yeah, man, I got a son." His face brightened slightly. "Besides that one, I got another one on the way."

Prince locked the door. "Whatever you got to say, get it over with, Preacher. We got some important business to take care of as soon as you finish."

Preacher nodded, then blurted out his news. "Man, it's all up and down the streets that the police have found Apeman's body. The wire that's out is that he was shot five times. Now, I don't know how much of this is true, but everybody that comes into the club is talking about it."

"The way this city is right now," Ruby broke in, "we can't afford to have someone kill one of our boys and get away with it."

Racehorse glared at her but remained silent. He understood what she was trying to do. She wouldn't be satisfied until the gunmen themselves were made to pay.

"The people in the know just about know what we are going to do about it," Prince replied. "The only thing they don't understand is how we are going to do it." Prince walked over and opened the door. "Preacher, I want you to have the members of the Rulers put on their outfits, 'cause there is going to be a hit made tonight. I want everybody who heard about this killing to know that we're getting ready to play payback before the night's over."

After closing the door behind Preacher, Prince turned to Racehorse. "This job tonight has got to be done in such a vicious manner, Horse, that even the hardest studs will be trembling at the thought of crossing one of my people."

"It ain't goin' be such a hard thing catching up with who's behind the killing, Prince. Frankie will more than likely be in her favorite bar partying tonight. The thing is, how am I going to get her out of the bar?" Racehorse rubbed his chin thoughtfully.

"Don't worry about that part of it, Racehorse," Ruby

said. "I can handle it, if Prince will give me the okay."
She stared at her man, awaiting his agreement. Her
eyes traveled quickly to Racehorse, then back again.
It would be a long time before she forgot all the bitches he had called her.

"You really want part of this job?" Prince asked her
slowly.

"I don't just want part of this job, daddy. I've
already figured out just how it can be handled, and
there won't be any complaints about it after I've handled it, either."

Racehorse glanced at Ruby, then back to Prince.
"What kind of crap is this, man? You think I'm going
on a job with a bitch?"

"Don't worry about her," Prince replied, smiling
slightly. "She can handle her end of it. She took care
of that job on Billy without anyone helping her."

Racehorse glanced at her nervously. "If she handled
that job I guess it's all right, but I still don't like the
idea of workin' with a bitch."

Ruby walked over to Racehorse and stared him in
the eye. "Before we're finished working with each
other, you'll realize I got a different name than bitch,
Race. That I promise you."

19

THE SILVER DOLLAR BAR was just beginning to get into full swing. The news of Apeman's death had put the bar's steady customers in a mood of gaiety, and the pimps and prostitutes were celebrating by buying out the bar.

Frankie could be heard over the roar shouting loudly and cursing. "Rack 'em back, goddamnit," she screamed at the top of her voice. "Give everybody a fuckin' drink on me."

Three older pimps at a table in the rear watched the proceedings with misgivings. "I don't know what the hell they're celebrating," one of the men said. "Just because that stud got waxed, that ain't goin' stop us from having to pay protection dues."

"That ain't the half of it," one of his friends replied. "Somebody's going to have to pay for that killing." He hesitated briefly, then added, "I hope to hell it ain't us."

The pimp who had started the conversation nodded in agreement. "I wasn't thinking about it in those terms, but now that you mention it, it's going to cost somebody more than a little piece of money."

The third man kicked the speaker's leg under the table. "Look what's coming through the door, man. You might just get an answer to your question faster than you realized."

Preacher, followed by four men wearing Ruler uniforms, came into the bar and stopped at the entrance. His eyes fell on Frankie, pounding on the bar with a beer bottle.

"What the hell is wrong with you, Sam?" she screamed at the bartender. "Didn't I say for you to give everybody in the joint a drink on me? Now let's get busy back there and serve it up if you want to make some money."

Sam hurried up and down the bar as fast as his short legs would allow, pouring drinks. "Okay, okay," he yelled back, "I can't work any faster, so take it easy."

"The hell you say," Frankie yelled. "If you can't work fast enough, I'll send one of my girls back there to give you a hand."

Sam stopped what he was doing and glared at Frankie. "The hell you will! I don't allow whores behind my bar. Bad enough my bar's full of them. If you want to get served, just hold your damn horses, you ain't in that much of a damn hurry."

Frankie noticed Preacher, and the whiskey caused her to throw caution to the wind. She glanced briefly at him, then said, "We don't get a chance to celebrate a punk's death every day, Sam, so hurry the hell up or I'll take my business across the street."

"You can take your girls any damn place you like, Frankie, only don't try rushing me."

Preacher spoke up suddenly. "Don't blow all your money across that bar, Frankie, 'cause you got to pay dues for them girls of yours if you're planning on sending them to work tonight."

A sudden silence fell over the barroom. Preacher turned away from Frankie and spoke to the crowd. "Because of that accident, everybody will be expected to pay double dues tonight."

Frankie flushed angrily. "You better hope you can collect the regular dues, boy, instead of talking about somebody paying extra."

Preacher grinned at her coldly. "You don't have to pay a penny, Frankie, if you don't want to."

"I know damn well I don't, and I ain't about to pay any either."

"Is there anybody else in here who feels the same way about this as Frankie?" Preacher asked, glancing around the room.

The silence had become so thick that you could hear the heavy breathing from a drunk in one of the back booths. Sam glanced around nervously. He knew just what was going on. He paid his protection dues, too, only they showed him a little more respect, like coming around early before many customers were in the bar. It was cheap, so he went along with it. He stared at Frankie and shook his head.

Preacher nodded at one of his boys with a notebook in his hand. "In that case, since no one feels like Frankie does, we can get on with our collection."

As some of the girls whose men weren't there lined up to pay off, pimps began to fall in line behind them. When one of the collectors came up to a tall, dark pimp, the pimp asked sarcastically, "How long are we supposed to go for this extra amount you guys have added on?"

Preacher spoke to the boy collecting the money. "Give him his money back."

The pimp stepped back from the collection table as though there were a snake on it. "Wait a minute, Preacher," he stammered, "that ain't what I meant. I don't want no money back, all I want to know is how long are we going to have to pay double rates."

Preacher looked at the man steadily. "If you want me to, Sonny, I could call up Prince and let you ask him yourself."

"That's all right, man," Sonny replied. "I don't want no trouble I can't handle myself."

Frankie's loud laughter rang out. She stared at Sonny as though he had just come from under a rock. "If that's what you whores call a man, this city is in real trouble."

Suddenly, the old-time saloon doors swung open and a tall, ebony-skinned woman walked in. The platinum blonde wig she wore bounced on her shoulders as she crossed the floor with the stride of an African queen. She was noticeably young under her brazen whore makeup, but she carried herself like a thoroughbred.

Frankie moved to the front of the bar and blocked her path. "Come on, honey, and join me. I'd hate for one of these lightweight punks to try and fire at you and end up running you away."

Preacher glanced twice at the girl before he realized that it was Ruby. To cover his astonishment, he spoke sharply to Frankie. "If I was you, Frankie, I'd make sure didn't none of my girls try and work tonight, 'cause they might run into anything if you don't come up with that money." He waited, then added, "You know what I mean, something like a sadist or some other kind of nut."

Frankie threw him a murderous look, then grabbed Ruby by the arm and guided her toward the rear of the bar. "One of you bitches give them punks some money," she said over her shoulder, glancing at her girls along the bar.

Ruby caught Preacher's eye as she slipped onto a barstool. Her tight black skirt rose up high on her thighs as she settled down, revealing a blood-red half-slip. With a small nod of her head, she motioned towards the door, before one of Preacher's men should recognize her. Preacher got the hint and started to leave with his followers.

One of Frankie's girls ran up and handed him sixty dollars. "It ain't but four of us working tonight, but if that ain't enough, you can send someone back later on. We should be done broke luck by then," she said, half belligerently.

Preacher took the money and started towards the door. "If we find out there's more girls working than what you said, I'll personally see to it that somebody kicks a mudhole in your ass," he told the girl.

Frankie moved from her barstool, then thought better of it and sat back down. The bar remained silent after Preacher had left.

Frankie broke the silence, turning to Ruby. "As you've heard, honey, they call me Frankie down here." She raised her hand and pointed to the girls at the end of the bar. "All of them are in my stable." She laughed abruptly. "It seems as though I'm just about the only person down here that really wears pants." She pointed over her shoulder at the pimps who were glaring at her. "You could say most of them are just punks in men's clothes." Her laughter rang out brazenly.

Ruby smiled. "All my friends call me Jamie, honey," she said easily. For a moment, she was fascinated by this loud, daring woman. She was well aware that it took a rare person to browbeat the pimps in this bar; they were all dangerous to a degree. When it came to taking any kind of shit from a woman, it hurt their pride. For Frankie to toss her contempt right in their faces was to skate on very thin ice. It wouldn't take but a slight nudge and the roof of the bar might fall in on both their heads. Ruby surveyed the place to see if anyone else might have recognized her.

After they had downed a couple of straight

whiskeys, using water for a chaser, Frankie moved closer and began to rub Ruby's leg. When Ruby didn't protest, she moved even closer and began whispering hoarsely.

"Listen, Jamie," she began, "I know where we can have a little privacy, if you'll agree."

"I don't know," Ruby answered hesitantly. "Where did you have in mind we go?"

Frankie tried to put on a nonchalant air. "It really doesn't make any difference," she said, "but I would kind of like to go up to my place for a few drinks."

Ruby pretended to be startled for a moment. "Oh no, Frankie, I couldn't go for that. Suppose one of your girls came in while I was there?"

Frankie waved one of her hands disgustedly. "That's your least worry, Jamie. Ain't none of my girls going to show up, and if one of them did, you wouldn't have to worry about her saying anything."

Ruby picked up the double shot of whiskey in front of her and sipped it slowly before replying. "I don't think I want to go to your place, Frankie…, but if you want to go over to my place, that would be marvelous."

Frankie's arm began to tremble with excitement as she ran it higher on Ruby's leg. Saliva formed in the corner of her mouth and began to dribble down her chin. With a backward swipe of her hand, she cleaned her chin and stood up. "Since you might want to come back later, honey, we might as well get the show on the road."

Ruby slipped off her stool and stood beside Frankie.

Ruby was tall for a woman, but when Frankie was beside her, she seemed actually short. The tip of her head barely cleared Frankie's shoulder. They walked out of the bar arm in arm. Frankie yelled at a passing cab in a heavy masculine voice. When they got in the cab, the driver looked twice and cursed silently.

Ruby called out the address to him, then sat back in the seat. "Wait a minute, baby," she said, pushing Frankie's hand from under her dress. "We got all night, so ain't no reason for us to rush this thing."

Frankie's breathing came heavy and loud in the silence of the cab. "I hope you mean that, Jamie, about us having all night. The last thing I want to do is come back and sit up in that goddamn bar the rest of the night." Frankie stared at her in the darkness. This would be one helluva cop, she thought. With a big strong whore like this in her stable, there would be pleasant nights ahead.

Ruby stopped Frankie from loosening one of the buttons on her blouse. She answered easily. "If you don't be so goddamn impatient, honey, I might let you stay all night with me. If what I'm going through now is a taste of what I'd have to put up with the rest of the night, I don't think I'll be able to stand it."

Frankie's eyes glittered dangerously in the dark. She made up her mind that, once Jamie was in her stable, she would take some of the smart-assedness out of her. She imagined beating her with one of her huge belts and grinned. Yes, it would be enjoyable to take some of the starch out of this woman.

The cab pulled up and parked in front of a shabby apartment building. The driver leaned over the back-seat and took the money. As the women began to get out, he spit out the door past them.

"What the hell is wrong with you, mister?" Frankie asked belligerently.

The driver ignored the remark and pulled away from the curb. As soon as the cab moved out into the light traffic, Frankie glanced at the building and spoke to Ruby. "You mean to tell me, Jamie, that as good as you look this is the best living quarters you could find?" She tossed a skeptical glance up and down the street, taking in the overturned garbage cans. "Hmph," she snorted. "It's plain to see you need somebody to manage your business for you."

"That's why I came down to the bar tonight, Frankie. I was hoping I'd meet someone who could show me where to work in this city. I haven't been here but a couple of weeks, and I don't really know where to go." Ruby hesitated, then added, "You know, the last thing I wanted was to hit the streets without someone able to bail me out if I took a fall."

"Don't worry," Frankie smiled. "You came to the right place, and you found the right person."

They entered the dimly-lit building and started up the stairway. On the first landing, a winehead came staggering down the stairs. He lurched into Frankie, almost knocking her down the steps. Before she could regain her balance, he shoved her out of his way. She crashed against the wall, but as he tried to stagger past, she reached out and grabbed him by the shirt.

Her right hand moved up and down in a blurring motion. The blows to his head sounded loud in the empty hall. With a sneer of disgust on her face, she tripped him and sent him falling the rest of the way down the stairs.

His screams were still in their ears as they reached the second floor. Ruby stopped at a door and stuck her key into the lock. She stepped aside and let Frankie pass in front of her. Frankie stopped in the doorway and shook her whiskey-filled head as though some instinct warned her not to go any further.

Before she could gather her wits, Ruby gave her a violent push from behind and she went stumbling into the room. Racehorse stepped from behind the door and hit her savagely upside the head with a nine-inch blackjack. She slowly crumbled up and fell to the floor.

The couple worked fast after that. In five minutes, Ruby emerged from the room and walked quickly down the hall to where a pay phone hung on the wall. After making a hurried call, she went back up the hall to the front window. She pulled back the filthy curtain that hung across the cracked pane, rubbed some of the dirt off the glass, and glanced out. She waited patiently until she saw a small boy ride up on a bicycle and stop under the streetlight. Then she retraced her steps and went back to the room.

"Here, Ruby," Racehorse said, handing her a large brown grocery bag.

"Did you clean everything up?" she asked in a subdued voice.

Racehorse glanced at her nervously. "Don't worry, Ruby. I took care of everything that needed taking care of."

"Well," she hesitated slightly, then started for the door. "I'm gone then, baby. I don't think you need me for anything else."

He didn't even bother to look up. "Okay, baby," he said, speaking more to himself than to her. "I think I'll go out the back door."

Ruby came out of the building and walked quickly to the kid on the bike. Her heels rang out loudly on the pavement. "Here," she said to him. "Take this bag up to the Silver Dollar Bar and throw it under the door. Oh yeah," she added, "there's no reason for you to be lookin' in the bag, and don't forget that somebody will be watching you at all times. If you stop somewhere and start bullshittin', we'll know about it."

"Don't worry," he said as he took the bag from her. "I ain't goin' stop nowhere, and I ain't goin' peep in the goddamn bag."

"Make sure you don't," Ruby ordered and removed a ten-dollar bill from her bra. "This is for you." She pushed the money towards him. "If you ever want to pick up some more easy money, make sure you do just like you're told."

Ruby started down the street as the kid went off on the bike. He rode for about ten ghetto blocks before the bag began to get heavy. As he went to change hands with the bag, something thick and sticky oozed onto his leg. He began to pump the bike faster as the bottom of the bag began to give way. As soon as he turned the corner into the next block, he saw a neon sign with a large silver dollar on it flashing off and on. When he got to the door, he stopped his bike and grabbed the bag at the bottom with one hand in order to stop it from bursting. With one hand on the top and the other on the bottom, he flung the bag under the swinging doors, then rode away. The blood on his hand added speed to his flight.

Inside the bar the bag rolled over and over and came to a halt in the middle of the floor. The people sitting at tables near the bar, and those at the bar, watched the bag bounce across the floor and come to a halt.

A young prostitute, not older than eighteen, let out a loud scream as the bag opened and Frankie's head rolled out and propped itself up on the severed neck in the middle of the floor. For the next ten minutes, the bar became a place of horror as pimps and whores alike screamed without stopping.

20

AFTER DONNIE LEFT the Roost he remained silent in the rear of the car. The news had already reached the kids in the clubhouse. Even though he hadn't known Frankie, he still felt a certain foreboding. It wasn't possible for them to continue getting away with wholesale murder. There was no doubt in his mind as to who was behind it either. He thanked his lucky stars that he only had to handle the homemade whiskey. That way, he reasoned, when the bust did come down, he didn't have too much to worry about. He figured the most he could get for the first offense was three years. And even so, he would still come out ahead of the game. Since he'd moved up in the organization, he'd been able to make enough money to buy his mother a house out of the slums; and for the first time in their lives, his brothers and sisters had enough clothes to wear.

Donnie relaxed and stared out into the early morning darkness. Whatever happened, he reasoned, he'd have to come out on top. Where else could he have earned enough money so that his mother would have fifteen thousand dollars stashed away. He still smiled at the thought of her face when he had dumped the money in her lap. There would be no more standing in line at the clinic or waiting for checks, or listening to sass from welfare workers. No more, he thought happily, would his mother have to wash other people's floors or accept hand-me-downs for her children. They even had insurance for each child in the family.

Suddenly the driver pulled up in the gas station that had been picked out for their meeting place. He glanced around quickly to make sure Danny hadn't shown up with the rental truck yet. "Van," he said to the young man Prince had given him for a personal bodyguard, "fill the gas tank up first, and if they ain't here by then, pull over by the pop machine and we'll sip on some pop until they show up."

The driver grunted and did as he was told. The boy sitting next to him in the front seat twisted around and spoke to Donnie. "How long you think it's going to take us to get this goddamn still set up?"

Donnie shrugged. "How the hell would I know? I ain't never seen no whiskey still as large as this one."

Donnie went back to staring out of the window. He didn't want to be bothered with stupid questions. His mind was too busy thinking over the money this new still would bring in. If everything went right, he'd be able to clear close to twenty thousand dollars in the next three months.

He prayed quietly, not really believing his luck could hold that long. "Lord, if you will only let me get in thirty more days.... I ain't hurtin' nobody, and just look at the good I'm doing with the money. Please, Lord, don't let nothing happen for another month, and I'll see to it that my sisters and brothers all be in church every week. In fact, Lord, I'll start going every Sunday myself, but just please, Jesus, help me to help these poor little black children that ain't never hurt nobody."

He caught himself and glanced around quickly to see if anyone had noticed. The two men in the front seat were busy talking about some girls they had lined up, so he bowed his head and said Amen.

At the same time across town, Fox, fresh out of prison, was making preparations to leave. He had had two warnings from the Black Cougars to stop selling dope, but because he was Prince's pipeline he had continued. He packed his bags with care. He glanced over at the two white envelopes full of money. Prince had given him ten thousand dollars to make another buy with, but he had decided that his buying days were over. He had eight more pieces of dope that belonged to Prince, but he was going to sell them outright and put that money on top of the ten thousand to take care of his traveling expenses. He grinned coldly, locked his suitcase, and placed it on the floor beside the other three. In a few more weeks, when Christmas rolled around, he'd be out on the West Coast with a pocketful of cash, while Prince ran around like a chicken with its head cut off, wondering whatever happened to his connect and his money.

Fox opened the closet door and took down his overcoat. He laid it on his suitcase, then glanced at his reflection in the mirror. He drew in his gut. It wouldn't be too bad in one of those swimsuits, he told himself, and a little black rinse would eliminate the gray hair on his head. Fox glanced at his watch impatiently. He wished the hell his customer would pick that shit up. He wanted to get out of the Motor City as fast as possible, although he kept telling himself that he wasn't afraid of Prince. As far as he knew, Prince didn't have the slightest idea he was getting ready to run. It was damn well time, anyway, he reasoned. The way things were going, it wouldn't be long before Prince's little playhouse came tumbling down.

Fox carried his bags into the front room and set them down beside the door. He glanced at his watch irritably. He almost decided to take the dope with him and forget about the sale, but his anger had been aroused by the Black Cougars telling him he couldn't sell dope in the city. He slammed his coat down and cursed. Wasn't no black sonofabitches goin' stop him from selling dope if he didn't want to stop, he raved to the empty room. Common sense told him to forget about the sale; he could always get rid of the heroin somewhere along the way. But he thought about the dopehouses the Black Cougars had closed up and cursed again. He wouldn't allow them the satisfaction of thinking they had run him out of town.

A sharp knock on the door snapped him out of his thoughts. He opened the door slightly, keeping the chain on the door. He saw the man he was waiting for and unhooked the chain. Before he could step out of the way, the door slammed back against him. Chinaman came in first, followed by the tallest man Fox had ever seen. Fox backed up swiftly, but he wasn't fast enough.

Before he could reach the shelter of the next room, the huge man caught him. The man's hands circled his neck, and he could feel his feet leave the floor. The hands tightened slowly as he wiggled frantically to break the hold. He beat like a child in the tight embrace of an adult. He kicked in vain as the black hands applied more and more pressure until he thought he had a band of steel around his neck.

He never even noticed when Chinaman picked up the dope he had left out on the table and carried it into the toilet. The sound of the toilet flushing came to him, but it was too late; he would never hear anything again.

Not a word had been spoken between the two men. They searched the apartment, then the body. The envelope inside Fox's coat was removed and each man took his share of the money. Then they left as they had entered, and only the sound of the winter wind broke the silence of death.

Donnie, still sitting in the backseat of the car, pointed at the truck cruising past the gas station. The driver of the truck hit his lights twice, then started to
speed up. The car shot out of the gas station and began
to follow the truck, unaware of the car already following the truck behind them.

Donnie leaned over the front seat. "Pass him, Van,
so we can lead the way." The driver pressed down
on the gas and Donnie waved out the window as they
passed. The driver of the truck raised his hand to
acknowledge the motion.

It took less than twenty minutes for them to leave
the west side and reach the north end of the city. They
pulled up in a garbage-littered alley, the lights of the
lead car picking up rats of every size and description.

Donnie's driver laughed as he turned into the back-
yard. The fence had been removed so that cars and
trucks could easily reach the house. The yard was barren of grass; it had been cleared out so that cars could
drive in without any problems. On one side, boards
and other rubbish had been stacked up out of the way.
Further back, there were traces of where a barn used
to be.

Van parked the car on the side, leaving enough room
for the truck to back up to the rear door of the small
frame house. The men in the car climbed out and waited until the truck driver managed to back in.

Danny jumped out of the truck grinning. "Goddamn,
man, we never would have found this joint out here

in the sticks."

Donnie returned the smile, but only with his lips. His grayish eyes glittered with anger. He still couldn't get over the idea of Prince sending Danny along. He needed men who would help carry the goddamn huge whiskey still inside the house, and he knew from past experience that all Danny would do would be stand around and play with his pistol as though he were Al Capone.

Donnie gritted his teeth and turned to the other men. "Okay, guys, the quicker we get the damn thing in, the sooner we can go home." His voice was mild, but he always got the results he wanted. Men liked to work for him because he would always work beside them. He never stood around and just watched.

The men opened up the back door of the truck. The huge cooker stood just inside the door. It was an old oil container, the type that can be seen in people's backyards or sitting behind farmhouses in the country. The only difference was that this one had been cut open, copper soldered around in the inside, then welded back together. Four of the men tried to lift it, but they just grunted under the weight.

Donnie walked up on the porch and spoke to the boy standing in the open doorway. "Bobbie, we goin' need all the help we can get. Is there anybody else in the house besides you and your woman?"

Bobbie, short and thin, shook his head. "My old lady ain't even here." He pushed open the door and came out. "We better prop the door open with something so we can carry that thing all the way in without stopping."

He jumped up on the truck while Donnie searched the yard for something to hold open the screen door. "Goddamn," Bobbie exclaimed. "I don't know if I want to try cookin' with this big bastard or not. If it should blow up, man, it'll take the whole fuckin' house with it."

"Don't worry about it," Donnie replied as he put a brick against the door. "As long as you watch it the same as you did the smaller one, it ain't goin' be no trouble. If you go to fuckin' around and don't take care of business, you might just end up gettin' blowed all the way to hell."

"I don't think he got nothing to worry about," Van yelled, leaning against the whiskey still, "'cause I don't think we goin' be able to get this big sonofabitch in the house."

"I guess ya'll won't get the motherfucker in the house," Danny said, sitting down on the porch, "if all you goin' do is beat your gums about it."

Donnie just rolled his eyes at Danny as he climbed up in the truck with the other men. "Van, you help me with the back of this thing, man. The rest of you try and pick up the front."

Bobbie and the other two men moved to the front of the oil container. "Why don't we push it to the edge of the truck, Donnie, then we can get under it and carry it the rest of the way in the house?" Bobbie asked.

The men pushed and pulled until they got it moving, then three of them jumped off and waited until

Donnie and Van got their end to the edge. Danny sat on the porch smoking. He grinned coldly as the men managed to get the still up and start for the porch, then stepped back as they made their way up the steps. They got as far as the door, then stopped. The still was too large to go in the door.

"The fuckin' thing is too big, man. It ain't about to go through that goddamn door," Bobbie yelled.

"Well I'll be a sonofabitch," Danny said sarcastically. "That's what I call being really bright. Here I am out here freezing my motherfuckin' ass off, and ya come up with some shit like this."

The men just gazed at the doorway as though looking at it long enough would make it wider.

Donnie glanced around at the nearby houses. "You guys keep your voices down. We ain't got no license to make whiskey, so just be cool." He stared up at the stars. It was still dark, but a tinge of light was beginning to break through. "We got to figure out some way to get it through that doorway before daylight." He glanced at his watch. "We still got a few hours, if we work fast. The squares that live around here won't be gettin' up before five-thirty or six, so let's get busy."

"Man, it's getting cold as hell out here," Danny complained, tightening his overcoat collar around his neck.

"Try doing some work, then," Donnie snapped, then spoke to the other men. "All we got to do is take the door frame loose. It should be wide enough then."

Suddenly a spotlight covered the porch. A loud

voice ordered them to stand still. "Don't move," the voice continued. "We got the place surrounded."

Before anyone could reply, Danny made his move. Donnie had started to raise his arms to surrender when gunshots exploded next to him. He glanced around stupefied. "You dumb bastard," he began, but something heavy struck him in the chest. He could feel himself falling from the porch as the night exploded in gunshots.

Danny leaped from the porch, his gun spitting fire. He took two steps towards the alley, then fell as bullets struck him from every side. The other men on the porch were caught in the crossfire. Two of them had guns, but it was useless. When the firing stopped, they were stretched out on the ground.

Donnie managed to climb onto his elbow. He could hear the sound of the policemen inside the house swinging their axes, destroying the barrels of whiskey mash. As his arm slipped from under him, he wondered idly what the noise meant. When the first policeman reached him, he had already left the world of fear and doubt. No more would he have to worry about the rent or whether he would be lucky enough to escape from the quicksand of his everyday life.

21

PRINCE SAT AT ONE of the front tables by the dance floor inside the Roost. The clubhouse was crowded and swinging. People pushed and shoved to get near his table, and he smiled benevolently at his admirers. Everything was going as he had hoped. His only concern now was what was holding up Fatdaddy and Brute. He glanced at his diamond-studded watch. It was getting close to four o'clock in the morning and again he wondered if he had made a mistake in moving against the highly organized trucking company.

Through the din in the club there came a loud thump on the door as if a drunk had fallen against it; then it was repeated. Some of the crowd stood poised, ready to run if it was a bust. Before anyone could move, the sound of a car peeling rubber as it left the curb was heard over the roar of the record player.

One of the doormen glanced out to make sure it wasn't a raid, then the other removed the bars from across the door. As soon as the door was opened, the bodies of Fatdaddy and Brute came falling into the clubhouse. A few mild screams were heard before the girls' companions could hush them up. Prince pushed his way through the milling crowd and stared down at the corpses of his two lieutenants.

"It looks like somebody beat them to death," Preacher said from beside him. There was no emotion in his voice; it was as though he were watching a movie on the late show.

Prince stared in shock at the men at his feet. "You three," Prince said, pointing his finger at three men standing near. "Take these bodies out the back way and drop them off. I don't give a damn where, just make sure they ain't found near here." He swept the crowd with his cold stare. "I want the rest of you to stay right here and keep on jamming as if nothing has happened. Sometime this morning you will get a phone call from me, and then you will go right into action without delay."

He stepped back to allow the boys to pass with the bodies. "Preacher, you come on with me and Ruby. We got a lot to handle before this day gets any older." He turned on his heel and walked out the door, followed by Preacher.

They stood on the sidewalk feeling the morning

wind blowing in off the river. "What the fuck is holding that bitch...." Prince was cut off by the roar of a powerful motor starting up. With the true street fighter's instinct, Prince jumped back down the cellar steps, while Preacher, caught off guard slightly, moved towards his car catlike. He dropped down and tried to roll under the car as a blast from a submachine gun awakened the neighborhood. Bullets ricocheted off the wall at the spot where Prince had been standing. As both men got to their feet, the dying sounds of the fleeing automobile could still be heard in the distance.

The cellar door opened and frightened faces peeped out. "What's happening out there?" someone yelled.

"Just close the goddamn door and keep on partying," Prince commanded. "It was just some friends lettin' me know they had me on their mind," he added, as Ruby ran up the steps.

As Preacher opened the car door, Prince took Ruby's arm and steered her inside. "No questions now!" he ordered.

Preacher started up the motor. He was a little shaken but no worse from the incident. He put the car in drive and pulled away from the curb. "Looks like someone is playing for keeps," he said over his shoulder.

"Don't let it worry you," Prince replied from the backseat. "I know just who the sonsofbitches happen to be."

"You do, huh?" Preacher asked, surprised.

Prince's eyes flickered with rage as he leaned on the back of the front seat to answer. "You better damn well bet I do, and before this day is over they'll wish like hell they never heard of my name." Even as he made the boast, a small voice seemed to warn him to back up, that things were getting out of hand, but he paid no heed.

Ruby spoke up. "I wasn't able to reach Danny or Donnie, Prince, but I got in touch with Hawk and Bossgame. They're both on their way, daddy."

He nodded and sat back against the cushions, his mind racing. If things continued as they were, he would soon be out of lieutenants, he thought coldly. Taking control of the city was getting to be expensive.

Preacher drove slowly down the side streets. By the time they reached the apartment, Hawk and Bossgame were just getting out of their car. They stopped on the sidewalk when they saw the Cadillac pull up, but Prince waved for them to go on in. The three occupants of the Cadillac glanced up and down the street nervously before getting out of the car and running into the building.

Bossgame stood inside the building waiting for Prince. He asked, surprised, "What's the matter, baby, the police chasing you or something?"

"I'll run it down to you after we get upstairs," Prince replied as he brushed past him and continued up the stairway.

After they were settled down in the apartment, Prince began. "There's no reason for me to try and hide the truth. I'll bring it right out in the open so everybody will know where we stand. The Mafia are behind the killings of Fatdaddy and Brute. Nobody else, just them."

"Just them!" Bossgame exclaimed. "Damn, that's too damn much right there! That outfit's too damn big for us to buck, Prince, we might as well face that right now!"

Prince glanced around at his top men. All he could see on their faces was agreement with what Bossgame had said. "What about you, Ruby, you feel the same way?"

Ruby glared around the room at Prince's lieutenants. There was nothing but contempt in her eyes. "I don't sleep with Bossgame and the rest of these so-called soul brothers, daddy," she replied drily. "Whatever you think is best, honey, you know I'll go along with it."

Prince's mouth twisted into a harsh smile. "Well, since I've got support from the thoroughbred in our organization, I do believe I'll play this thing the way I feel. First of all, I'd like to pull your coats to something I've always believed. The Mafia ain't shit in the ghettos, and I'll tell you why. If they come down here fuckin' around, we'll know them as soon as we see them. Ain't no 'woods coming around asking for no information without us knowing about it, so all we got to do is stay in our black neighborhoods and wait. If they try and hire some mean brothers to do the job, they'll have to hire an army, 'cause that's just about what we got." Prince stopped to let his words sink in.

In the silence Ruby spoke up. "Even if they try and hire some brothers to do the work, they'd have to go out of town to get them, 'cause ain't no niggers in their right mind here in this city goin' try and step on our toes."

Prince could see that their words were having an effect on his men. "Preacher," he said suddenly, "I want you to have all your boys down in front of that warehouse in the morning before the first truck rolls in." He pointed his finger like a gun. "Bossgame, you and Hawk see to it that every gang we have at our disposal is down there too, and don't accept no excuses. Tell them I ain't having no shit about this, I want every goddamn one of them there. I want at least five hundred boys and girls milling around there when those trucks start pulling in. I want you to pass out the order that not one of those trucks is able to pull off after you're through with them without the aid of a tow truck. Is that clear and understood?"

He waited until his men nodded in agreement. "I don't want not even one to be able to drive away from there without the help of another truck! Then we'll see how the Mafia likes it." He stared at his men, driving his words at them so they could feel his confidence. "I don't believe that the Mafia, or anyone else for that matter, besides the police, can muster enough men to stop us if we stick together."

The men started to talk among themselves. With the aid of the whiskey and reefer that Ruby passed out, their nerves were soon built up to such a point that they believed nothing could go wrong. It seemed foolproof, now that Prince had shown them how it could be handled. As they left, they were joking among themselves about how the Mafia took it in the hip, or under the arm. They went out into the streets, full of confidence, and did their work well.

When dawn broke over the city, the first out-of-state trucks to enter the waterfront section were stopped two blocks from their destination. The drivers were removed forcibly from the cabs and the trucks completely wrecked. As the driver of the first truck fell into the milling crowd, he was kicked and stomped. In one hour, over forty trucks were stopped and their drivers beaten. The police arrived on the scene, but the first two cars to show up were given the same treatment as the truck drivers. As soon as the police swarmed over one area, the crowd moved to another block and continued to fight.

Ruby, from a vantage point away from the fighting, made a quick phone call to the Black Cougar headquarters and told them that blacks were being beaten up all over the waterfront. The Cougars rushed men to the spot to help out their brothers, and soon they were committed to the battle because the police never changed their strategy. Their operation was simple: if it had a black head on its shoulders, try to knock it off.

What had started out as a gang war had now turned into a rioting mob. Scores of teenagers broke into the neighborhood's warehouse and fought their way through the yards. "Loot" had become the password, and as the boys fought, the girls would disappear with the goods, taking to the alleys they knew so well.

Police began to arrive with dogs and riot guns. It

took them a good hour to begin to restore order because, as soon as they broke up the fighting on one street, it moved to another. A state bus arrived, then another, as the police began rounding up the gang members. Even inside of the buses they kept fighting in the aisles until the police fired warning shots at the ceiling. As the loaded buses pulled away, bodies of truck drivers could be seen up and down the street.

Fire trucks moved back and forth trying to stop the fire blazes before they could spread. Ambulances pulled away one after the other carrying the dead and injured. Sometimes they carried police, more often teenagers or truck drivers.

Morales shook his head sadly. "They tell me that five truck drivers are dead, and before it's over they figure to find at least three more in the same condition."

Captain Mahoney nodded. "That's the same count I got."

Lieutenant Gazier came running up, out of breath. He waited a second until he could speak. "Well, I guess this about brings our case to an end. We picked up at least six different gang leaders, and before it's over, we'll probably have six more. With that many in the tank, somebody's got to start singing."

The captain nodded. "Yes, you're right about that. When one starts, they'll fall over each other trying to outtalk the next one." He stared around for a moment, then spoke to his two lieutenants. "I want a first-degree murder warrant taken out on Prince, and each gang leader in our custody will be arraigned on the same charge. Find out just what gangs are locked up. If we don't have the leaders in custody, put out warrants for them, too."

Lieutenant Gazier grinned coldly. "All right, Captain. It looks like that punk has finally made a mistake he won't be able to wiggle out of, huh?"

"That's just about it," the captain answered harshly. "This is one jam five lawyers couldn't get him out of." There was a flash of bitterness in his voice. "Morales," he said, "each one of you better pick up another partner, that way you can cover more territory. I believe you two boys know more about these punks' hideouts than the rest of the department put together."

Gazier left to report the pickup on Prince, and Morales and the captain started back to their car. "Just look at the damage these punks have done." The captain pointed at two trucks still smoking from where gas had been poured over them and set on fire. "Morales, I'd bet it's over a hundred thousand dollars worth of damage to the trucks alone, without counting what's been done to their cargo."

"Say, Pat," Morales said, stopping and pointing. "Look over there, will you. Looks like one of Prince's top boys on that stretcher." The policemen hurried over and stopped the men with the stretcher. The kid lying on it had a bandage around his head that didn't quite cover the gaping wound. While they stood looking down at him, one of the male nurses stepped forward and pulled the blanket over his face.

"Well, this is one that won't be in any more street

fights," the nurse said flatly.

"That's the end of Bossgame," Morales said. "What do you think happened to him?"

"I don't think, I know," the nurse replied. "We found the truck driver who swung the iron pipe right next to him. His friends took care of the truck driver, but he made sure before they got him that he would have plenty of company in hell." The nurse nodded towards the stretcher coming up behind them.

Morales walked over and pulled the cover from the second kid's face. He quickly covered it back up and turned away to avoid being sick. "There's no reason for you to look, Pat," he said when he regained his composure. "That's Little Larry on that one. Looks like he would have been better off staying in jail."

Morales started walking towards the car. Captain Mahoney caught up with him and grabbed his arm. "There's no reason for you to let this upset you, Morales. If the boy hadn't been here fighting, this would have never happened to him."

"It's hard to think that way, Pat, when you see a kid not even eighteen years old with his whole face bashed in."

"Before you go and get soft-hearted, Morales, think about that poor truck driver who probably had two or three kids at home. Try thinking about what you'd tell his wife."

"Pat, I know these kids are in the wrong; don't think I'm trying to find excuses for them. It's just that I hate to see kids throwing their lives away at such a young age."

"They're old in their way," Mahoney replied unrelentingly.

"Yes, I realize that they're old, Pat. But the way things have been going—three murders last night, and now this—we might as well put on their epitaph when we bury them: the old die young."

Mahoney rubbed his nose with the back of his hand. "Lieutenant, if we don't catch up with Prince soon, we're going to bury a whole lot more of these kids, 'cause it's a sure bet that the Mafia won't take this without some kind of retaliation."

"Don't worry, Captain, we'll get him, and it won't be long."

"I got a feeling you better make it real quick, son, real quick."

22

IT WAS AFTERNOON now and the streets had been cleared of the wreckage. The fighting had been over for some time, but the warehouse across the street from the trucking concern was still smoking. Inside the teamster office, a big man smoking a thin cigar was pacing the floor. Every time he glanced out the window he became angrier.

"I'm going to give you one more chance, Ed. You and Bill fucked this deal up, so I'm going to see if you can straighten it out." He gestured impatiently with his cigar when Bill tried to interrupt. "I don't want any more damn excuses. You're not dealing with nothing but some young punks, and your stupidity is going to cost us over three hundred thousand dollars worth of damage."

"Boss, it's not how you think it is," Ed replied, his voice trembling. "The kid that gives these punks their orders is smart."

The cigar was pointed again. "Of course the kid is smart. Maybe I should give you over to this kid, then let him take care of your job. Now just shut up," the bossman roared. "I've said I don't want any excuses and I mean it. You got three days to get that boy, three days! This time make sure you don't knock off any small fry like those two you killed and started all this trouble. I want you to get the top man in three days, or we'll replace you with someone who can do the job."

Across town in Tony and Racehorse's penthouse, Prince sat brooding over the day's events. Every time the television came on and his photo flashed across the screen, he realized bitterly that he had made an awful error. His organization had come tumbling down around his head. If he had only thought out the matter more carefully, things would have been different. All he would have had to do was back up, forget about what happened to Brute and Fatdaddy. Common sense should have told him he was over-reaching. Now the only course left to him was flight. With his picture on everybody's mind, he'd have to leave the damn country.

Tony got up and switched the television back on. The newsman was just wrapping up an announcement on the arrest of some Black Cougars during the riot. He continued to speculate on a possible alliance between the Cougars and the organization behind the latest outbreak of killing.

"That's good for them bastards," Ruby said, laughing harshly. "Now all we got to do, Prince, is get us on a big iron bird and fly the hell away from here. In another week or two, the white folks will be done forgot all about you as they nail them Cougars' black asses to the fence."

"I see that bitch is still trying to think for you, Prince," Racehorse said arrogantly. His contempt for his associate was barely concealed. It showed in his laugh, in his attitude, as he continued. "In fact, baby, you ain't really got no problem. If you'll just stop listening to your woman for a minute, I'll explain something to you."

"Maybe you got something there," Prince replied slowly, hiding his rising anger. He smiled, but his eyes were chilling. "You go on and explain it to me, Horse, but leave my woman out of it. How we get along with each other doesn't concern you."

Racehorse laughed. "Maybe you're right about that," he said easily. "You can get out of this shit with your ass still in good shape, Prince, if you don't mind spending a few dollars. I got a connect in Florida where the guy will smuggle you across to Cuba in his boat, but it will cost you a nice piece of change."

"I got a few hundred dollars hid away," Prince answered.

"Your ass!" Racehorse snorted. "If you and Ruby

ain't got over fifty grand hid away, you ain't got a penny."

"If we got a hundred thousand hid away, it ain't none of your motherfuckin' business!" Ruby said loudly. If looks could kill, Racehorse would have been dead. "This sonofabitch thinks he's smart, Prince. We don't need no tellin'. If the bastard has a connect that will help you, that's cool, but ain't nobody got to kiss his black ass to get along with him."

Racehorse threw up his hands. "See, that's what I mean. Your bitch has got too much mouth. What she needs is a good old-fashioned ass-kickin', then she'll be in her place."

Tony spoke up before the argument could get out of hand. "All this arguing ain't going to help anyone. Whatever you say ain't going to change the fact that you got big problems, Prince. If Racehorse has a connect for getting you out of the country, you'd better listen to him, because you're hot as hell."

"That makes sense, Tony," Prince said softly. "I'd like to see an end to this fussing as much as anyone else." He got up and walked to the window. "It's a sure thing we won't be able to make a move before it gets dark, though." He stared out of the window quietly, filled with bitterness. He promised himself that he'd never allow them to put him behind bars again. No, it would be better to hold court in the streets, no matter where they stopped him.

He turned back to the room. "It won't be much longer before it's dark. Then, Ruby, you can slip out and pick up the money. We might as well try to get away tonight."

"The man would like to get his hands on Ruby just about as bad as he'd like to get hold of you, Prince," Racehorse said. "I don't think there's any heat on me and Tony, though, so why don't you pull our coat to where the money is and let us pick it up for you."

Ruby laughed sarcastically. "I wouldn't trust you with my mammy's bloomers, let alone a big piece of money, Racehorse."

"I don't know what makes you say shit like that, bitch," Racehorse answered quickly. "You should know we wouldn't burn Prince. Why, we couldn't afford to. He's the only person who could bust us, so you know we'd treat him right."

"Tell me the blind can lead the blind, or that a fly can fuck an elephant," Ruby shot back, "but don't bring us this weak shit about who you won't burn. You'd burn your mammy for her last days on earth if you thought you could get them, so take that bullshit to someone whose head screws on."

Racehorse glared at Ruby. "The hell with what that bitch is talking about, man," he said angrily. "What do you think about the idea, Prince? Damn what your cunt is talking about."

Before Ruby could reply, Prince cut her off. "Shut up, Ruby, I'll handle this." He turned to Racehorse. "Whatever she said, Horse, I'll just about go along with. What's to keep you two from running off with the money once you get it? You done told me you got a connect to get into Cuba, so what the fuck?" He waved his hand to avoid an interruption. "I'll tell you how we can do this. I'll give you twenty grand for going with Ruby to pick up the money, Racehorse. And to make sure you don't burn me, leave your gun here."

Racehorse cursed. "Fuck that shit!"

Prince shrugged. "Ruby, take a hundred dollars and buy you a wig; maybe you can slip into the apartment that way. It will be a helluva lot cheaper."

Racehorse changed his mind quickly as Ruby stood up. "Okay, baby, I'll go for it." He removed his pistol and held it out to Prince.

Prince gave the gun to Ruby. "When he goes in the apartment, honey, I want you so close to him you'll look like you're part of him, understand?"

She nodded her head. "Okay, daddy, but I'll still stop and pick up that wig before we go to the apartment."

Prince sat back down. "Okay, baby, do it like you want to. Just make sure you take care of the business. We ain't got no room for mistakes this late in the game."

"Don't worry, honey," she answered as she followed Racehorse from the room. "I'll be back as soon as possible."

Across town in another apartment, Preacher was rushing his wife. "Hurry up with that goddamn packing," he yelled. "I done told you we ain't got no time. Just bring what you can for now. You can have your mother pick up the rest of the stuff." He glanced at his watch. "Hurry, goddamn it!"

His youthful, brown-skinned wife came running out of the bedroom with a suitcase in one hand and a small child in the other. She put down the suitcase in the middle of the floor, next to two others. "I ain't got but one more to pack, honey, just wait a minute," she said and started to turn around.

Preacher snatched her arm. His eyes were wild. "Can't you get it through your head, woman? We got to get the fuck out of here now! Not later, but right now!" He pulled her by the arm and pushed her towards the door.

She stumbled, then straightened up. As she reached the door, there came a thundering knock from the outside. Preacher dropped the suitcases in the middle of the floor as his woman backed away, her face filled with fear.

Suddenly the door came crashing in. Preacher's wife began to scream in terror.

As the policemen came rushing into the room, Preacher raised his hands and screamed, over and over, "Don't kill my wife, don't kill her. She ain't did nothing. Don't kill her."

The first policeman to reach him knocked him to the floor. "If you move, nigger," he growled, "I'll kill you." The officer stood over him with a gun pointed at his head.

Preacher's wife raced across the room and grabbed the policeman's arm. "Don't kill him," she screamed, trying to knock the gun from his hand.

"Goddamnit," the officer cursed, trying to fight her off with one hand. Before one of his partners could step in to help, the gun went off. The slug hit Preacher in the middle of the forehead. He fell onto his back, dead before he reached the floor.

In the ensuing silence, one of the officers cursed. "I'll be a sonofabitch," he said to no one in particular.

Preacher's wife fell across his body and began to sob. The officer who had pulled the trigger kept repeating, "I didn't mean to shoot him, I didn't mean it." The rest of the policemen stood dumbfounded. It had taken everyone by surprise.

Ruby took her time picking out a strawberry-red wig. When she had finished making her purchase, she strolled around the store slowly so that, when she left the shopping center, it would be dusk-dark.

Racehorse sat on the passenger side of the Cadillac chain-smoking. "Goddamn it, you didn't have to take all fuckin' night, did you?" His voice was edgy from the strain of waiting.

She slid under the steering wheel without bothering to answer. Racehorse stared at the expanse of beautiful black thigh as her skirt inched up higher. "I thought the only thing you liked was snow, Racehorse," she said coldly, glancing at him from the corner of her eye. "My thigh ain't nowhere near white, nigger, so you might as well stop fiendin' on it."

He laughed shortly, then reached over and put his hand high up on her thigh. "You know, Ruby, you and me might be able to work something out." He waited to see if she would interrupt, then continued. "I know there ain't no heat on me, and I don't think there's too much on you." Racehorse stopped talking and worked his hand higher on her thigh.

Ruby dropped one of her hands from the steering wheel and removed his hand from her leg. "Whatever you're trying to say, you might be able to say it better if you would just try concentrating on it instead of trying to stick your hand under my dress."

"Well now, I might at that, but I enjoy it better this way," he replied as he began to feel her leg again. "Ruby, have you ever thought about pulling up on Prince?"

She shrugged her shoulders. "What woman hasn't ever given in to the thought of leaving her man?"

The ambiguous answer seemed to satisfy Racehorse. "Why don't you try thinking about it now then? When we pick up that money, Ruby, ain't nothin' between us and the airport but air." The idea of pulling up with the money had occurred to him the moment Prince had told him to go along with Ruby to pick it up. The idea of taking her along was only a temporary measure until he could get his hands on the gun. Then he'd make other arrangements. The thought of making love to Ruby was pleasant enough, but the idea of staying with her was madness. He couldn't stand a willful-minded woman.

She grabbed his hand again, but this time she clawed it deeply with her fingernails. He snatched it back with a yell. "Next time, find you something else to paw on," she said, spitting the words out. "I told you once, nigger, ain't nothing about me should remind you of snow, and since you're so mad about white bitches, you'd better find you one of them to put your funky hands on."

Racehorse moved across the seat and stared at the scratches on the back of his hand. They made the rest of the trip in silence, and he thought of how to get his gun away from her. He wanted that money, as well as the joy of killing Ruby.

She parked the car a block away from her apartment building. They walked together up the sidewalk, each involved in their own thoughts. When they reached the building, Ruby pointed the way to Racehorse, then followed him up the stairs. She gave him the key and stood back as he opened the door. Before he could move out of the way, she kicked him in the back, sending him falling through the open doorway.

"Well, now, pretty boy," she said slowly as he lay at her feet. "You done any thinking on how we should rip my man off for his money? Any *more* thinkin', that is, 'cause that shit about you and me didn't work out too well."

He pushed himself up on his hands and glared up at her. The pistol in her hand didn't waver. It was pointed directly at his head. He stared up at her. Her eyes were black chips of ice. They glittered with an unholy light that made him tremble uncontrollably.

"Wait a minute, Ruby. I was just kiddin' with you, girl. You know I know you ain't goin' leave Prince. I was just playin', woman, that's all."

She started laughing, a wild, almost hysterical

sound. She walked past him and picked up a cushion. Before he could raise any higher than his knees, she whirled back around. The sound of the shot was muffled by the cushion, but she fired twice more.

Racehorse slipped back to the floor, trying in vain to raise his hand. Blood gushed from the corner of his mouth as he lay stretched out on his back. All of the gunshots had hit him in the chest and stomach.

Ruby watched him for a minute, then disappeared into the bedroom. She came out carrying a black bag. She stared down at the body once to make sure he was dead, then slowly let herself out the door. She glanced up and down the hallway making sure no one had been drawn by the noise. Her high heels mingled with the noise from the other apartments as she ran downstairs. A chill wind was blowing as she stepped out on the street, and she clutched her collar around her neck.

The black doctor's bag she carried was stuffed with money. As she neared some dilapidated storefront buildings, she clutched the bag tighter. Wineheads and junkies loitered in front of the stores. Normally the sight of gangs didn't disturb her, but because of the large amount of money she carried, her nerves were on edge.

After the first glance, the junkies ignored her and went back into their nods.

As she neared a group of men who were passing a wine bottle back and forth, a young drunkard staggered into her path and tried to wrap his arms around her. Removing her hand from her coat pocket where she held the gun, she gave him a hard shove in the chest.

The unexpected push sent the man down hard. He climbed back to his feet, cursing, as his friends laughed. He shook a clenched fist after her, but it was too late. She had forgotten about him before he was out of her sight. Her real concern had been the addicts.

Ruby relaxed and breathed more slowly after she reached the car. She jumped in and locked all the doors. She glanced idly at the black bag. For the sixty thousand dollars inside that bag, the addicts would have killed their mothers, let alone her.

23

PRINCE STARED MOODILY out of the window. Ruby should just about be on her way back, he thought impatiently. The sound of a phone ringing came to him sharply. He listened absentmindedly as Tony talked into the receiver.

"Just a minute," he heard Tony say before he hung up. He went into the bedroom and closed the door behind him.

Prince stared at the closed door. Tony's curious behavior hadn't escaped his notice. From the corner of his eye he had seen the fleeting glances Tony sent his way. He started for the bedroom door but stopped. If something had happened to Ruby, his barging in wouldn't do any good. If Racehorse has hurt her, I'll hunt both of them down if it takes a lifetime, he promised himself. As he stood in the middle of the room undecided, he heard Ruby's soft, arranged knock. He rushed over and opened the door.

After finishing his conversation in the bedroom, Tony hung up the phone. He walked over to his dresser and slowly pulled out one of the drawers. It was unbelievable, he told himself. Luck didn't generally fall his way this easily. His uncle, a higher-up in the Mafia, had called him. They were trying to find out where Prince had holed up. They wanted him so bad they were willing to pay fifty thousand big ones for whoever made the hit on him. Tony grinned coldly. That was fifty thousand Racehorse wouldn't be up on. He'd handle this himself. With everybody in the city searching for Prince, he had the man under wraps.

When Tony stepped through the bedroom door he was surprised to see Ruby, but it didn't cause the pistol in his hand to tremble. He held the gun lightly, pointed in Prince's direction. "Well, well, I see we have our little lady back," he began. "What happened to old Horse? I'm surprised he allowed you out of his sight with all that money."

"What's the gun for?" Prince asked sharply. "I thought you were too big to start playing cops and robbers."

Tony glanced down at the gun. "No, no, I wouldn't say I was playing kid games. Let's just say this is the instrument I'm going to use to get big stuff." Tony grinned, revealing beautiful teeth in his tanned face.

"To begin with, Ruby, you bring that bag of sweet green things over here."

That was as far as he got. Ruby glanced up at Prince before firing through her coat pocket. The bullet struck Tony high in the chest. As he fell back, the automatic in his hand went off. Prince lurched from the impact. Ruby came out of her pocket with the gun and fired again, this time hitting Tony in the face. As he slid down the wall, she pulled the trigger twice more, but the gun snapped on empty cylinders.

"Baby, baby, you all right?" she asked frantically as she turned to Prince. He was clutching his stomach and leaning against the door. She stared at the slowly spreading blood, her eyes wide. "Just hold on, daddy, I'll get something to bandage it up with."

"We ain't got the time, woman," he managed to say. "We got to get the hell out of here. Those shots must have been heard by someone in the building."

She nodded. "Okay, daddy, I won't take but a moment." She ran into the bedroom and snatched the sheet off the bed. As she came out, she bent over and retrieved Tony's gun, slipping it into her coat pocket.

They left the apartment together. Prince had his arm around her neck for support. A few people glanced out of their apartments as they passed, but no one tried to stop them. Prince pressed the bundled-up sheet against his wound as they made their way to the street. Ruby helped him into the Cadillac. After getting him settled, she walked around to the driver's side, glancing up and down nervously. "Damnit," she swore under her breath, "I'll still have to get rid of this goddamn car." She frowned, troubled. She'd have to get Prince somewhere safe before even attempting to pick up another car.

Prince rolled over on the car seat, holding his stomach. He listened to Ruby's words but didn't hear them because of the pain, the burning fire inside his stomach.

Ruby glanced down at him as she drove. He had to have help fast. But how? Her brain raced with only one thought: how could she help her man?

Time, she reasoned, was precious. She didn't have time for aimless driving, so why was she doing it? She turned onto a side street and parked between two cars. She leaned over and examined the wound.

It was the first close look she'd had of the wound. "Oh daddy, please daddy, what I'm goin' do?" She was a lost woman, clutching at the only thing she believed in in life, her man. "Tell me, daddy, what?"

He could hear her voice, he understood. He could feel her hands on his face. She kissed him, clutched his head to her bosom, almost smothering him in her fear. Tears ran down her face.

"Can you understand me, darling?" she murmured in his ear. "I'll get you a doctor, daddy, don't worry. I'll have one as soon as I find one."

She fingered the gun in her coat pocket. It wouldn't be impossible to walk a doctor out of his house. That was her least worry. She rested his head against the door.

"Daddy, daddy, I got to take you out to your grandmother's. Prince, you hear me, daddy? I got to get you to your grandmother's, so I can go get the doctor." Her voice was husky. She prayed fervently as she drove. Feverishly, she picked out gaps in the traffic and sped through the night.

Prince managed to regain consciousness enough to speak. "It's up to you, mama, it's up to you," he murmured, his voice drifting off.

She stared down at him, her face glistening from the steady flow of tears. "Don't worry, baby, don't worry," she managed to reply.

She pulled up in front of the old house and parked. The street was deserted. The winter wind had driven most of the inhabitants inside. The isolated people she saw were scurrying for the warmth of their shabby dwellings.

Ruby managed to get Prince's arm around her neck. She was able to support most of his weight as they made their way to the porch of the run-down house. She pounded on the door, her eyes searching the street for prowling police cars.

"Child, child, what done happen to you?" the elderly woman cried as she came out the door. Together, the two women managed to get Prince inside and stretched out on the sofa.

Prince's grandfather watched the proceedings with a cold stare. He cursed suddenly and stood up. "I told you, ma, when we was watchin' TV and that boy's face came on the screen, that he done went and got in more trouble than he could get out of." He walked over and looked down at Prince. There was no compassion in his face. "I done spent ninety years in this world and I ain't never been inside no jail."

Ruby stood up and spoke to the old woman. "You will watch him for me, won't you? I got to get out of here and run down a doctor somewhere."

"We don't need no nigger here that all the police department is lookin' for." The elderly man ran his fingers through his kinky, snow-white hair. "Ain't havin' no trouble out of no white folks 'cause of that boy there."

Ruby glanced at the old woman. "Don't worry, child, I'll take care of him. Don't you worry none on what that old fool is saying. He know I'm goin' take care of this boy. You just hurry and get that doctor. That's what you do. You just hurry on along."

Ruby leaned over and kissed Prince. When she got up, she pecked the old woman on the cheek. "I'll be back as soon as possible." She glanced again at Prince before going out the door.

As the sound of the closing door faded, Prince pulled himself up and clutched at his grandmother's arm. "It hurts so," he gasped. Then he lay back and died. There was nothing heroic in his death, just the passing of a boy who would never have the chance to see twenty-five. The two old people began to weep, tears of frustration and despair coursing down their cheeks. For the grandfather, it was the last of his bloodline. The youth he had treated with such callousness was gone. For something to do, he picked up the black bag Ruby had left behind and threw it into a corner, out of the way.

Lieutenant Gazier was quiet as the detective car moved in and out of traffic. The trouble was coming to an end, yet he hadn't been able to find that incident that would bring him the recognition he longed for. All it would take was a small break. Whoever got the opportunity to arrest Prince would make all the headlines, and that would guarantee a boost to his career. Suddenly he sat bolt upright in the seat. He turned around and stared at the white Cadillac they had just passed.

"Turn around and catch up with that Caddie," Gazier ordered. The uniformed officer quickly threw the car into a U-turn and fell in behind the Cadillac.

Ruby watched the movement in her mirror. She knew at once that it was a police car behind her and quickly ran over her chances of escaping a bust. If it was an officer who didn't know her, she had a chance. To try to escape in the Cadillac was insane; the police car was smaller and faster. She decided to bluff; she didn't believe there was a pickup out on her. She pulled over and parked with the motor running.

The police car came up, passing slowly. Ruby stared hard at the officers, trying to see if she could recognize them. She couldn't see their faces, but the officer driving was in uniform. Her heart skipped a beat, it might be the break she'd been looking for. She waited for it patiently. That was all they needed, one good break, and she and Prince could still pull out of trouble.

When she was just about to believe they were going to leave her alone, the police car stopped. Ruby reacted. As the officer on the passenger side jumped out, she removed the pistol from her coat pocket and rolled down the window.

Lieutenant Gazier almost ran around the police car. He thought he had recognized the driver. He didn't want to believe his luck was so good. She would be even better than her boyfriend, because with her he would end up with both of them. Woman or not, he promised himself, he'd get his information from her before they got to the station.

He was still smiling when he reached the Cadillac. Ruby, recognizing Gazier, fired point blank into his face. As the body of the detective fell beside the car, she plunged her foot on the accelerator. The car leaped away. Before the other officer could react, the Cadillac was almost past him. He drew and fired wildly. Two of his shots crashed through the side window. The car swerved and struck a fire hydrant.

Silence prevailed for a brief moment. Even the streets seemed to be bidding farewell. Ruby twitched on the car seat, blood gushing from a head wound. For one brief instant, life held her, and she thought: What will my man do now?

Donald Goines
SPECIAL PREVIEW

STREET PLAYERS

This excerpt from Street Players *will introduce you to "Earl the Pearl," a ghetto spawn who clawed his way to the top and fights like hell to stay there. He views the street from his penthouse and is everybody's mellow fellow, a big spender, the toast of the inner city. He's as cool and sharp as an ice crystal. Even Joe Chink can't touch him. Then somebody puts the heat on, and his friends start dropping like flies, threatening to take Earl with them. But he bounces back...for awhile.*

I

EARL'S APARTMENT WAS elaborately, tastefully and expensively furnished. The three young men lounging on the floor had completely disregarded the plush gold velvet couch and matching chairs to stretch out on the high-pile, red wall-to-wall carpet. Charles, a tall Negro with brown, bumpy skin and a high natural, began crawling towards the coffee table while Earl and the others watched listlessly. "Anybody want me to roll them a joint?" he asked.

"You can twist me another, as long as you're at it, man," Billy, a slim, dark-complexioned black man called from the far corner. Billy pushed the cushion from beneath his head and rose to a sitting position, patting his hair lightly, pushing the process back in place. He eyed Earl, who was standing across the room looking out of the picture window. "Say, Earl," he said, "let's call up some square bitches and have them come over and dig this penthouse of yours, man."

Earl, tall and brown-skinned, ran his fingers across his moustache, smiled, and walked to the glass-topped coffee table where Charles was busy twisting reefers. He picked up a joint and pointed it towards Billy before lighting up. "That's the reason I *got* this penthouse, Billy, instead of some run-down, cold-water flat across town," he said.

"What the hell you mean by that?" Duke, the fourth member of the group, asked as he came over and joined the men at the table. He accepted one of the joints Charles held out to him.

Earl took a slow drag from his reefer before answering. "I'd feel like a damn fool if we had some square bitches sitting around getting high and one of my whores should happen to come home," he said.

Billy picked up a cushion and tossed it over beside the table so that he could kneel on it. "What difference would it make? You're supposed to be the one doing the pimping, Earl, not one of your whores."

Duke laughed loudly. "I ain't got nothing to do with it, Earl, but Billy is pulling your coat to the real."

"Pimping is my livelihood, nigger, so I don't need any goddamn instructions!" Earl replied sarcastically. "Neither you nor Billy would give me a goddamn penny towards my rent or car note if I blew my whores, so don't worry about how I take care of *my* business."

"Goddamn, baby," Billy replied, jokingly. "If someone who didn't know us heard you talking, they wouldn't believe we was real cool with each other."

"That's right," Duke yelled, putting his two cents in. He removed a large bankroll and began counting hundred-dollar bills on the table. "I'll gladly loan you any parts of this case, if you need it, man. Go ahead, take what you want."

Charles twisted up the last reefer. "Why don't you motherfuckers quit bullshittin'. If it wasn't for them bitches Earl got out on the track, he couldn't borrow five dollars, let alone some big stuff. That ain't nothing but neck—and the side of it at that—that you're talkin' out of!"

Earl spoke up with the youthful gaiety and irresponsibility of a young man who didn't care what others thought of him. "Ain't nobody asked your greasy black ass to loan me no money, so you can quit flashing that little roll of yours. You sure in the hell ain't impressing nobody with that A-D-C trap money."

Duke stuffed his bankroll back into his pocket. "Okay, nigger, I hear you rappin'. Just 'cause you got this pad up here, you must think that makes you one hell of a pimp."

Earl laughed harshly. "They rent these penthouses to anybody, Duke. All you got to do is be handling."

All of the men laughed, while Duke sneered, revealing a perfect set of evenly spaced, well-kept teeth. There was a constant undercurrent of competitiveness

between the men in the apartment. None really trust-
ed the others, not where their women were concerned.
It was great sport for one to end up by taking one of
his friends' girls.

Duke continued his harassment. "I still don't know
how you went about getting this place, Earl. You sure
don't look like no peckerwood. What did you do, send
one of your white girls up to rent it?"

Again the men in the room laughed. Earl adjusted
his pants and straightened his shirt. "Whatever I did,
Duke, you can bet I did it like a player. In fact, if you
should want a place here and can't get it because of
your extremely dark man-tan, you can let your white
girl rent it, and you put on a white jacket and carry
her bags in for her.

"That ain't nothing but bullshit ya keep kickin' back
and forth," Billy said suddenly. "I don't understand it,
but every time you two get together, it always ends
with both of you trying to drop lugs on each other."

Charles nodded in agreement. "That's right. Instead
of pimps, you act like two bitches."

Earl and Duke glared at the other two men. Neither
man actually wanted to discontinue the light
exchange. Both men had a hidden dislike for one
another, and yet they ran together almost every day.

"Let's ride down on the whores and see who's catching them the biggest," Duke said suddenly as he stood
up.

A dry, bitter laugh escaped from Earl. "Since you
ain't got no whores down on the track, how in the
hell are you goin' find out who's catchin' what, and

how?" Earl grinned at the other men, then added, "Unless what you really mean is, let's ride down and see what them thoroughbred bitches I got are doing."

"Not really, Earl. You know you ain't the only person in this room who happens to have a soul sister working down on the track."

"Bravo, bravo!" Billy shouted, clapping loudly. Earl watched Billy with the attitude of a man well aware of the deceitful nature of the people he deals with.

Charles bent over and knocked the ashes off his joint. "Well, all the reefer is gone now, so let's do something."

"Here," Billy said, tossing a small package on the table. "Let's snort this little bit of poison up before we pull."

Earl stared at the package as though someone had tossed a snake on his table. "Well I'll be damned, Billy. You mean to tell me you've been carrying all that smack around in my car all day without me even knowing about it?"

"You didn't have nothing to worry about, Earl, and besides, it ain't nothing but a fifty-dollar bag," Billy answered.

Duke bent over the table and tore off a piece of matchbox cover. He quickly creased the torn piece down the middle and stuck one end of the quill into the white powder. With an adept motion, he picked up some of the white powder with his quill and quickly stuck it into his nose. Snorting loudly, he looked around the small group. "What's the matter, baby?" he said directly to Earl. "Is a little bit of money really making you get shitty?"

Earl spoke up sharply. "You can call it anything you want to, Duke, but I don't want you or Billy or any goddamn body in my house, car, or just in my company carrying no dope without me knowing about it!"

Charles tried to relieve the sting of Earl's words. "That's about the way Dicky-boy will feel about drugs by the time he gets out of prison," he said quietly.

His words put Billy on the defensive immediately. Everyone in the house knew just what he was saying. "What you're talking about ain't shit, Charles," Billy stated loudly. "That dope that was found in Dicky's car belonged to the white bitch, Pat. If he hadn't had the funky bitch sitting damn near in his lap, the dope wouldn't have been found at his feet."

There was a slight tightening of nerves, and the tension in the room could be felt. "Well, all of you were in the car together, my man," Earl said sharply, staring at Billy's flushed face. Before Billy could reply, Earl continued. "And I know for a fact that Dicky didn't fuck with no junk, so it sure didn't belong to him, and he's the one that got five years for it."

"That's bullshit and you know it!" Billy exploded. "They gave Dicky all that time because they knew he was driving a Cadillac that his white whores had bought for him. They been wantin' the man for years, and they got the chance and just socked it to him."

Earl stared around the room at the other men. He was young, strong, and full of confidence. "Well, that may be the case," he said, "but for the record, I want you to know that I don't want any drugs in my car unless you done pulled my coat to it."

"Aw, man, why you come up with that weak shit?" Billy asked, then added, "You act like I ain't got no Cadillac of my own, baby. I just ain't got to ride in yours."

"Well, you said it, Billy, I didn't. But since you stated it, I think that's the best thing I've heard. I know you ain't goin' do right, and every time you get in somebody's car, you're going to be carryin' some kind of drugs—for either you or your woman. So, you know, take your own weight."

"That's cool," Billy answered while in the process of snorting up some dope. "I guess you remember I left my car across town when I got in your car with you and Charles."

"You don't have to worry, Billy Banks," Earl replied. "I'm going to drop you and Duke back off at your car when we leave. I just want you to let me know when you get into my car if you're carrying dope on you. I like to be careful. I hate to have the police find a package of stuff on my floor when I don't really know how it got there."

The men stared at each other. Billy was far from being a fool, but he didn't really get angry over what Earl had said. If push came to shove, and he was in Earl's car and they got stopped, he knew in his heart that he'd stick the dope down in one of the cushions if he hadn't had the time to throw it out the window. Anything, just as long as he got rid of the dope so that the police couldn't take it out of his pocket. With the dope found in the car, he'd never have to worry about going to prison, not on a rap like that. Maybe Earl would end up losing his Cadillac, but that would be far better than getting a few years behind bars.

The phone rang,. Charles was sitting right next to it; he got Earl's nod, then picked up the receiver.

"It's long distance, Earl," he said, holding the phone out as Earl reached for it.

"Hi, honey," Earl said, then hesitated and began to listen. He picked the phone up and started to walk away with it but changed his mind. "What's the name of the doctor you're seeing?" he asked suddenly. He waited, then continued. "Well, if the doctor thinks you should go into the hospital, honey, then you do what he says. Female trouble can become a problem if you don't take care of it. How much money have you got? Four hundred. Well, that should be enough. Get you a private room, and if the bill should run over that, let me know. But what you try and do is tell them you'll pay the rest, if it should turn out to be more than four hundred dollars. As soon as you get back to work, you should be able to take care of that yourself, Lill."

He nodded his head at something she said, then hung up. "The bitch done come down with female trouble," he said to no one in particular. Earl turned his back and walked over to the window and stared out. His mind was busy with how to handle the problem that had just come up. While his girl was in the hospital, he would miss the money that came regularly from the whorehouse in Pennsylvania, but the money wasn't his real problem. What he was pondering was whether or not he should send another girl up to fill the place of the one going to the hospital. If he did that, then when the one in the hospital got out, there would be confusion between the women. Lill was a good prostitute, but she couldn't get along with any of his other girls. That was one reason why he kept her working out of town. Whenever she came back to Detroit, she managed to always get into some kind of scrape with one of his other girls.

"Damn, baby," Duke said loudly. "You sure believe in blowing your money, don't you?"

Earl turned from the window and stared at him. "I don't know what you mean, man."

Duke smiled, revealing yellow spots on his teeth. "I mean by blowing all that money on a hospital bill. All you had to do was have her check in a general hospital somewhere and, when she got well, just leave. Ain't no way they can make a whore pay no bill." He grinned widely at his own cleverness. "Yeah, baby, if she was mine, I'd of had her mail that four hundred, maybe lettin' her keep fifty or something like that. But she'd never have blown all that money for no doctor bill."

"Yeah, I see what you mean," Earl replied, then laughed harshly. "That's the difference in pimpin' and simpin', man. I let all my ladies go first class, all the time. That's why I got a stable of good young whores instead of some dopefiend bitches that shoot up all the profit."

"You can call it simpin' if you want to," Duke continued, determined to get his point across, "but I'd be four hundred bucks richer sometime today if I had been in your place."

"Fuck all that shit!" Billy said loudly, as he snorted up the rest of his dope. "I'd have asked you to take a blow, Charles, but I know you don't want your *big chief* Earl to know that you like a toot now and then." He glanced up at Earl, "Hey, man, how about running us back over on Johnny-R street so I can pick up my car?"

Earl picked up the vest that went with his mod walking suit. He walked into the bedroom to see if the brown silk outfit was fitting him properly. When he came out, he was ready to go. The rest of the men got up and followed him to the door.

Billy laughed loudly as they walked out into the hallway. After closing the door and shaking it to make sure it was locked, Earl caught up with the group at the elevator. He spoke directly to Duke. "Everybody seems to have a lot of advice about how somebody else should treat their whores, but when it comes down to the real, all a nigger will find out is that all his so-called friends have but one thought in mind, and that's how to steal one of them whores from his stiff ass if he lets his game get funny."

The elevator door opened in front of them. Earl stepped in before Duke could reply. There was an elderly, well-dressed couple already inside, so they discontinued the conversation.

2

AFTER DROPPING DUKE and Billy off, Earl, known in and out of all the craps-houses and after-hours joints in the city as "Earl the Black Pearl," decided to drive up on Twelfth and see what kind of action he could find on the corner so early in the evening. He didn't bother to ask the quiet man riding next to him if he wanted to go.

Slumped down in the front seat, Charles stared out of the wide Cadillac window. "You know what we should do for this coming holiday?" he asked suddenly, his voice a deep bass and seeming to rumble as he spoke.

"I don't know what we *should* do," Earl replied easily, "but I got a damn good idea of what I'm going to be doing." The news came on the radio, and Earl quickly switched on the tape recorder.

Charles stared at the slim, dark-skinned man behind the steering wheel. Some black men seemed out of place behind the wheel of the expensive automobiles they drove, wearing work clothes, factory outfits in a ten-thousand-dollar car, but Earl appeared as if the car had been made for him. The white on the white Cadillac fitted him to perfection. The diamonds that he wore glittered as his hand moved over and flicked the button to let down the electric window a crack.

He lit up a stick of reefer. "That don't mean that I won't listen to a good idea for the coming holiday, though. Run it down, baby, I just might go for it."

"Naw, man, that's okay. It wouldn't have made no sense no way." Charles shrugged his shoulders and straightened up in the seat. "We just passed the Man coming out of that alley."

Earl nodded and continued to smoke the weed. Every now and then, he'd check out the mirror. He started to speak, then caught himself. He didn't think he could get Charles to understand just what he meant, and he might just give the wrong impression. It was just that he got a nervous feeling whenever he passed policemen. It wasn't a fear; it was more like a danger signal. In them, he saw the constant threat to his way of life.

As he drove along, the neighborhood began its subtle change. He turned right on Twelfth, a one-way street, and pawnshops and nightclubs began to appear on each side of the street. Farther on, one could see the devastation of the sixties' burning and looting spree. It was everywhere. Here a gutted building, next door a large lot with the debris of past fires scattered over its barren surface.

They stopped for a red light, and the early evening breeze drifted lightly around the car. Everywhere they looked there were the clusters of people that the good weather brought out; they pushed against each other in the cluttered entrances of open doorways to apartment houses and poolrooms and shine parlors. Girls with shortened skirts stood in the darkened doorways, while their counterparts patrolled the sidewalks in revealing hotpants outfits.

Charles stared at one of the younger prostitutes hungrily.

"I'd bet money, Charles, that you'd turn a trick with that young girl if you wasn't shamed she'd come back up on the corner and tell it," Earl said, tossing back his head and laughing. It was a deep sound, one full of mirth, with the kind of heaviness coming through that aroused women. It was also a practiced laugh, one that could be turned on and off at will.

Charles joined in the laughter. He knew it was true. He'd never make a successful pimp of himself; he loved to groove too much. He fell in love with his woman's hips, and that love-joy was his downfall. Earl called it "having a tender dick."

"That's right, boy, you need to laugh," Earl said. "If there's any man who's guilty of following his dick, it's you. For a hard-on, Charles, you'll fuck around and drive five hundred goddamn miles, get there, get the cock, and never bother to ask about the trap money." He laughed again and stared at his husky partner. Charles was by nature a thug. He took his by wit or pistol. Ever since they were childhood friends, Charles was a strong-arm man. At that step in their development, Charles was the boy most of them looked up to. He was the fighter, going to the gym at night, taking up boxing.

How the worm turns, Earl thought coldly. He had been one of the cool ones during this period, always standing back against the wall, posing, and at all times as sharp as his wardrobe would allow him to be.

Another red light caught them. As they sat at the light, two brown-skinned girls crossed the street, flirting openly with the men in the Cadillac.

"Boy oh boy," Charles exclaimed. "You sure get a lot of action when you ride in a hog!"

Earl's laughter rang out sharp and clear. "It don't have to be the Caddie, baby; it just might have been me they were giving that action to, man."

"Shit!" Charles said loudly. "It was the Caddie, baby, that's what it was. Them bitches was lookin' at the ride. It wouldn't have made any difference if two apes was sitting in here!"

"Okay, baby," Earl replied easily. "I ain't about to start arguing over it with you, but one day you'll find out. It ain't always the car, but sometimes it helps out." He laughed again, this time softer.

Another red light caught them. As they sat waiting for it to change, a long, gold Eldorado turned the corner. The driver recognized Earl and blew the Eldorado's deep horn.

Earl waved at the driver. "Old Bobby Spencer," he said, speaking more to himself than to Charles. "That old man has handled more money than any four niggers in this city," he stated.

"I guess so," Charles answered. "If I had the good coke connect that he's got, I'd handle the same kind of money myself."

"Maybe. That man has been selling cocaine for over twenty years now, Charles, and he ain't got busted yet. Now that's what I call a smart street nigger."

"It ain't that he's all that smart, Earl, or that he can't get busted. He's just been lucky that them bitches that he's got dealing for him ain't never switched around on him and cracked him downtown. Shit, every time one of his broads gets busted, they take the weight themselves. Ain't none of them ever gave him no trouble." Charles fell silent, waiting for Earl to agree with him.

"That ain't luck, Charles, that's business. It shows the man knows what's happening. He must tell his women just how to handle it, 'cause if you don't explain it to a bitch and leave it to her to handle, she'll fuck it up every time."

"I don't know," Charles mumbled. "It seems like luck to me. If it was me, the bitch would get downtown and tell it all."

"I'll agree with that," Earl said. "More than likely, you'd have left it up to the woman to handle it, never taking the time to sit her down and explain just what to tell them white folks downtown whenever the bust came. So when the bitch got busted, she'd be feeling on her own and she'd try shifting the weight. It's all in being a top-notch player or just another mediocre-ass nigger out here in the streets."

After the exchange, they rode on in silence, neither man bothering to break the quiet. Each man sank down in his own thoughts, Charles thinking that he was right, that it was just a matter of luck, and Earl knowing that he was right, that it was just a matter of taking care of business. He saw a parking spot in front of a small barbecue restaurant, pulled over, and let his white convertible top down.

As the top went back slowly, four young girls standing in the front of the greasy spoon restaurant stared at the occupants of the car brazenly. In their glance, there was an invitation that needed no words to explain. The weather was warm, the evening was young, and a ride in a convertible would beat the hell out of standing in front of a dirty restaurant. The girls were more than eager. They were ready.

Without seeming to, Earl steadily examined the women. Suddenly, there was a quick movement to his eyes as they focused on one of the girls in particular. "Hummmmmm," he murmured. "What a lovely creature that is."

Before he had time to make a move of his own, Charles took the play out of his hands. "Come here, baby," he yelled, not picking out any particular girl.

Two of the young girls moved away from the window and walked over to the car. The beauty that Earl had noticed was one of them. When the girls reached the car, Charles began to fidget. Now that the action was right in front of him, he was at a loss for words. Earl watched his friend, amused, and his lips turned down in a cold sneer that he was unconscious of.

The girls were amused by Charles' seeming inability to follow up on his bold approach. "Uh," he began, "uh, ain't you got a sister, girl, that works out of the Honey-bunch Bar?" he asked, trying the break the cold silence.

The tall brown-skinned girl, to whom he had addressed the question, put her hand on her hip. "No, baby, I'm afraid you've got me mixed up with somebody else." She answered frankly, her eyes shifting over to Earl. It was obvious that she wasn't interested in Charles.

The slight rejection stung Charles, and he became nasty. "Bitch, I ain't got you mixed up with nobody. Your sister is whoring out of the motherfuckin' bar, so you ain't got to lie about it!"

Now she gave Charles her full attention. She stared straight into his eyes and answered. "If I do have a sister working out of there at night, I don't see why you should be concerned with it, 'cause she sure ain't got no stiff-ass nigger like you for her man." She rocked back on her heels, spreading her legs so that the tight, tiny skirt seemed about to burst.